The Witches We Are

TALES FROM BRIAR VALE
BOOK ONE

FELICITY KYLE

This is a work of fiction. Names, characters, business, events and incidents are the products of the author's imagination. Any resemblance to actual persons, living or dead, or actual events is purely coincidental.

ISBN 978-1-962738-00-2 (paperback)

ISBN 978-1-962738-01-9 (ebook)

Published by Lost Sleep Publishing LLC

The Witches We Are

For P

and everyone who wishes that the world
had a bit more magic

Contents

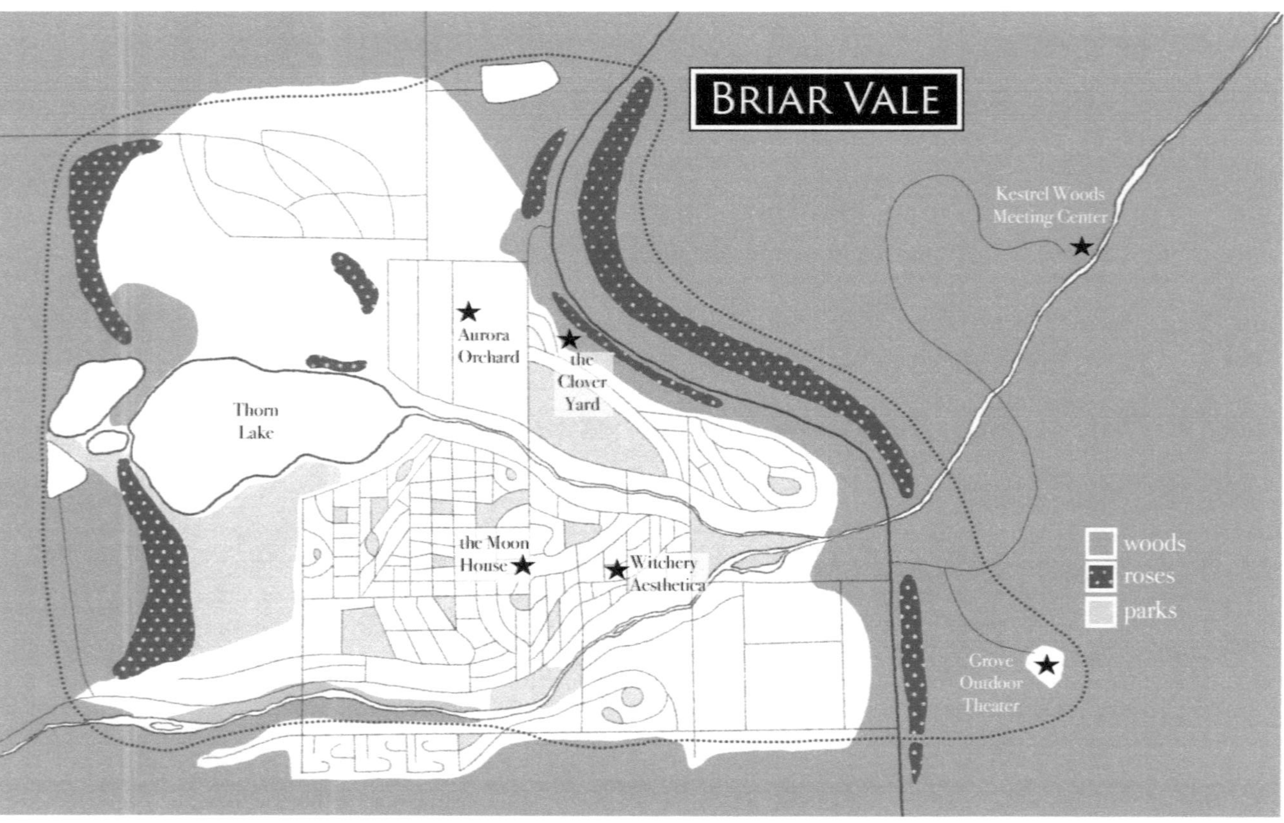

BRIAR VALE
Kestrel Woods Meeting Center
Aurora Orchard
the Clover Yard
Thorn Lake
the Moon House
Witchery Aesthetica
Grove Outdoor Theater
woods
roses
parks

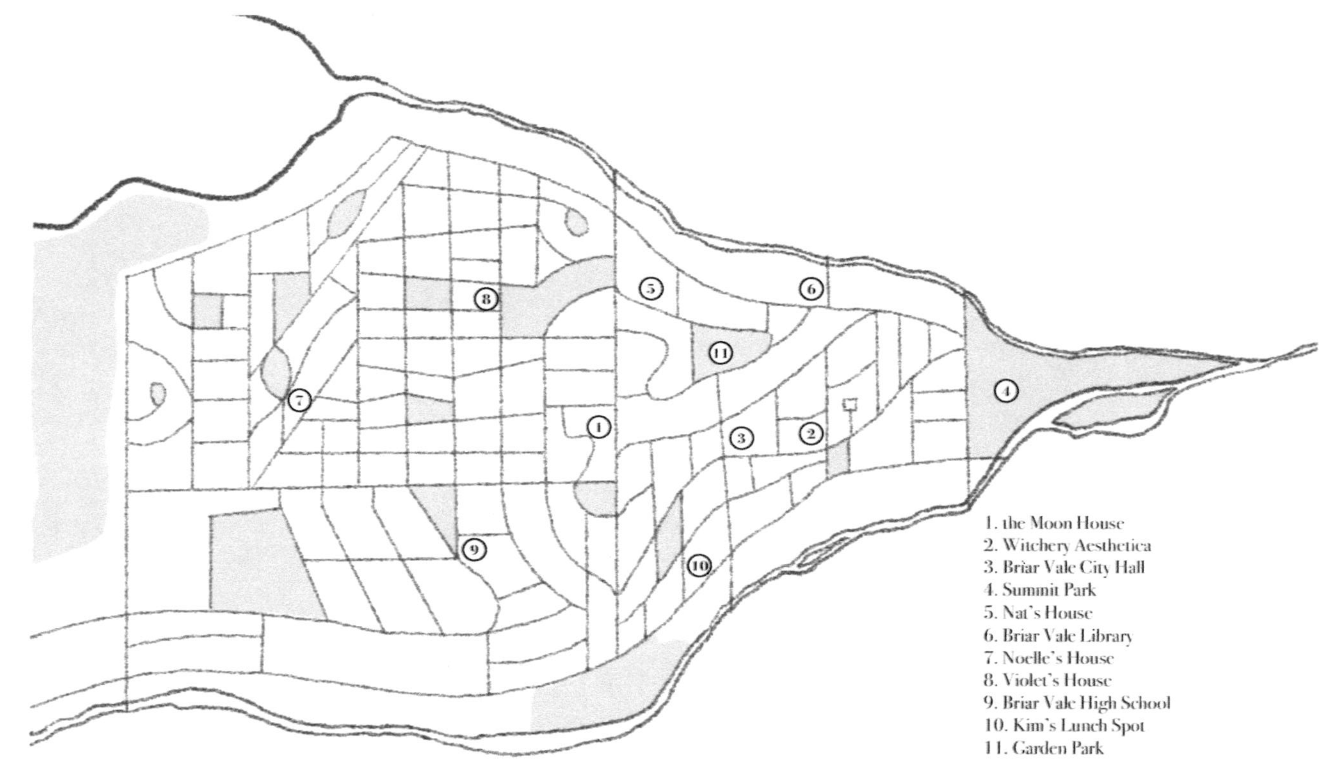

1. the Moon House
2. Witchery Aesthetica
3. Briar Vale City Hall
4. Summit Park
5. Nat's House
6. Briar Vale Library
7. Noelle's House
8. Violet's House
9. Briar Vale High School
10. Kim's Lunch Spot
11. Garden Park

One

ON THE GORGEOUSLY SUNNY morning of September 5th, Brenn Maren cracked her knuckles, straightened her shoulders, and drew in a deep, fortifying breath. And promptly started choking on her own spit.

She took a sip of her coffee and her coughs turned into a hiss of pain as the too-hot liquid burnt her tongue. "Ouch, ouch, ouch," she gasped as she fanned her open mouth.

Her familiar, Mayhew, a large black crow, swooped through the doorway. He landed on her desk, hopping over to drop a stack of band-aids in front of her. He threw his head back and let out a cawing noise that sounded suspiciously like cackling.

"Very funny," Brenn muttered. "What a hilarious guy you are. Listen to me chortle in glee." She swept the band-aids into a drawer. Setting her coffee aside to cool, she cleared her throat several times. "Fifth time's the charm?"

Mayhew cocked his head. "Maybe," he croaked. He looked from her face to the deck of cards she held in her hands several times. "You try."

Brenn thumbed through the deck, making sure she hadn't shuffled in an unpainted card from the pile she kept next to her brushes. Dozens of images flashed past as she flipped through the entire stack. Since she'd turned sixteen, about a month before each solstice and equinox, she would have a dream she couldn't remember, and when she woke up, the vision of a divination card stuck with her until she painted it. At this point her deck was a more personal record of her life than any album of photos from the same time could have been.

"Okay," she said to herself. "One. Is that big thing still coming?" She laid a card face down on the table. "Two. Is it going to affect me directly?" Another facedown card next to the first. "And three. Are you done throwing whatever weird tantrum this is?" Brenn gently slapped the third card onto her desk.

Charles, her other familiar, leaned over with his paws resting on a pile of books on the corner of the desktop, craning his neck to watch her. The sleek white ermine looked at her with a hint of concern in his eyes, and chittered softly.

"Yeah, I know. I'm just going to do it." Brenn stretched her fingers, her knuckles popping again. "I'm just going to flip these over and get my answers, and it will be like the last four days never happened." She chewed her bottom lip. "Yep."

She sat there tapping the back of the leftmost card with her fingertip, unable to make herself turn it over. Mayhew clacked his beak at her.

Brenn shrugged at him. "If I don't do it, then I never have to know."

He made a sound of disgust and flew out of the room. Brenn called after him, "Fine, okay. You're right."

She squinted, peering through her lashes barely enough to see where the cards were. Huffing a heavy breath through her nose, she flipped them over in quick succession.

Blank. Blank. Blank. Just like the last four days.

"Noooo," she groaned, dropping her forehead to the desk with a clunk. "Fuck, fuck, fuck."

All through the entire month of August, her cards had warned her something big was coming. Something life changing. Then on September first, they showed her nothing. That was the day her magic started faltering.

Now every card she pulled was blank, even though she checked the deck obsessively before she used it. Brenn didn't usually put a lot of stock in harbingers, but this felt too big to ignore. One time, sure, she could write that off as a strange little hiccup, but day after day? And it wasn't only her cards. Her magic had been glitchy too, reliable spells not working the way they should or even outright backfiring.

Brenn twisted her hands together under the desk, her eyes squeezed tightly shut. She could feel goosebumps rise on the back of her neck, and she clenched her body to try to stop her shivers. Her stomach twisted uncomfortably as she tried to remember if this had ever happened to anyone she knew. Talking to her family about her issue was not an option. Her oldest sister, Noelle, was obnoxiously self-assured and had never failed at anything in her entire life. If Brenn went to her, she would never hear the end of it. Sasha and Carl Maren, her parents, were semi-famous in the witching world for the prestigious magical advancement conferences they had developed when Brenn was a baby. They were embarrassed enough by the way Brenn used her skills in her business, Lost Seas Procurement and Persuasion; if she confessed she was magically deficient, they might try to whisk her off to some sort of secretive magical rehab. And Cleo, her younger sister, always expected her messes would be fixed if she called Brenn.

Normally, Brenn would go talk to her Auntie Violet, who had been her confidant since her childhood. However, every year Violet went on retreat with her coven, arriving back mid-September. They had a strict no-contact rule, which was extremely inconvenient for Brenn this year.

No, she had to figure it out on her own.

Feeling determined, Brenn sat back up quickly, startling Charles into leaping from the stack of books he had been dozing on. Unfortunately that made Brenn flinch, and her now-cool coffee was so close to her arm that she knocked it over. As she scooped up her divination deck out of the rapidly spreading puddle, she said her usual spill-cleaning spell. The coffee hovered in the air as a wiggly sphere for a few seconds then splashed itself down, missing her mug entirely and soaking a box of charms she had to deliver to a client this morning.

"You have got to be kidding," Brenn said to the mess in front of her. She massaged the spot between her eyebrows as she sat looking at the sodden cardboard. Maybe she should go back to bed.

Instead she crossed the hall to her storeroom, rummaging in a cupboard for a box to swap for the coffee-saturated one in her office. As she checked the contents of appropriately-sized containers, she mentally ran through the healing spells she knew. One of her great-great-multiple-great-grandparents had been a doctor and kept a thorough record of their knowledge and magical experiments. She loved reading about how her ancestors approached magic.

Brenn sat back on her heels. She had an entire bookcase of her family's grimoires, handed down and added to by each generation. Surely she wasn't the first person to have a case of magical incapacity.

She dashed into her office to drop the box she held on the desk and nearly fell as she spun around to hurry down the hall-way. Charles stared at her from the foyer table where he sat smoothing his fur with his paws.

"Got an idea," she shouted as she rushed past.

A few hours later, Brenn was sitting on the floor in her library, stacks of well-worn leather journals scattered around her. She was concentrating so deeply on the page she was reading that she didn't hear Mayhew the first few times he spoke.

"LATE," he yelled at her, landing on her knee.

She blinked at him.

He pecked gently at her watch. "Witch late," he said at a slightly lower volume.

It was nearly noon, which meant she had been poring over her books for almost three hours. "Oh, fuck," she spit out as she jumped up. Her first client had expected her thirty minutes ago.

She ran into her office, grabbing the box on her desk and tossing it in a bag with the rest of her deliveries for the day. "Thanks, Mayhew," she called as she tried to shove her feet into her boots and snag her keys off the foyer table at the same time. Brenn caught herself before she could tie her boot laces with magic, and hastily did them up by hand. "I'll see you guys later. Don't move the grimoires. Charles, just stay out of the library entirely."

AS SHE PULLED onto the gravel drive of Aurora Orchards, she brushed a lock of unruly hair out of her face, scowling at her phone as it buzzed for the seventh time since she got in the truck. Cleo again. Her younger sister almost certainly wanted her to come fix something or other. Brenn made a funny little circular gesture above her phone. "Silenced," she said firmly. A stinging spark of static electricity bounced from her phone to her fingers. Instead of silencing, it started blasting her 'sad girl in the bath' playlist. She sighed deeply, shaking the feeling back into her fingertips as she eased into a parking spot.

Elise Matthews waved and began talking before Brenn had a chance to get out of her truck. "Hey, Brenn! We missed you at the last couple of Spell Dev meetings. Everything ok?"

Damn. She forgot that there was a Spell Development meeting last night. She really was off her game. Not that she would have gone anyway, what with every spell she attempted lately fizzing out, but that did make three in a row she'd missed.

"No yeah, I honestly forgot last night. I've been dragging a bit this weekend. You know how it goes." She rummaged in her truck for the box of harvest charms the Matthews used to keep their trees docile during the tourist rush. Last year, a particularly mischievous tree had goosed every person that walked near it, and they couldn't spare an employee to watch the tree full-time this year. The box had shifted to the bottom of her tote, and she pulled the other orders out to get to it.

Elise followed her around to the other side of the truck. "You getting enough sleep? Vitamin D? You want a cup of coffee?"

Coffee. *Coffee.* Her hands stilled as she remembered the disaster in her office this morning. "Oh, for crying out loud. I don't have your delivery."

"You can't find our delivery?" Elise wobbled a little on tiptoes, peering into Brenn's truck.

"No, I know exactly where it is. I spilled my damn coffee all over your box, and I was going to switch it with this un-coffee-soaked box, but I got distracted. And then I was running late and rushing and grabbed this box without actually transferring your charms to it. Unless you want this box of..." She opened the lid. "Color-shifting miniature mice figurines." Her shoulders slumped the tiniest bit.

"Nah, we're good." Elise's sarcasm always came out slightly sweet, lessening its impact. "We aren't going to need the charms until the end of this week anyways, so swing back by when you get a chance."

"Thanks, Elise. I'm so sorry. I don't know where my head is."

"No worries. You know, Mina's been working on her teas and made one for luck. You want some?"

She pushed the door shut and leaned against the back of the truck. "Luck tea? I don't know that that's going to do much for me."

Elise gave her a grin. "Honestly, I think it just gets you a little high, but if it makes you stop overanalyzing every situation, well. Something to be said for that."

Brenn thought about the sticky spots of coffee she still had to clean off her desk, her possibly-fried phone, her deck full of mysteriously blank cards, her burnt tongue, the newest mess she would have to deal with for Cleo, and gave into her base impulses. "Yes. Yes, please, I'd love some tea today."

～

SHE WAS FEELING SLIGHTLY BETTER as she headed back through town towards her house. Sure, it was a little hot for this time of year; the weather should have been showing the first stirrings of autumn, but it was a lovely, relentlessly sunny day. She stuck her arm out of the window as she drove, letting her hand ride up and down on the breeze, admiring the way the golden light highlighted the warm undertones of her brown skin.

Aside from the four years she spent at MSU getting her business degree, Brenn had spent her entire life living in Briar Vale. It was a small town, around 9,000 people, and had grown up out of land that held an excess of magical energy. Like most other magic towns scattered around the world, every resident had some degree of magical ability.

The Vale was quaintly charming, tucked into the forests of western Michigan, with a vibrant downtown area of small businesses and restaurants and strange little hotels and inns. Two rivers framed the town, one leading into the largest of the three lakes on the west side. Tourists enjoyed the festivals and events that were held every few weeks or rode the vintage steam train that circled the town to marvel at the scenery. And in every direction a person looked, there were huge tangles of wild roses, the namesake of Briar Vale, in any color imaginable. And some beyond that.

Her phone pinged again, another 'hey I need you' text from Cleo. Well, at least the thing still worked.

Glancing over at the tin of tea Elise had sent home with her, she decided to keep ignoring Cleo and push the rest of her work to tomorrow. She'd take this afternoon to herself, bliss out with Mina's luck tea, and after some rest, her magic was sure to work normally. She hoped.

She dismissed another text notification from Cleo.

WALKING BACK through the door of the Moon House, she stroked the door frame. "Hello, house." Her keys almost made it into their regular place as she tossed them across the room. Mayhew cawed as he swooped down to pluck them off the floor and dropped them in the novelty caldron Brenn used as a key bowl. Charles ran up her arm as she bent down to untie her boots. "Thanks, Mayhew. You guys want a snack?" Charles chirped quietly as she stroked the downy spot of fur under his ear. The three of them walked down the long hallway to the kitchen at the back of the house.

Sunlight streamed in through the mullioned windows that stretched the length of the kitchen. Brenn pulled her smallest teapot from the armoire in the corner, careful to shut the door with her hand and not a flick of magic. The last thing she needed was blasting her cupboard to smithereens. She filled the electric kettle with water and turned it on. She decided that after the tea kicked in, she would try for another divination card vision. That bothered her the most about her magic not working properly; she was overdue to make her next card by nearly two weeks. When the cards had been behaving normally, she thought maybe she had to first deal with the big thing they had said was coming.

Now she had a sneaking suspicion her lack of visions correlated to her magic being off.

As she waited for the water to heat, she was struck with a horrifying thought. What if the visions disappeared not because of her faulty magic, but because her deck was complete? Acid crawled up the back of her throat as she considered that. She was not ready for whatever milestone that would mark.

A gentle squawk from Mayhew broke her train of thought. He cocked his head to the side inquisitively, his shiny black feathers gleaming like an oil slick in the sun. "Work?" he croaked as he hopped closer.

"I'm taking the afternoon off." But that did remind her she needed to reschedule everyone she was going to skip.

The ledger with the day's delivery list was still lying open on her desk. Ignoring the three missed call notifications from Cleo, she called each client, distributing appointments to the rest of the week. Yawning, she stretched, wincing as her joints cracked. She scribbled a note to re-up her yoga pass the next time she was near her gym and tossed it on a pile of other hastily recorded notes.

She set out her card supplies in the lying room. A nice cup of mildly enhanced tea, a doze in her lying room, her 'vision time bitches' playlist, and she should be set to rights. Seventeen more days until the equinox—that gave her plenty of time to dream up her card. Simple. The kettle whistled in the kitchen, and she pushed herself up from the floor.

In her rush earlier, she had knocked some of the photographs in the hall askew, and she straightened them absently as she walked back to the kitchen.

She shrieked as Cleo appeared from around the corner. "Oh good, you are home. We need you to come—"

Standing in the broken glass of the picture frame she had just knocked off the wall, Brenn glared at her younger sister. "Cleo, what in the fresh hell!"

Her sister scoffed, then looked at someone Brenn couldn't see. She could, however, hear her older sister Noelle speaking bossily in the background. "Look, Brenn, can you come down to the store? We need you to find out some information for us."

"I just put the kettle on for some tea, and I pushed work off until tomorrow so I can rest this afternoon. There's gotta be someone else around who can help you. Or I can come by tomorrow between deliveries." She stretched over to the console table to grab a couple pieces of junk mail to scoop up the worst of the glass.

"No, Brenn, we need you *right now*. I'm not leaving until you agree to come down, and Howie is here. You know you can't break his projections."

Cleo had her in a corner and they both knew it. Brenn couldn't counterspell Howie's uncanny astral calls. She definitely wouldn't manage it today. A truly impressive magical working, he could send a real-time projection of a person to any location within five miles of himself. Both the projector and projectee could fully see and hear each other. It could be very irritating, and he knew it, which is why Howie didn't often do it. Except when Cleo asked, because nearly anyone would do what Cleo asked.

Brenn swallowed a frustrated scream. "Fine," she huffed. Cleo gave her a steady look, pointed at her, and disappeared. Brenn let herself have one little irritated howl and stomped into the kitchen to turn the kettle off.

LUCKILY FOR CLEO, there was plenty of parking in front of Witchery Aesthetica when Brenn pulled up. This month Cleo had a display for celestial witches in one window, with little mobiles of stars lazily orbiting a precarious-looking stack of lunar-themed goods in the middle, and a cozy cottagecore scene in the other, with teacups charmed to send up little columns of steam. Inside, the shop was a large, nearly circular room divided into sections devoted to two dozen different kinds of witchy aesthetics, with six separate counters in the very middle arranged in a hexagonal formation. Above the counters hung a gigantic chandelier composed of hundreds of tiny twinkling lights like a cloud of golden fireflies.

As Brenn wound around tables piled high with witchy sundries, she grudgingly admired how Cleo had spelled each section to create an atmosphere appropriate to the goods featured. The bright and cheerful garden witch segment smelled like tomato leaves and peaches, with Vivaldi's Four Seasons playing gently. Dark academia smelled like old books, and instead of music, customers could barely hear pages turning and people murmuring in the background as if they were in a library. Gothic witches were treated to a mix of The Cure and Soiuxsie and the Banshees and a loamy, stony scent under dimmed lighting, like shopping in a forgotten corner of a castle courtyard. Brenn found walking through the different departments both relaxing and oddly stimulating at the same time.

The finishing touches that drew the most customers in, however, were the photo walls Cleo had scattered throughout, set up and spelled so that every picture taken turned out perfectly, every video had a dreamy, polished quality. There was a group of people gathered around the rose wall in the botanical section. Brenn caught a glimpse of her younger sister's blue curls as a couple of people shifted. She made a beeline for her.

Cleo and Noelle flanked a white teenage girl with bright copper-colored hair in two long braids and a port wine birthmark over her left eye and cheek. A lurid purple-green bruise stood out starkly on her forearm, her skin translucent in that way redheads sometimes have. She was staring at the floor with an uncertain but slightly defiant look on her face.

Brenn pushed past a pair of gossiping people. "Cleo? What's going on?"

"Brenn! Great!" Cleo moved them to the edge of the small crowd and spoke in a hushed tone as Noelle kept interrogating the girl. "We need to find out what this girl's name is and where she came from."

"Why?" Brenn asked, trying to tune out Noelle's voice. "Who is she to you?"

"She's been here since we opened this morning, like three hours. She wouldn't talk to anyone about what she wants, and I thought maybe she was stealing, but then I saw the bruise on her arm. So I called Noelle."

"Ugh, Cleo." Brenn made a disgusted noise.

"I know," Cleo hissed. "But I didn't want to jump straight to child services, and she works with kids. Who else was I gonna call?"

Brenn made a face at her. "And *this* is somehow better?"

"It's done now, so deal with it." Cleo turned back to address the girl. "If you can give us some basic information, sweetheart, we can figure out how to help you."

The girl met Brenn's eye. "I just need a place to stay for the night. I have a little money, or I can work to pay for it," she said quietly.

"I think it's best we go down to city hall and talk to a social worker, and they can find you a place to sleep tonight and a doctor to look at your arm," Noelle said briskly, like it was already done. "Then tomorrow, we can arrange to get you home." She addressed the group still standing there. "She's much too young to be on her own."

Cleo looked at the girl with sympathy. "Sweetheart, I agree with my sister. You can't be more than, what, sixteen?"

The girl's wide-eyed look darted between the three of them. "No, but—"

Noelle gave a resigned sigh. "There you go. You shouldn't be wandering around an unfamiliar town without a parent with you.”

Brenn could feel the situation slipping sideways. “Cleo. Noelle. If she’s that young and managed to come *here* on her own, there’s probably a reason for it.” She moved to reach a hand out to the girl, but Noelle put her own hand on Brenn’s wrist, holding her back.

“Brenn, I don’t know why you’re here, but now that you are, could you just get her name?”

Most of the people around them made sounds of assent, Cleo included. Brenn felt a sudden flash of irritation that she was not unused to feeling around her sisters. “Hey, *you* called *me*. She’s not going to talk to anyone if you all keep overwhelming her like this.”

“I didn’t call you. And I have five kids, Brenn. I think I know how to handle this.” Noelle shot her own look of annoyance at Brenn. Cleo stepped between them.

“I called her,” she said to Noelle. To Brenn, she continued, “Sorry I dragged you down here. All we need is for you to persuade her to talk to us, and then you can get back to your ‘restful afternoon’.”

Brenn could hear the air quotes in Cleo’s voice. She drew in a deep, steadying breath and looked away before she was tempted to say something rude to her sisters. As she did, she locked eyes with a short Asian woman slouching by the bohemian witch photo wall one section over, hands tucked deep in the pockets of her oversized canvas jacket. She held Brenn’s gaze for a long second and then gave her a flicker of an eye roll.

Biting back a smile, Brenn turned back to the group arguing over the girl. “Look, let me take her to get some lunch, just the two of us—”

“Brenn, if you can’t get her to tell us her name and where...” Noelle interrupted, then trailed off. The quiet woman had pushed off the pillar she was leaning against and walked over to join the group.

"Didn't she," the woman gestured at Cleo, "call her for a reason?" She indicated Brenn with a nod of her head. "Lot of effort wasted, looks like."

Noelle looked taken aback at being questioned by a stranger. "And who exactly are you?"

"Nat," the woman said mildly.

Cleo snapped her fingers. "I thought I knew you! I've run into you at The Clover Yard before, right? The solstice committee meeting? I appreciate you trying to help, but my sisters and I can take care of this."

Nat took her hands out of her pockets, palms out, fingers up, shrugging. "You asked for her help, why not let her give it to you?"

Exasperated now, Noelle spoke firmly. "Look, we don't need any more opinions here—"

Brenn saw her opportunity and cut her off. She put on her innocent voice. "Nono, isn't Willa done with kindergarten right now?"

Noelle glanced at her watch and sighed heavily. She looked authoritatively at Brenn and then Cleo. "I will be back in twenty minutes. Do not go anywhere."

When she left, the group lost steam, drifting away. Brenn spun around to Cleo. "Thanks for that, Cleo. For crying out loud."

"Whatever. You know why I called Noelle first." She fluffed an errant curl back into her fauxhawk. "Your whole thing with her isn't my fault."

Brenn pointed a finger in her baby sister's direction. "I'm not interested in any more from you." She turned to the girl who was standing like she was trying to melt beneath the floor. "Hey, sorry they were treating you like a helpless child." She pointedly ignored Cleo's indignant 'hey' and held her hand out for the girl to shake. "I'm Brenn. Can I buy you some lunch or a coffee or something?"

The girl seemed slightly less mortified. She glanced around to make sure they were alone but still spoke softly. "Audrey. Lunch would be good."

"Okay, good. Let's get out of here before my nosy sister rushes back." Out of the corner of her eye, she caught a tiny smile on Audrey's face. A little feeling of accomplishment glowed in her for the first time all day. And her taking off with the girl would annoy Noelle like nothing else. Maybe her luck was turning.

As the two of them walked out of Witchery Aesthetica, Nat stood from the bench on the sidewalk. She walked over to them, smiling at Audrey. "Brenn? Could I have a minute?"

"Oh. Uh, sure." Brenn motioned to the bench, asking Audrey to wait for her there. "What can I do for you?"

"First, I wanted to apologize for pushing into your conversation. I didn't intend to overstep." Her eyes twinkled. "But your sisters seemed very...set in their interpretation of the situation, and I have experience in redirecting that sort of energy."

Brenn's mouth twisted wryly. "Yeah, they can be a lot. Thanks for interrupting." She took a step towards her truck.

Nat stopped her with a hand on Brenn's arm. Her voice low, she said, "I actually wanted to say, I was on my own a lot when I was a teenager. If you ever need to talk, or insight, or any help at all, feel free to call me." She handed Brenn a business card with a phone number written on it.

Brenn held the paper for a minute, feeling a little tingle in her fingers. "I, um. Thank you. I was only planning to take her to lunch, but I'll keep this in mind." She punctuated her comment by tapping the card on her other palm before putting it in her pocket.

Nat gave her a strangely knowing smile. "Sure. Well, just in case."

Two

AS BRENN TOSSED a pile of invoices behind the passenger seat so Audrey could get in the truck, her stomach clenched. Was she doing the right thing? Maybe she should have waited for Noelle.

Then Audrey slid into the seat next to her and gave her a shy, relieved smile. Nope, forget Noelle. "Is there anything in particular you'd like for lunch?" Brenn asked as she started the truck.

"Anything is fine." Audrey seemed almost embarrassed to have spoken at all, much less express a preference. "I don't have any allergies or anything."

Brenn replied briskly, sweeping away the awkwardness. "Well, I think we should probably get out of downtown so Noelle doesn't barge in." Cleo mentioned The Clover Yard earlier. That would be a good choice. Wide range of food and across the river on the far side of the fairgrounds. She might be able to ward them before Noelle tried to figure out where they were. "Actually, I have a place in mind. You buckled?"

Audrey nodded, and Brenn steered the truck out onto the street.

She covertly watched Audrey as she drove, trying to gauge her reactions as they travelled through town. Audrey seemed interested in looking around but sat hunched like she wanted to avoid anyone noticing her. "So I don't know how much you know about our town, but it's named Briar Vale because it's set in a valley filled with roses. Almost the entire town is surrounded by giant thickets of roses." She chided herself a bit, as if a teenager was going to care how the town was named. That feeling faded quickly as Audrey said that was neat and asked what park they were driving past.

"That's Summit Park. On the far east end is where the rivers split. We're going to drive over the Thorn River, and the Bramble River runs along the south side. You probably went over that one as you came into town."

She risked a full look over at Audrey. Keeping her voice light, she asked, "So, how did you get to Briar Vale?"

"Oh, I got a ride with some ladies coming for a candle making class."

"You hitched with strangers?" Brenn tried very hard to not sound judgmental. She wasn't sure how well she succeeded.

Audrey didn't seem to notice. "Yeah, they were okay. I told them I was meeting my cousin, but her car broke down so she couldn't pick me up."

"Clever. How'd you choose Witchery Aesthetica?"

"It's on social media? The photo walls? Everyone tags their pics, and Cleo seemed super nice when she comments on them?"

Ah, that made sense. Cleo spent a lot of time curating the shop's social media presence. Every month she came up with yet another wildly popular hashtag for her fans to use on their posts. The thought of doing that much marketing for Lost Seas made Brenn want to immediately take a nap. "She can be very nice when she's not texting you one million times and invading the sanctity of your home."

Audrey cringed a little. "I'm so sorry. I didn't realize—"

"Oh no, no, how would you? I'm sorry. It wasn't your fault."

Brenn felt like a jerk. "Cleo texts me every other week to fix problems for her. Plus, I was already having a day." She snapped her mouth shut. She did not need to whine about her bad day to this kid she barely knew, and she definitely wasn't going to divulge anything about actual magic until she had a better understanding of why Audrey had shown up. Fortunately, regular people tended to brush off things they didn't want to see, like magic.

They turned onto Crabtree Road, and she gestured out her window. "If you look between the motels, you can see the fairgrounds. There's an open-air market all year round on Sunday mornings." She pressed herself back against the seat so Audrey could see around her body.

As they passed the end of the row of motels, they were pulling up to The Clover Yard. It was a strange little restaurant, a tiny yellow building housing the kitchen, with a bathroom on the far side and fifteen tables scattered outside around a clover lawn. Each table sat under its own brightly colored, fringed four-post tent, like a beach cabana. In the wetter and cooler weather, there were transparent plastic walls that rolled down to shield diners from rain and snow and wind, boosted with a few charms. Along the edges of the property, beds of zinnias exploded with riotous color.

Brenn felt Audrey straighten and heard her say a quiet 'wow'. Smiling to herself, she parked and stretched her arms over her head once she was out of the truck. The scent of roses hung in the air, somehow enhancing the delicious smells of the restaurant. She was pleased to see Audrey taking a deep breath and then relaxing her shoulders. This was a good plan. And she could worry about what possessed her to take on this kid after she got some food in her and figured out why Audrey was here in the first place.

"Hello! Two for lunch?" a server chirped, leading them to a

small table. "I'll give you a minute to look at the menu. If you have any questions, wave me down, k?"

Brenn watched Audrey's brow furrow a little. "Hey." Once Audrey looked at her, she continued. "I invited you to lunch, so I'm buying. I want you to order what you feel like eating and to get enough food for you."

She nodded, her braids bouncing a little with the motion. "What's your favorite thing to eat here?"

"I like the watercress BLT. I order it pretty much every time I'm here." She was pleased when Audrey ordered a BLT plus a polenta bowl and a pear salad without hesitating. Once the server left again, she leveled a serious look at the girl. "Okay, so this is the part when you start telling me things." She suddenly remembered Noelle.

"Actually hang on a second." Brenn unscrewed the top of the salt shaker on the table and spilled a little pile out. She smoothed it flat, carving a sigil out with her fingertip, repeating the process at each corner of the table. Touching the first sigil firmly without smearing it away, she said, "Shielded." When she felt the shield snap into place correctly, she sagged a little in relief.

Audrey tilted her head quizzically. "What was that?" she asked. "It feels kinda weird."

"We'll get to that in a bit. Let's make a trade; you answer my questions, I'll answer yours." She paused as the server set out their food, careful not to disturb her sigils. Another plus for this place—attentive and, more importantly, conscientious staff.

"I think we should start with basics. What's your last name? Where do you live? How old are you actually?" Brenn put a finger up for each question.

Audrey swallowed the giant bite of polenta she had shoved in her mouth as soon as the plate touched the table. "My full name is Audrey Vega, I don't live anywhere, and I'm fifteen." She shoveled more food in her mouth, salad this time.

Brenn put two of her fingers down, brows raised at the dramatic answer. "I'd like a little more specificity on the second question, please."

"I left the last place I was living, and I'm not going back. If you aren't going to help me, I can leave again." She paled. "Please. Please don't call CPS."

This was apparently more serious than Brenn had expected. But she definitely wasn't going to send the kid back into a bad or dangerous situation. She felt the anxiety coming off of Audrey and slowed down a bit. "Where was the last place you lived?"

"Lansing."

"Is that where your family lives?"

"No."

Brenn kept up a steady stream of gentle questions that Audrey answered with one or two words as she practically inhaled her lunch. Are you in danger there (maybe), do the candle ladies you hitched with know where you lived (no), is there anyone I can call to tell that you are safe (please no), are you enjoying your lunch (yes), why do you think no one would be worried about you (I was in a group home). Brenn's gaze softened. "Are you a foster kid?"

"Yeah, I guess."

"Can you tell me a little more about that?"

"My parents are dead, and I've been in twelve different foster homes. I got kicked out of the last one, and they put me in a group home."

"I'm sorry to hear that." Brenn waved the server down and ordered one of each dessert they had. "Will you tell me why you had to leave your last foster family?"

The sheer uncontrollable panic on Audrey's face made Brenn's own heart speed up. She desperately tried to think of a way to calm her down. She couldn't rely on her soothing spells to work properly; she honestly got very lucky with the shield. The kid was so skittish she was sure Audrey would bolt if Brenn touched her. Damnit, Noelle *was* more qualified to deal with this kind of thing. She ended up looking Audrey directly in the eye, waving her hands around helplessly. "Hey, it's okay. I'm not going to do *anything* until you tell me what's go—"

Audrey squeaked and pointed at the table. There suddenly were dozens of little chamomile flowers growing out of the table, as though Brenn had flung seeds down when she was waving her hands. "That's—what's that?" Her finger shook. "How did you do that?"

Brenn sucked in a deep breath. "That is something I will explain to you in a minute. I will. First though, Audrey, I need to know why you left your last foster home." She let the silence stretch.

The girl wrung her hands, opening and shutting her mouth several times. Finally, she started talking, the words spilling out faster as she went on. "I don't know what happened, I kept getting sent back from fosters because I was too weird. You know? Things happen when I'm around, weird things. Like one time all my foster family's bikes ended up stuck high up in the tree in the front yard? Or all the doorknobs in the house would switch sides, or all the food in the fridge would turn hot pink? And they all thought it was my fault 'cause it didn't happen before I got there, and I guess it stopped when I was gone, though my caseworker wasn't supposed to tell me that. But I found out anyway? And then at my last one, there was a bunch of storms, and their house flooded twice, and a tree fell into it from wind once, and it got hit by the electrical wire outside and caught on fire once too, and each time it was when their son was being mean to me and I was upset and then the last thing—" She stopped talking, clapping a hand over her mouth.

"That sounds like you've been through a lot. What was the last thing, Audrey?" Brenn could feel the space in Audrey that needed a push, and she searched for the right way to put a little pressure on it. "I need you to tell me, and then I'll answer every question you have, I promise." She held out her pinkie, crooked.

Audrey stared at it, then looked at her, then back at her finger. She cautiously hooked her own pinkie around Brenn's. She nodded, more to herself than to Brenn.

"So their bio kid? James? He said he was going to cut off all my hair and I better hope that's all he was gonna do with the scissors. I don't know what happened. He grabbed my arm, and then all of a sudden, he smashed into the side of their garage." She held out her arm and gestured from her wrist to her shoulder. "He had burns all the way up his arm, bad ones. They thought I burned him with a firecracker or something and pushed him into the garage wall, but I was in the neighbor's yard. It was really far away." She wiped tears from her eyes. "The neighbor's camera showed there was lightning or static electricity or something, but they sent me to the group home anyways. So that's why I left, I'm a freak, and I thought maybe the magic store might have a book or something that could tell me what I did so I don't hurt anyone again, and maybe I could find a job to support myself."

"Oh, honey. I know what's going on." Brenn took her hand. "There is an explanation for what happened to you."

Audrey pulled her hand away with a whimper. "But I didn't tell you the worst part yet."

"What's the worst part?" Brenn made her voice as quiet as possible without whispering.

"I wanted to hurt him. I wanted to blast him as far away as I could. I meant it. I made it happen." She sat very still. "If you want me to leave, I understand. I'm an awful person."

Brenn looked at her with sympathy. "No, I don't want you to leave. And while, yeah, wanting to hurt someone on purpose isn't great, you definitely aren't alone in wanting someone who is hurting you to come to harm themselves. You aren't awful.

You were under an unimaginable amount of stress and dealing with more than you were aware of."

The server noticed an opening and rushed over to quickly drop plates of dessert on their table, handing each of them a fork with a flourish.

Brenn thanked the server and waited until Audrey started eating tiny bites of the French silk pie. "So, answer time. You found your way here because you were called here. And you felt called here because you have an affinity for magic." Audrey gasped and started coughing little crumbs of pie crust onto the table in front of her. Brenn ate her own dessert until the girl stopped coughing. "Yes, that means you have magic. Magic is real. That's what threw that jackass kid into his garage and likely what caused all the other weird stuff. That's why you felt strange when my shield went up and why the chamomile started growing out of the table."

She could feel Audrey trying to keep herself from bursting out with questions. "Magical ability shows up in kids around the age of seven and is pretty unpredictable until they turn twenty-one. That's when your magic settles, and it's likely that you'll feel a pull to a particular style or talent that is natural to you. I'm very good at finding things, physical items, but also the particular things that will persuade someone to answer my questions or do what I ask."

Audrey blinked at that.

"Yep, that's why Cleo called me down. I could have used my abilities to force an answer out of you, but I generally avoid using it like a bludgeon, which is why I didn't. Every person who lives here has some kind of magical ability or affinity, though they are better off than you because they know what is going on and have been trained properly."

Audrey looked unsure at that. Watching her fidget, tentative and fluttery like a baby rabbit, Brenn's heart twisted.

Brenn felt a rush of affection and a teeny bit of kinship for

Audrey. With the way her magic was acting lately, she knew a little of what the girl was going through. Sending her back to the normie world, untrained and unsupported, would be a disaster. Plus, maybe teaching someone else the basics could help her fix her own nonsense.

Without letting herself think too deeply about the consequences, she blurted out a question. "Do you want to come stay with me and learn how to be a witch?"

Ooh, Noelle was going to be *pissed*.

Three

AUDREY LOOKED DISBELIEVING, and then slowly delight took over. "Yes! Can I? Really, that's okay? You can teach me?"

Brenn laughed. "Yes and yes and yes. We'll go to my house and set up the guest room, and I can give you some basics. And introduce you to Charles Mayhew."

"Charles Mayhew? Who is he?" Audrey asked.

"They, actually. They're my familiars, Charles and Mayhew. I got in the habit of thinking of them as a unit I guess, because they are almost always together. Thus, Charles Mayhew." Brushing the salt sigils off the table, she got up to leave. "You'll see when you meet them. And then tomorrow, we can take a tour of the town and get you some supplies and things. Sound good?"

"Yes, thank you!" she nearly shouted, bouncing a little with excitement.

Brenn kept up a steady stream of information about everything they passed as she drove them to the Moon House.

She felt more than heard Audrey gasp in wonder. The Moon House was a Queen Anne-style home, two stories tall, with gingerbread trim curling along the edges. The clapboard was painted a light robin's egg blue, and the verge was done in darker shades of grey-violet and Brenn's favorite blue-greens. A tower rose three stories from the southeast corner of the house, a set of bay windows on each floor. On the second floor of the campanile, the middle window was made of gleaming stained glass with a creamy white crescent moon in the center. In the middle of the house, there was a front door seldom used by Brenn now or her family when they had lived there. Tangles of late-blooming wisteria climbed up the porch that covered the front door and ran around the side of the house. Brenn let the garden grow how it wanted, and now at the end of the summer, it was lush and wild.

Around the left side of the house, next to the porch, the dark brick driveway led to a detached garage. Parking outside the garage, Brenn ushered Audrey up another brick path onto the porch outside the door at the side of the house where, three hours earlier, she had been ready to wallow by herself all evening. She stroked the door jamb, greeting the house as they walked in. Mayhew flew down from the banister at the top of the stairs to land on her shoulder. "This handsome fellow is Mayhew."

"Hello, hello," he croaked, staring intently at their guest.

"Hi, Mayhew." Audrey seemed surprisingly relaxed at his greeting. "Can I pet him?"

Brenn shrugged. "Ask him." Her shrug bounced him off her shoulder onto the back of the chair she sat in to remove her boots. "You can leave your shoes under the console table there for now."

Audrey stopped stroking Mayhew's head to slip her sneakers off and let her backpack slide to the floor. At the slight thud, Charles peeked his head around a doorway down the hall. Brenn gestured for him to come closer.

"This is Charles. Charles, Mayhew, this is Audrey. She's going to be living with us for a while." He sniffed the girl's outstretched hand cautiously. Apparently liking how she smelled, he crept up into her palm. "Great, everybody's acquainted. Tour?"

Audrey nodded and stood up, lowering her hand so Charles could hop down.

"So, this is the foyer. That door is a bathroom, and down the hall that way," she pointed to the front of the house, "the living room is on the driveway side, and the library is on the tower side." Taking a few steps across the foyer, she waved a hand at the open door next to her. "This is my office. I'd rather you stay out of there for the time being. Some of my clients prefer their orders stay confidential."

Audrey peered in for a moment. "Should we keep the door closed then?"

"I assume you have self-control. This room is storage for my business. You can look at the things that are out but leave the stuff in the cupboards and closet alone. Most of the stuff on the shelves is safe to handle gently." She flicked the light on. The room was fitted with floor-to-ceiling shelves on three sides and locking cupboards on the wall with the closet door. There was a large scarred wooden table in the middle of the room and mismatched filing cabinets shoved up against it on one side. Audrey's eyes widened at the shelves stuffed to bursting with jars and bottles and boxes. Brenn gave her a minute to take in the entire room and then tapped her arm to get her attention.

"That's the dining room," Brenn flapped her hand at the room across the hall. They moved to the next door. "And this is my lying room, which you are welcome to use whenever you'd like. Oh, hang on."

She scooped up her painting supplies and stepped around Audrey to drop them in her office. When she walked back into the room, she found Audrey standing just inside the door with a bemused look. "What is a lying room? Is that a magic thing?"

"Ha. Not really, it's more a me thing. I don't do great with traditional meditation, so I come in here and, you know, let my mind drift." She bent over and turned a switch on a small black machine with a spherical prism at the top. Soothing colored light washed over them. "This is an aurora machine. Like the northern lights. And that is obviously a speaker. So I turn on a playlist and lie on those cushions and just watch the light." She pointed at the cushions. "Lying room."

The kitchen of the Moon House was cozy and welcoming. A huge slab of live-edge walnut topped the island that dominated the center of the room. Windows ran the length of the north-west wall, above the sink and stove that were set among the lower cabinets. At the back, there was an oddly shaped alcove that functioned as Brenn's pantry and held the refrigerator. Next to the door they entered from was an armoire filled with tea cups and pots and mugs, and along the last wall were glass-fronted cupboards.

Each wall, including inside the pantry and the cabinets, was hand-painted with a bright, cheerfully chaotic pattern of branches and leaves and fruits and flowers and butterflies. There were punched-copper sconces on the walls and a pendant light in the middle of the room made of a large branch, each leaf a tiny glass bulb. Audrey stood next to the stools with worn cushions pushed up to the island, turning in a slow circle. "This is the best kitchen I have ever seen."

She ran her hand along the edge of the walnut, gently touched the cushions, peered into the cupboards. "Can I help you cook in here?"

"I'm counting on it," Brenn said. "I can cook the basics all right for myself, but it would be nice to have some incentive to make more exciting food." She went to the fridge and grabbed two sparkling waters. She handed one to Audrey and twisted the cap off hers as she walked them onto the back porch. It was dim, even on such a sunny day, with a deep overhanging roof and lilac bushes grown up outside most of the screened windows. The furniture was more patches than anything else after the decades it had served the Maren family, but still inviting and comfortable. A ceiling fan turned lazily overhead. "That door will take you to the backyard, obviously, and the garage. Until the house decides you are a permanent resident, don't let that door close all the way or else you'll be locked out." She showed Audrey how to twist a small latch so it held the door open a crack.

"So that's this floor. Basement is that door." She pointed as they crossed the foyer. "And now you can pick which room you want—" She was interrupted by her phone vibrating off the console table where she had left it and onto the floor. Groaning loudly, she pointed to the living room. "It's Noelle, and if I don't answer it, who knows what she'll do. Go hang in the living room, and I'll come get you when I'm done."

She waited until Audrey was out of sight. Noelle's voice came blaring out of the speaker as soon as she hit 'answer'. "Brenn! I thought I told you not to leave Cleo's shop."

"You did—" Noelle kept on talking over her.

"And then you shielded yourself! I have told you so many times that you can't run away from everything that makes you uncomfortable!"

"That's—"

"Where are you now? I can't believe how irresponsible you are being with this child. You don't even know anything about her! I'm sure her parents are frantic! We need to—"

"Noelle." Brenn practically shouted. Her sister sputtered out, and in the quiet, Brenn continued. "I have told you at least three hundred times that I am a grown adult, and I will make my own choices. You are not my mother."

Noelle sucked in a breath, and Brenn winced. She could feel her gathering steam into another big sister lecture. But then, oh happy day, there was a murmur in the background and a quiet noise of reluctant assent from Noelle. "You're right, you are an adult." The slight edge in her voice grew sharper. "But the adult thing to do was not run but stay and talk about our options like grown people."

"Well, no one has to worry about options anymore. Audrey is going to stay with me for a while, and since she has an affinity for magic, which is *why she found her way here in the first place,* like I thought, I will teach her how to be safe with it."

"Audrey? You got her name?"

"Yep. And enough details about her life that I am confident this is the best way forward."

"Uh-huh. Give me her full name and details, and I will make some calls and get this figured out. You don't need to be a care-giver for this girl. There has to be—"

"Absolutely not." She tapped the edges of the pile of junk mail on the table until they were perfectly even. There was a line of dust and fur on the bottom of the mirror above the table that she wiped away with a fingertip. If she was going to have another person living here, she would have to be better about cleaning. She wondered if Charles would be insulted if she asked him to dust once in a while.

"What do you mean, absolutely not? Brenn, this is ridiculous."

"I mean exactly that. It's not like I'm adopting her or going to be her new mom. I've been wanting to give back to our community anyways, and taking a desperate teenager who just learned she has magic under my wing seems like a great way to do that." Brenn fist-pumped discretely. Playing up the commu-nity angle always got Noelle. And it was doubly great because Brenn actually meant what she said. It wasn't solely a convenient argument. "She needs an experienced adult to help her, so she's going to stay with me, and I will help her figure out her magic. This is not a situation for you to negotiate. This is what is happening. She doesn't have anyone else."

Noelle was silent for a minute, and there was more soft

conversation in the background. With suspicion, Brenn asked, "Do you have me on speakerphone? Is that Jasmine?"

"It is. I thought it would be helpful to get her perspective since she would be affected too if we took the girl in for a few days until we could get her home."

Brenn closed her eyes as she *listened* to her sister. There was a sliver of a gap in Noelle's resolve. Holding the phone away from her face, she hummed through a scale until she found the right resonance to push into that gap. She drew a circle bisected by a vertical line over her lips and whispered 'authority'. The spell didn't feel as powerful as it should, but she hoped it would be enough. Pulling her shoulders back, she put a little steel in her voice. "She isn't going to stay with you. Besides, you have five kids and a wife to think about, and, as you love to remind me, I have no responsibilities but myself. I am a good option. And Nono, I am not budging on this."

"But—"

"Noelle, it's not like you'll never see us. You can keep an eye on how she's progressing *when I invite you to*. You live barely a half mile away." With another circular gesture in the air and a whispered 'agree', Brenn pressed on. "This is a practical plan. You can call me again in forty-eight hours to check in, okay?"

"Well, I guess I hear that you aren't going to change your mind," Noelle said, a hint of superiority in her voice. "I will be calling you on Thursday. I expect you to be available."

Wanting to get her off the phone, Brenn valiantly managed to let Noelle's demand roll off her back. "Fine, I'll talk to you on Thursday, goodbye." She hung up before Noelle could say goodbye herself.

Since Brenn could remember, Noelle had been the perfect child. When they were kids, she always did her homework directly after school and never forgot to turn it in. She practiced her clarinet every day. She had immaculate adult-like manners when talking to their parents' friends and clients. Following graduation, Noelle went to the University of Michigan, left with a master's in education, and, after only two years of teaching, landed the position of principal of West Pleasant Middle School. A couple of years after that, she started dating Jasmine Hughes, the daughter of family friends, and two years later married her. A passel of adorable children followed: Isadora and Conner, their now thirteen-year-old twins, nine-year-old Savannah, five-year-old Willa, and finally Theodore, now three years old, who completed their family.

With their parents on the road so often running their seminars, Noelle had taken her role as the eldest sibling a little too seriously, acting with authority more suited to a parent than a sister. When she came back after finishing college, she had a hard time accepting that her sisters weren't small children anymore. There was less friction between her and Cleo, as Cleo lived at home while she attended Briar Vale Community College, and Noelle was present for her transition into adulthood. Brenn, however, was leaving for MSU right as Noelle was moving back into town, and her older sister seemed unwilling to think of her as anything but a feckless teenager. Brenn sometimes wished she had lived up to the reputation Noelle created for her in her head. At least it would have been fun.

Whatever. She'd worry about Noelle later. Much later.

A laugh rang out from the living room. She bit back a smile. Audrey had found the trick to her miniatures.

"Figured it out?"

Audrey startled at her question but grinned at her. "These are amazing. Did you make them?"

"Some. I did enchant them all myself though." On every flat surface, there was at least one miniature scene. The coffee table had a slab of amethyst upon which a woman in a ball gown spun while a snake danced around her in the opposite direction. The half bookshelf next to her armchair had two miniatures on each shelf and three more on top. One featured a group of people trying to pull a gigantic monster from a lake and toppling over when the rope broke, just to be reset and do it all over again. There was a tiny astronaut that zoomed around on a comet, a grandmother baking cookies and shooing teeny mice away from her tiny oven, a Sasquatch stomping through a shopping mall, lemons that fell from a twisted tree to roll on the fake grass to spell out 'you're the best'. Brenn was extremely proud of the enchantment she built for them—if a person complimented them out loud, the animation would be triggered and complete five full loops before stopping.

She was a little sad to realize the only other people to see them in all their glory were her Auntie Violet and the woman who fixed her chimney. Those kinds of thoughts always made her feel too small inside her body, like she would evaporate into thin air if she admitted the loneliness she felt sometimes.

"Can you show me how you make them move someday?"

"Sure thing. You want to go upstairs and pick out a bedroom now?"

"Yes!" Audrey scooped up her backpack as they crossed the foyer again.

Brenn showed her her own bedroom, in the tower room with the stained glass crescent moon, the room Charles and Mayhew shared next to hers, and then the two spare bedrooms at the back of the house that shared a bathroom between them. Audrey chose Cleo's old room, still sporting a night sky mural across the ceiling. The bed had a diaphanous chiffon canopy that Cleo had bedazzled when she was eight so it sparkled in the nightlight she had always turned on before bed.

Stifling a yawn, Audrey flopped down onto the mattress. Oh. It was late afternoon, and the poor girl had had an emotional day. Brenn tactfully gave her an out. "Why don't you take a shower, and then we can put sheets on, and you can take a nap if you want. I can whip up a quick dinner when you're ready."

Audrey mumbled a yes as she got up and rummaged in her backpack, and the bathroom door clicked shut behind her.

~

WHEN SHE EMERGED in a cloud of steam (an hour later—Brenn hoped her water heater was up for the task of a teen in the house again), Audrey looked decidedly perkier. She asked Brenn where to leave her dirty laundry and then caught the corner of the sheet Brenn tossed to her. As they made the bed, Brenn jumped right in.

"So magic. Magic is partly a specific kind of energy that works throughout the world in its own way and partly innate understanding of how to communicate with and use that energy. Magic just is. It does stuff by itself, and it can be manipulated also.

"You've known people who are naturally good at things? Some people call it beginners luck, or talent, or if you are really good at doing the thing, prodigy. In magical parlance, we refer to that as affinity. Some unconscious part of you is in tune with magical energy in that specific way." She smoothed a thin quilt over the bed. Tossing a pillowcase to Audrey, she proceeded to wrestle the other one onto a plump feather pillow.

"You become a witch when you start to learn how to intentionally use magical energy. And there are a lot of different ways to communicate with magical energy. Like when you go to make an apple pie, maybe you peel your apples in long strips with a paring knife, or use an apple peeler machine, or slice the apple and then peel each chunk, or if you have serious chaotic energy, just throw them in unpeeled. Some techniques are more refined or require more effort or must be done in a certain sequential order, but as long as you get a reliable end result that everyone's okay with, it doesn't really matter."

"So that's like spells and stuff?"

"Exactly. A spell is like a recipe, or choreography, or a song. And sometimes it's like muscle memory, and you do the thing without consciously thinking about it." She glanced around the room to see what was missing. Hangers. Audrey needed a few hangers for the closet in her room.

As Brenn went out to the hallway closet, Audrey leaned around the doorframe. "In your lying room? With the lights? Why don't you use a spell for it?"

"Because magic takes energy and the machine is easier. Look, it's like laundry—I'm perfectly capable of washing all my clothes by hand and hanging them to dry, but it takes a hell of a lot more effort and time and space than just using the washer and dryer. Tools are a good thing." She handed the hangers to Audrey. "After dinner, let's make a list of what we need to pick up for you tomorrow."

BRENN COULDN'T REMEMBER the last time she'd enjoyed making a meal as much as her first homemade dinner with Audrey. They had a great time talking about easy things, like their favorite TV shows and if it would be easier to escape a vampire or a werewolf. Wiping tears of laughter from her eyes as Audrey claimed she absolutely would give herself heavy metal poisoning to take a werewolf down with her if the circumstances were that dire, Brenn surprised herself by asking if she wanted to learn an easy spell. "I think you probably could manage lighting a candle."

"Seriously?" Audrey sat up perfectly straight, practically vibrating with eagerness.

Brenn tossed a wadded-up napkin at her. "Yeah, seriously. That's the point of you being here."

"I guess a part of me didn't think you were for real? But I definitely, definitely want to learn," she assured her.

"K, come on." Brenn led her into the backyard. Twilight made the garden feel mysterious, heavy with possibility. And honestly, atmosphere can adjust a spellcaster's frame of mind very effectively, and Brenn wanted to stack the deck in Audrey's favor. There were a couple of votives still in the lanterns lining the small stone patio next to the house. "So you need to feel like you are *in* your body. Do some jumping jacks or something to get your heart rate up."

While Audrey leapt haphazardly around the yard, Brenn shoved the patio chairs and table out of the way. She sat criss-cross-applesauce on the stone, putting two votives in front of her. "All right, that's enough jumping. Come sit down."

She took deep breaths until Audrey started to mimic her. "Feeling alive? I want you to take that feeling and visualize compressing it into a single point on the wick of the candle. When you think you've got it solidly, snap your fingers over the wick and tell it to light." Audrey drew in an excited breath as Brenn demonstrated with one candle.

It was a full two minutes before Audrey said, "Light!" Unfortunately, it wasn't the candle wick that went up in flame but a leaf that had blown between them.

"Whoops," Brenn said, making a plucking gesture to extinguish the fire. "Did you get distracted at the end by the leaf?"

Shamefaced, Audrey admitted it. "I thought about it at the last second, I'm sorry!"

"That's why we're out here, where there's less to immediately damage. The fact you could even produce the fire is a great first step. Try again." Over her next four tries, she set another leaf, Brenn's cuff, and two weeds aflame.

"Ugh, why can't I do it? I see it but it. Won't. Go!" Her voice raised in frustration.

"Hey, this is the first time you've ever tried to use magic on purpose." Brenn tapped the girl's knee with a finger. "Let's try it backwards. I'll light the candle, and you draw the fire from the wick to put it out. Imagine pulling the flame off the candle and it falling apart in the air as you do it."

She lit one candle and tapped it closer to Audrey. Brenn's eyes crinkled at the corners watching Audrey scrunch her face up in concentration.

"Okay, okay. Fire out," she said under her breath. "I can do this."

And she did.

Staring at her fingers in disbelief, she looked at Brenn. "Yes! Do it again?"

They practiced it over and over until Audrey could extinguish the flame almost as soon as Brenn had it lit. "Now, try lighting it again. Could you feel the magic in your fingers when you put the fire out?"

"Yeah, it, like, buzzed? Like when you vacuum a big room, and you can still feel the vibrations after you're done."

"Exactly. I want you to focus on that feeling and on lighting the wick at the same time. It should be easier now that you know what it feels like."

Audrey snapped her fingers and whispered, "light." And both candles lit at the same time. Her eyes shining, she beamed at Brenn. She practiced lighting and then dousing the candles until full dark fell and Brenn made her go to bed.

CLEANING up the last bits of their dinner mess, in her quiet house, Brenn tried to untangle her feelings. There was pride that Audrey took to the spell work so rapidly, and a weird satisfaction at having another person in the house, glee that she'd be able to prove Noelle wrong, relief that she could still light a damn candle, and wrapped all around that, fear. Fear that she would fail as soon as Audrey needed to be taught magic that was more than muscle memory Brenn had developed as a kid. Fear that she would screw the girl up more, fear that she would disappoint her, fear that Noelle was actually right, that her family had been right about her her whole life, that she herself just wasn't *enough*. Fear that she hadn't thought this through, was insane to have invited a vagrant teenager to live in her house, and that all these feelings were happening too quickly. And worst of all, the deepest, strangest panic that if she failed, Audrey would be taken away from her, and it would somehow feel like missing a limb.

She ran her fingers over the list they had made together, her handwriting spiky and impatient, Audrey's round and hopeful. Well, she would have to make sure she didn't fail.

Yep. Simple.

AUTUMN at last showed her face on Wednesday morning. Or at least poked a fingertip around the door. The morning was sunny, with the barest thread of chilliness weaving through the air. And then, breaking the fragile magic, there was a cacophony of crashes and a very annoyed "damnit, ow, yuck yuck *yuck*!"

Brenn wheeled a very dusty ten-speed bike out of the garage, an air pump tucked under her arm. She let the bike tumble into the grass and frantically picked cobweb remnants off her face and shirt. Gross. Spiders were so *gross*. Yeah, she knows they're helpful. Whatever. They were still supremely gross. Especially when a tower of boxes Brenn swore hadn't been there minutes before tipped what seemed like several years' worth of old webs directly on her head. She was extremely grateful she had tied a scarf around her hair before she went digging in the dark recesses of her garage.

"Blech," she made a gagging motion, slamming the porch door open to go get a rag to wipe the bike down. And possibly a flamethrower to clean out the spiders in the garage. Audrey sat at the island, a glass of orange juice in front of her. She was pressing her lips tightly together, clearly trying to not ask annoying questions as Brenn stomped into the house. "Do you need help with anything?" she asked carefully.

Brenn growled a bit as she stomped down the hall.

It took several minutes for Brenn to clean herself off, and then she grabbed a couple rags from the basket under the sink. She gave one to Audrey as she walked back through the kitchen. "Can you ride a bike?" she asked.

"Yeah. Not fast, but I can stay up." Audrey drained her juice and hopped up to follow her.

Out in the yard, Brenn got her rag wet with the hose. "Good. We need to wipe this down and fill the tires, and voila! You have a bike."

Audrey paused on the doorstep. "Wait."

Brenn stopped wiping the bike frame. "I have an extra helmet and a bike lock. I wouldn't let you ride without protecting your head."

Audrey shook her head. "No, I mean, I've never had a bike of my own. Do I need to wait for you before I use it?"

"What? No, not after we get you a map of town so you don't get lost. Which we are going to do this morning." She pushed the kickstand down. "Finish wiping this off while I get my bike and our helmets out."

A mere ten minutes later they were cruising down the street towards downtown Briar Vale. "Is there anything you wanted to add to the list?" Brenn called to Audrey as they pedaled.

"Can we stop at a bookstore? I want a book about being a witch, and maybe a book about this town too. If that's okay?"

"Sure. Bellwether Books is probably the best place for that. We can do that first."

Bellwether was the largest bookstore Briar Vale had. Audrey cupped her hands around her eyes and peered through the window while they waited for the shop to open. The sunlight slanting through the huge windows made the blonde wood shelves gleam, highlighting the rainbow of spines on each one. "This looks great. Do you think they will have both things?"

"I'm confident," Brenn said, snapping the lock closed on their bikes. She handed Audrey a small key. "Here. We'll need to get you a keychain too."

Audrey shoved the key in her pocket. "Thanks. Hey, what is that noise? Is there like a wind chime store around here?"

"What? Why?" Brenn asked.

"I swear I've been hearing bells all morning."

"Bells? Really?" Brenn started to smile.

Audrey gave her a weird look. "Yeah, bells. What's going on?"

Brenn guided her into the middle of the sidewalk. "Close your eyes and start turning in a circle, slowly. When the bells get louder, stop."

If Audrey's eyebrows could have shot off her face, they would have. Brenn's smile widened. "I'm serious. Do it."

Audrey sighed and dutifully shut her eyes as she turned a half-step to her left.

"Whoa. They are louder that way." She opened her eyes and pointed down a crooked alley between buildings across the street.

Brenn nodded in satisfaction. "You're going to love this. Let's go." Audrey had to stop and spin and listen twice more before they came out to a tiny park tucked inside a block lined with buildings. There they found an intricately painted cart stuffed to the brim with books, a sign that said 'For Whom The Tome Tolls' stretching over the shelves, and a handful of bells tacked up around the inside edge of the roof, ringing busily.

Audrey breathed rather than asked, "*What?*"

"Mmhmm," Brenn replied. Once they got within a few steps, the bells abruptly silenced. Audrey stopped short. A soft groan greeted them as a tall black man unfolded himself from the captain's chair next to the cart. He stretched and yawned, and rubbing his hands briskly on his face, started talking. "Welcome to For Whom The Tome Tolls. The cart has decided that you in particular need—" he stopped as he looked at them directly for the first time. "Oh, hey, Brenn. Didn't expect this was for you."

"Arlo. Come on. I read." They both snorted a laugh. Audrey just stood between them, confused. "This is Arlo. Arlo, Audrey. She's looking for a couple books."

"Uh, hi," Audrey said, distracted. A book was slowly pushing itself out from the shelf and tumbled down to the counter that circled the cart. A small grey head peeked out of the open spot, chittered at Arlo, and disappeared back between books. Audrey's mouth hung open.

"What was that?" she asked with a horrified fascination.

"Something in between a gremlin and a pixie. They won't actually tell me what they call themselves or where they came from. So I call them Gary, Larry, Sherry, Merry, Harry, Barry, Terry, Fuzz, Thurston, Vivica, and Kevin." He tapped each corresponding cart creature shown in a photograph that was taped to the side of a shelf as he rattled off the names. "Vivica named themself."

Audrey made a choking noise.

Arlo picked up the book that Gary or Merry or Thurston had pushed off the shelf and held it out to her. "*Fundamentals of Witchcraft*, huh? Baby witch?"

She stood there, dumbly looking from the book to Arlo to the cart. Brenn laughed again. "The cart is sentient and knows when someone needs a specific book. The cart creatures get Arlo and let him know where to go, and the bells call the recipient until they come pick up their book."

"What?" She barely noticed as Arlo put the book in her hands. "The cart is sentient? That means it's alive?"

"Well, kind of. It doesn't need sustenance or much besides someone to keep it in working order and to wheel it around." Arlo stroked the smooth wooden counter. The cart shook a little and made a noise like a purr. It gave Brenn the impression it was preening. "It is very affectionate, though."

Audrey gaped. "What?" she asked again. "I mean, how? I mean, this is amazing."

Arlo chuckled. "No idea how. It just showed up one day, and here we are fifteen years later." He cocked his head to the side. There was a faint pounding noise. "Sounds like your order has another couple of books." He walked them around the cart, where two more books stood out several inches from their shelves. "We've got a *History of Modern Witchcraft* and *The Mystic Arts for Interested Parties*. Wait...and...*Briar Vale: A Compendium*."

He tapped a little door set into the bottom shelf. Another tiny grey face poked out. "Is this the last one?" he asked, holding up the Briar Vale guide. A spindly grey arm swung around and pointed up over their heads. There was a sonorous chitter, and the door slammed shut. A pocket-size folded map shot off the cart and fell onto the ground. "Okay, that's the rest of your order. Do you want a bag?"

Brenn pulled a rolled-up shopping bag from one of her pockets. "We're good. You going to be at Spell Dev next week?"

"Are you?" He asked with a significant look. "Don't think I missed that you've skipped the last three."

"I actually just forgot the last one." He scoffed. "I promise you. I did skip the other two, though." She pulled a guilty face.

Audrey wandered to a nearby bench while they chatted, buried in her new books, shopping bag forgotten next to her. Arlo watched Brenn gaze at her and bumped into her to get her attention. He lifted his chin in her direction. "What's the story?"

"Lots of innate magical affinity. She's a foster kid, got kicked out for the last time, and managed to get here, thanks to Cleo's obsession with social media."

"Lucky. How did you end up with her?" His voice held a

healthy amount of skepticism that made Brenn bristle ever so slightly.

"Oh, thank you so much." He immediately started to apologize, but she waved it off. "Noelle tried to take charge of the situation. Howie was there. You can get all the gruesome details from him."

"Oh boy. Say no more."

"I wasn't planning to. You going to be here much longer?" Brenn asked over her shoulder as she went to get Audrey.

"Maybe an hour or two? For Whom still feels a little worked up, so we're likely getting another customer."

Brenn flashed him a thumbs up. Audrey stopped trying to unfold her map and turned her attention to him. "Thank you for the books. Did Brenn pay for them, or do I need to?"

"It's taken care of. Enjoy them, and if you have a burning need for any more, I'll see you then." He gave her a wave as he settled back into his chair.

～

AS THEY WALKED BACK out to the street proper, Audrey kept picking at a string hanging off the handle of her bag. "Brenn? How much do I owe you for the books? I brought the money I have, so I can give it to you now."

Brenn had started to turn right out of the alley but abruptly turned left instead at Audrey's question. "I've got you covered. But thanks for reminding me there is one more thing we have to do before shopping."

At first glance, the Briar Vale City Hall didn't even look like a municipal building. The brick was a strange yellow-grey color. The main entrance was a set of Dutch doors, which were half open in the balmy morning. On either side of the doors, there were three deep-set bay windows, punctuated with two tall, very skinny windows between. Two wings stretched off to the left and right, also with bay windows, which gave the impression the building was undulating. The deep grey-green roof sported dozens of bronze dragon statuary, each with a light patina.

Brenn led Audrey to an office on the first floor. The person at the desk glanced up at them with interest, holding a finger up in a 'wait a minute' gesture as they finished a phone call. "Hello! What can I do for you ladies this morning?"

"We need to set up my friend's financials."

"Great! The new account forms are on the table in the hall. Fill it out completely and bring it back when you're finished." They picked up the phone receiver again.

"Oh, sorry, no, I need to put her on mine. She's not sixteen yet." Brenn leaned to the side as Audrey tugged on her shirt sleeve.

"Brenn, I don't think you should put me on your bank account," she whispered urgently.

Now Brenn looked confused. "This isn't a bank." This was obviously City Hall, so why would Audrey think—oh. Account. Right. Briar Vale was not like the normal world. She explained to Audrey in a hushed voice. "We do things a little differently here. Every business in town charges to our individual accounts, so we don't have to use physical money. At the end of the year, this office does an audit to see where things need balancing and who might need extra assistance, that kind of thing."

She squeezed Audrey's arm. "I'm adding you to my account so you don't have to worry about money. You might think you're on your own, but I volunteered to take care of you while you're here. That includes getting you the things you need. Clothes and toiletries and supplies, of course, but also a little autonomy."

"No, that's too much. I couldn't—"

"It isn't, and you definitely can. When you turn sixteen, we'll come back and set you up with your own account, and then you can fully manage the responsibility of being a citizen. Now fill out this section." She pointed to a bit on the form.

After the clerk scanned the form, they presented Audrey with a shiny plastic card. Her name and line drawing likeness of her face were printed on the dark purple card in raised gold foil. "Fancy." She held it up next to her face, and Brenn gave her a silly quiet golf clap.

~

FOUR HOURS LATER, Audrey had enough clothes to get her through the week, some rudimentary spell-casting supplies, and a newly cut key to the Moon House. Brenn went down the list they made last night, checking off the last couple of items. She checked her watch. "I need to make a couple of deliveries this afternoon. Do you think you'll be okay on your own for an hour or two?"

"I guess? Should I go back to your house?"

"You can, you have a key now. But you can hang out downtown as long as you want. Let me see your map." Pulling a pen out of her pocket, Brenn marked a few spots on the map. "So that one is the Moon House, that's Witchery Aesthetica, and that one is my friend Dani's shop. Her daughter is a year ahead of you." School. She would definitely have to get Audrey in school. She paused, considering her afternoon. "Yeah, no, we'll enroll you in school tomorrow."

Audrey curled her lip in disgust. "Can't we wait until I'm more settled?"

"Nice try. The semester started yesterday, so if we get you in tomorrow, you'll only have missed two days." She flagged another location on the map. "That star marks the best candy shop in town. We will talk about your spending limits on my account later, but right now, go get a sickening amount of sweets. Tonight we can binge a trashy TV show and gorge ourselves."

Audrey tried to grimace, but the lure of sugar was greater than her resolve. "Fine." She stretched the word into several syllables in the way teens are particularly skilled at.

Brenn just shook her head. She watched until Audrey turned the corner, then she pulled up her list for the day. Three of her clients were downtown, and their orders were small enough that she had been able to stuff them in the pockets of her cargo pants. If she could get these done in the next hour, she would have enough time to finish the ones she'd need the truck for before dinner time.

BRENN'S BUSINESS was called Lost Seas Procurement and Persuasion. She had a particular knack for finding items that were difficult to locate, or discovering the specific reason that would persuade a person to do what she wanted. She had started a proto-version of the business when she was a teenager, finding spell components for her neighbors and convincing other kids' parents to let them stay out late or teachers to give extra time on assignments. That version had blossomed into a thriving business after she'd graduated from college. A few years after opening officially, Brenn had been so busy she had to limit her clients to local residents only. Even with that limitation, her schedule was almost always full.

Her last order downtown was a serenity charm for Brian Conrad, who functioned as a sort of public mediator/peacekeeper, since Briar Vale had no police force. Mostly he dealt with out-of-town visitors behaving badly. Brenn found him on the street across from Summit Park, standing there between two tourists sniping at each other. He was a tall, square-ish white man with an impeccably groomed Ron Swanson mustache and an impassive look on his face. Brenn watched his blinks get longer and longer as the tourists kept talking over each other; the last one held for a full count of six. He said something to the one on his right and asked a question of the one on his left, which set them off yelling again. She caught his eye, held the packet up between two fingers, and waggled her eyebrows. His mustache wiggled ever so slightly. She motioned to the door next to her with a jerk of her thumb and went inside.

The Curio Cabinet was one of her regular clients, so she was intimately acquainted with much of their inventory, but she always enjoyed poking around to see if there was anything new on their shelves. Brenn waved hello to the woman behind the counter, who gave her a quick smile over the head of the customer she was assisting. Brenn made it through the entire left side of the store before Brian arrived.

"Hey, Brenn, sorry about that." His eyes looked tired. "I will be so happy when the first of November gets here."

Briar Vale was a popular destination all year round, with its quaint downtown oozing with charm and picture-perfect weather no matter the season. They did have a few times throughout the year when the steady stream of tourists eased, like the handful of days immediately following Halloween.

"Don't worry about it." Brenn handed him the paper-wrapped charm. "The instructions are on the inside of the wrapper, so don't toss it." She studied him for a minute. "Maybe you need a vacation, or to hire some help, instead of relying on charms and potions."

Brian sighed. "In a perfect world. I set up a meeting with the mayor about amending town funds to get me additional help, but Mayor Ackerman really isn't interested in change."

Brenn made commiserating noises and offered a few other suggestions before taking her leave. She was heading back to her bike when she started hearing bells tinkling. Dammit, no. She didn't even want to know what the cart had for her. She ignored the ringing and walked faster.

Somehow the bells kept getting louder. And now they sounded like someone calling her name in a deep voice she was all too acquainted with.

Arlo caught up with her, and in the sudden silence, she blushed. Face hot, she whirled around and held her hand out wordlessly. He put two slim books in her hands, not saying a word. She shoved them in her bag.

He made a gesture somewhere between a wave and a salute and pushed the cart past her.

Once he was out of sight, she dug the books back out of her bag. The top one wasn't much of a surprise, *You and Your Teen Witch*, but the bottom book, oh no. Gaping in horror, she stared at the cover, which blared *Managing and Mending Your Middle-aged Magic* for just anyone to see. "Middle-aged?!" she screeched.

She clapped a hand over her mouth, scanning the street to see if anyone had heard. By some miracle, Brenn had the sidewalk to herself. She hid the books away again, her face burning in absolute mortification.

Five

STIFLING A YAWN, Brenn glared at the slim book sitting so innocently on her kitchen island in the watery predawn light. She was so irritated at For Whom's jab she had barely slept last night. She was *thirty-six*, for crying out loud. Middle-aged, her ass.

But that goddamned cart was never wrong.

"Fine," she whispered viciously. She skimmed a chapter of flowery garbage about embracing the changes she was going through, gave up, and flipped to the table of contents. There was a chapter about mindset, one on proper practices, one on tools and methods, blah blah. She ran her finger down the list until she hit 'Stifled Spellwork.' Perfect.

The beginning of the chapter was all meditation, which Brenn needed no help with, thank you very much. That's what the lying room was for. She turned the pages until she found an actual exercise to try, a path to find the source of her block so she knew what she was dealing with. It was an easily prepared tea that apparently performed best at sunrise. That worked out nicely.

She put the kettle on. She dropped the mint leaves that were the base of the tincture into three separate teacups. Running her finger down the page, she mouthed the instructions. Boiling water, mint leaves, three slices of fresh ginger with a word that represented what might be stymieing her magic, and an incantation—easy enough. She grabbed a knife and collected a knob of ginger from the pantry.

Every single thought she ever had flew out of her head the minute she put the tip of the knife to the ginger slice. How was she supposed to articulate what might be affecting her magic when she had no idea in the first place? The sun was almost peeking over the horizon, so she hurriedly carved the words 'self', 'family', and 'health' into her ginger and tossed them in the teacups. That would cover a good range of possibilities.

She had to let it steep for five full minutes while speaking an intention for clarity three times, once over each cup. Then, facing east, she'd have a swallow of each one, and whichever tasted like only ginger was the root of her issues.

She took a sip of one, then the other, and the third. Huh. All tasted the same. She tried sipping in the opposite order. Tasted the same. She speed sipped, one two three. Same.

Brenn scowled. She tipped the dregs down the drain and quickly washed the cups. As she was drying the last one, she heard Audrey ambling down the stairs. Reaching over the island, she opened a drawer and swept the book in. She definitely did not need Audrey seeing that book.

"Morning," Audrey said, bleary-eyed. "Can I have some cereal?"

"Sure. Orange juice?" Brenn tossed three different boxes of cereal on the island, pointed to the cupboard with her bowls, and grabbed the juice and the milk. Charles scurried onto the counter, sitting a respectful distance away so he could watch Audrey eat.

"Is this an okay outfit to wear? I didn't know if there was a dress code." She slid off the stool so Brenn could see her whole body. Her hair was pulled into a ponytail, and she had paired a tee that had a constellation of grinning stars with grey pants that hung loose on her frame.

"I'm pretty sure that's fine, especially for your first day. You got your backpack ready? You want to pack a lunch or get one at school?"

"Get one, please," Audrey said through a mouthful of cereal. She picked a piece out of her bowl and slid it across to Charles. He chittered his thanks and ran into the dining room to eat it.

"Use your account card, but it should mostly be covered by the school. I'm going to go change, and then we'll head out." Audrey gave her a thumbs up.

BRIAR VALE HIGH SCHOOL was a ten-minute walk from the Moon House. Brenn chose it for Audrey mostly because it was closest and she had matriculated there herself, but also, her friend Daniela's daughter attended there and was only a year older than Audrey.

"Hello," she said cheerfully to the woman behind the front counter. "This is Audrey Vega, and we need to enroll her today."

The woman bustled up and gave Brenn a stack of forms to fill out. "Hi, Audrey. Can you please put your hands on mine so I can verify a few things?" She clicked her mouse several times, then pulled a small microphone out of a drawer and set it on the counter.

Outstretching her hands, she waited for Audrey to step forward. "Okay. This is the record of Audrey Vega, new student, birthdate...April 26, 2008. Born...Royal Oak, Michigan. Ah, a novice. Entering as a sophomore. Recommended for craft exploration elective classes and student alliance buddy program."

Brenn and Audrey stared at her. "Oh, dears, that's my knack. No need to be afraid. I only get a bit about a person, birthdate and place, that kind of thing." She held her hand out to Brenn, who put her own out slowly. "Let's see, September...25. Mid-eighties." She winked conspiratorially. "Happy birthday a couple weeks early!"

"Thanks," Brenn responded weakly. The woman beamed at her.

"So, Audrey, next door is our school counselor. He can help you choose your classes, get you a building map, and set you up with a student buddy. When you are finished with that, come back, and I'll have your student ID ready, okay?"

Audrey nodded. "I guess I'll see you after school."

Brenn squeezed Audrey's hand. She felt her shaking a bit. It had been a long time since she had been surrounded by strangers, but Brenn could remember keenly how nerve-wracking it could be. She felt a rush of sympathy, but not wanting to embarrass Audrey, she tried to play it cool. "Do you want me to walk back here to pick you up?"

"No, I'm alright." She waved awkwardly as she walked out of the office.

"They grow up so fast."

Brenn jumped a little as the woman behind her spoke. She had forgotten she wasn't alone in the office.

"I wouldn't know, actually. She just started staying with me a couple days ago." She ignored the silent question posed by the woman's raised eyebrows. "Is there anything else I have to do?"

"Nope! The school day ends at 2:30. We'll send her home with a student handbook, which you should probably also look over, and next Monday, there's an activities fair. We encourage parents and guardians to come with their students for that event." She slid a card with a list of dates to Brenn. "It's the second item on this calendar. Feel free to call us anytime if you have questions!"

Brenn heard the dismissal and did her own awkward wave as she left.

INSTEAD OF WALKING STRAIGHT HOME, Brenn went to the Pink Petal, a coffee shop that was two blocks past her street. She had desperate need of a gigantic cup of sugar and caffeine and maybe a croissant sandwich. For protein. Not because she was lazy and didn't want to make her own breakfast.

How could that have only taken fifteen minutes? She thought about the six hours she had before Audrey got home, mildly confused at how that was so much time and yet so little simultaneously. Running through her to-do list, she started organizing what she wanted to get done in descending order. For Lost Seas, she had two pick-ups and a half dozen deliveries, including going back up to Aurora Orchards. Thursdays, she took Charles and Mayhew to Summit Park, but she wanted to wait for Audrey to do that. At least one more exercise from her book. Two would be better. She would be fine for the rest of September, but if Audrey needed help with homework further in the semester, Brenn needed to get her shit together and her magic fixed posthaste.

She chewed on the straw of her iced almond-caramel-chocolate latte, convinced she was forgetting something. She could feel whatever it was looming over her like a cloud of doom. Her phone rang. Noelle.

Yep, doom, in a cloud, no longer only looming.

"Good morning Noelle." She barreled on before Noelle could get more than a 'hello' out. "I am walking back home after enrolling Audrey at Briar Vale High. She is fine and healthy. I added her to my account, she has the things she needs for the time being, Charles and Mayhew love her already. What else? Oh, she took Cleo's old room. I think she liked the sky mural."

Noelle got two words in before Brenn kept going. "Right, I'm going to get her a pediatrician—they still see pediatricians, right? Until eighteen?"

"Yes, Brenn. Though you can take her to your physician if you want. What about—"

"She also has a map and a bike. With a helmet."

"That's all great, but I still think you are not the best fit for her. I've been in touch with our child protection services here since Audrey does have magic. There are several suitable homes here in Briar Vale where she could stay, or we could look in Birch Grove. Or farther, if she doesn't want to stay in Michigan."

"I...come on. You can't be..." Brenn sputtered to a stop and clenched her teeth, livid at her sister's overstep. She ground her jaw, grasping for the right words to make Noelle understand. "Are you doing all this because I made a choice without giving a PowerPoint presentation to convince you it's a good idea? Noelle, I'm a stone's throw from forty. I have a suitable home. I can look after a largely independent teenager."

"Of course you're capable of it, but Brenn, I simply have more experience than you." Ooh, she hated when Noelle used her placating-parents voice. She bit the inside of her cheek to keep from being snotty as Noelle kept going.

"I don't want to upset you anymore, so I'll check in with you at the beginning of next week. Good job getting her in school, though maybe we should think about moving her to Fairweather High. It would be a lot easier for me to keep an eye out if she was just down the street."

"Nope. Thanks, Noelle, talk to you next week, bye!" At least Brenn enjoyed her new style of signing off conversations with her sister. Just plowing through and promptly hanging up was going to save her so much time.

AFTER CONSOLING the disappointed Charles Mayhew that she had arrived home alone, Brenn reluctantly retrieved *Middle-Aged* from the drawer. The book fell open in her hand, displaying practices to increase casting strength. She certainly wasn't opposed to that.

This one had her put items of increasing energy into charged circles on the floor and attempt to lift them out of the circles one at a time. There were plenty of things to choose from in her storage room, and a full hour slipped away from her as she rummaged. She looked at her watch and cursed under her breath. She tossed her supplies on the rug in the foyer. Mayhew goofily hopped over with a stick of chalk held in one foot. "Thanks," she said as she took it from him. "Okay, fellas. You guys need to back up a bit." They both sat on the edge of the console table, watching her like two very adorable gargoyles.

She flipped the rug half up and sat on it, drawing circles on the hardwood floor in front of her. In the first circle, she put a blank slip of paper. No particular energy at all from that. Nodding, she felt good about that one. Next was a downy white feather, then a quartz tumble, dried beetles, a freshly picked dandelion, and a sliver of dragon scale calcite. She had brought out a tiny jar filled with rain that had previously been part of a rainbow, but that was difficult to collect with precision. If something went wrong, she didn't want to lose it recklessly.

She got up to put it back in the store room.

She flopped back down, squirming around until she scooched the rug into a more comfortable position. Propping it up on one of her boots, she squinted at the book's instructions for charging a circle. She couldn't remember the last time she had cast a containment. Ghosts and spirits and such were not her bag. She carefully followed the directions listed. There was a faint 'ting' as the first circle charge snapped into place. Five more followed in quick succession.

The book was a little vague on how exactly to pull the items through the barriers. She wasn't sure if she should try to break the circle or create an opening. Staring into the air, she absent-mindedly twirled one of her curls around her finger. Mayhew clacked his beak to get her attention, then tapped it on the small tea tin on the table next to him. Oh, brilliant, she thought. A few months ago, Elise had taught Spell Dev members a precision summoning spell that moved objects by weaving the air under them. That might work.

She hummed an incantation to lift the slip she had placed in the first circle. The paper rose slowly. Brenn moved her fingers as if she were braiding the air, building a bridge for the paper to hop through the circle's boundary. Her motions got tighter and smaller as she concentrated. "Yes," she hissed through her clenched teeth. "Come on, break the circle." The paper started to crumple in on itself. It bounced against the invisible edge of the field. She kept her fingers steadily moving, trying to infuse more power into her bridge. There was a slight crackling sound, and then the crumpled ball of paper shot out of the circle and across the room.

Brenn threw her head back and cackled dramatically. The cart was never wrong. She flexed her fingers with a cascade of popping noises and wiggled back into position. Starting all over again with the feather, she lifted it from the floor, braided the air, and pushed her will into the bridge she created. The edges of the feather singed a little as it began to breach the barrier of the circle. By the time she got it fully out, it was burning. She plucked the fire out. The book hadn't had a warning about things catching on fire in the process, but she did go rogue by powering the bridge with extra magic.

The solidity of the quartz added a new difficulty. She had to braid even more tightly to keep the rock from dipping towards the floor and probed the circle for a thin spot. Brenn's teeth felt like they were buzzing inside. The quartz violently slammed against the circle's edge and then exploded into bits of burning coal. The other three items followed in sudden succession, scorching the hardwood. She jumped, her leg colliding with the empty first circle, which caused a percussive blast of air that rolled her backward into the wall. She lay there stunned for a second, then frantically twisted around to make sure Charles Mayhew were fine.

They were watching her placidly from the safety of the top of the mirror. She let her head thump on the floor. "What am I going to do?" she moaned, her voice muffled by the rug. "I am not giving Noelle the satisfaction of being right about me."

Charles patted her ear with his paw, chirping at her. She lifted her head. "Yeah, they'd take Audrey away." He ran in a tight circle and chittered. "If I can't help her with her magic, there's no reason for her to stay."

Mayhew called from his perch on the mirror. "Make stay. Say yes. Fix witch."

"I'm trying, man. Give me a minute to clear this up, and we'll do a different chapter." She swiped her finger through each of her chalk circles to break their charge. The exploding items left a pile of grit on the floor. Maybe she should get the vacuum out.

Her phone vibrated in her pocket. Dropping the cloth she had put in her pocket to clean the marks from the floor, she hit answer and tucked it between her ear and shoulder. "Lost Seas, this is Brenn."

"Brenn? This is Nat, from your sister's store the other day?"

"Oh, hey. What can I help you find? Actually, hang on, let me get a form first." She scrambled up.

"I don't need anything. Well, I do, but not from your business." Brenn frowned. She switched her phone to her other ear as she sank into the foyer chair. Nat continued. "I was wondering if you would be interested in joining the coven I'm forming?"

"A coven?" Brenn had never even entertained the idea of joining a coven. Partially because she wasn't sure anyone would want her. Though it was known that casting as a coven increased each member's power. If those effects lasted, she might not even need to attempt more rituals from *Middle-Aged*. Putting the book away permanently was not a sad thought. She rolled the end of a curl in her fingers while she listened to Nat explain her plans.

"...and I've only been here a few months, but I miss casting with my old coven, so I thought I would start my own here. Ideally, I'd like seven witches, so five more besides you and me. I have three other people in mind. Do you have one or two friends who might be interested?"

Brenn bit her lip as she thought about it. Definitely not her sisters. Out of all the Spell Dev witches, she was the only one not in a coven already. Even Arlo belonged to one, and his brother Howie had never been into the whole thing. Maybe Dani would want to join; she had complained about the sad state of her social life the last time they had gone out together. "I think I have one person who is free and might be into that."

"Great! Will you ask if they will bring a friend too? I was thinking we should have an informal introduction meeting at my house in a week. Can you make it Thursday night?"

Brenn assured her she could make that work, and they discussed logistics for a few minutes more. After she hung up with Nat, she sank into the foyer chair. Mayhew sat delicately on her knee. "Say yes. Good girl," he said.

"*That's* what you were talking about? It would be nice if you would share things with me a little more explicitly." She picked an almond out from the stash she kept in her pocket and held it out to him.

"Coven, coven, coven," he repeated before carefully taking the almond. Charles chirped and spun around.

"Yeah, fellas, I guess I'm joining a coven." Brenn repeated it softly to herself. "I'm joining a coven."

Six

THE SMELL OF PENCIL SHAVINGS, apple crisp, and teenager washed over Brenn in a wave of nostalgia as she wound around the tables dotting the cafetorium. She and her sisters all had attended Briar Vale High, as had their parents and grandparents, and so on throughout her family tree. She had performed on the stage on the far end in the yearly talent show and eaten lunch every day in the cafeteria half of the room. She hadn't been back since she'd graduated, yet it still smelled exactly the same, even if everything was smaller than she remembered.

Daniela leaned over to give her a hug as she reached the table. "So, friend, I hear you have some news to share with me? A full week after the fact?"

"I know, I know." Brenn handed her a container with some of the chocolate molasses cookies she and Audrey made the day before. "Here, a peace offering."

"Yes, you *can* buy my love." Dani immediately opened the container and took a huge bite of a cookie. "But seriously, how did this happen? You just decided, hey, I want to house a wayward teen, sounds like fun?" A few sugar crystals flew into the air as she mumbled around her treat.

Daniela Flores-McCormick was the proprietor of Phoenix Apothecary and Brenn's closest friend. They had met in a professional capacity first—Brenn going on a chaotic goose-chase for a cord of raspberry wood Dani swore she needed immediately for potion making. Brenn was sure she would hate the woman on sight, but her breezy charm won Brenn over instead. They had become fast friends that day.

She thought back. It had been more than two weeks since she'd last talked to Dani, unusual for them. The beginning of the school year was always busy, but she knew she was avoiding Dani because of the weirdness with her magic. She squeezed her friend's arm. "I'm sorry. I haven't been around much the last couple weeks. And now you know the reason."

Brenn glanced around the room, looking for Audrey. She pointed. "So the redhead over there with Lydia is Audrey, which I'm sure you already know." Lydia was Dani's only child and very close with her parents as a result. "Cleo called me down to Witchery last Tuesday because she just wanted me to do the thing and get the girl's name. And then Noelle got under my skin, surprise, so I took Audrey to lunch and then somehow ended up moving her in with me."

"Ah, Noelle. Suddenly this makes so much more sense."

"Wow. That makes me sound like such an ass." To be fair, initially, she *had* acted so impulsively as a reflex to Noelle's blithe arrogance. "Honestly, I did take her to lunch because I was so annoyed at my sister. But then Audrey told me what had been going on, and, I don't know, I felt like helping her was the thing I was supposed to do."

"Well, Lydia likes her, so she can't be that bad."

"We've been getting along. She won Charles Mayhew over from the word hello." She grabbed a cookie for herself, narrowly avoiding Dani's slap at her hand. "I think the house likes her too. Oh, get this. Her second day, we were out getting her some more clothes and things, and For Whom the Tome

Tolls called her, like, immediately. You should have seen her face. Amazing."

"What an introduction. You both are settling in okay? You need any help, you can call me. I am an authority, you know, having lived with a teenager for the past three tumultuous years."

Brenn snorted. "Like Lydia isn't the most perfect child to ever exist."

Dani rolled her hand in a flourish, bowing in acknowledgement.

"I do have something I wanted to ask you, though." Dani raised one eyebrow. Brenn searched for the right words. She didn't often ask people for help, much less a favor as big as joining a magic circle that would be a lifelong commitment once it was sealed. Thinking about it that way in stark terms made her apprehensive herself, actually. She rushed the question out. "How do you feel about covens?"

Dani sat back in her chair. "That is not what I was expecting. I guess I like the idea of them? I've always been curious." She ran a fingernail along a groove in the container in front of her. "I'd probably go to an initial meeting, get a feel for the witches involved."

"Well, today's your lucky day! Or, at least, Thursday will be your lucky day!" Brenn did jazz hands.

"What are you on about?"

"I've been invited to join a coven, and the woman organizing it asked me to bring a friend along."

"You're serious?" Dani watched Lydia and Audrey giggling together at a booth for the Merfolk Appreciation Society. "She's not going to care I'm nearly fifty?"

"For crying out loud, you're forty-five, not a decrepit crone. Plus, who wouldn't want a crone in their coven? The institutional knowledge alone!"

Dani kicked the leg of her chair, and Brenn wobbled for a few seconds. "Okay, okay. I am serious. You are the only person I know who would be interested and doesn't already belong to one and is not one of my sisters."

"Brenn, you can be truly pathetic at times." She smiled to soften the comment. "But yeah, I am definitely coming with you. Do I need to bring anything?"

"I don't think so. Well. Actually. Do you know another witch who might want to join? I'm supposed to bring two people, but I'm coming up dry."

Dani pursed her lips, her eyes darting back and forth like she was reading a list. "I may have a lead. Who is this mystery woman with the open coven?"

"Her name is Nat. Let me give you her number." She fished Nat's card out. Brenn had transferred it from pocket to pocket every day, so it was always with her, like a good luck charm. It was embarrassing. She feigned nonchalance as she read the numbers off for Dani, but when she was done, she shoved it back into her pocket so quickly she bent the card in half.

THURSDAY NIGHT SAW her frantically texting Dani about what to wear to the first meeting of their potential coven. Audrey was lounging on Brenn's bed as she tossed outfits out of her closet. Audrey held up her phone. "Lydia says you should wear what is authentically you, so your new friends can see you at your most comfortable."

"Well, tell Lydia thanks for the advice, but I don't know if I should go strutting into Nat's house in a work jumpsuit with frayed cuffs and boots that have been beaten to hell and back." She grabbed her own phone as it pinged. Dani sent a photo of her outfit, which unsurprisingly was amazing. She dramatically fell face-first onto the bed. "Why isn't this any easier as a grown-up?" she shouted into the mattress.

Audrey gingerly patted her head. "I'm sure they aren't going to judge you. Cleo always says make your outside match your inside. Maybe you should text her?"

Brenn looked up. "I am not texting Cleo for help." Rolling off the bed, she grabbed the first thing under her hand. Olive green cargo pants. Could be worse. She shimmied into them, standing in her walk-in closet, and then put on a clean and minimally wrinkly button-down that had sunset-colored pastel stripes.

She cuffed the shirt right below her elbow and made one concession to vanity with a chunky hammered silver bracelet her aunt had given her last year for her birthday. "Good enough." She spun around for Audrey, arms out.

"Yeah, that's not bad. Don't wear your boots."

Brenn smacked her with a pillow before she left the room. Audrey's giggles followed her down the stairs.

RUNNING A FEW MINUTES BEHIND, Brenn parked on the street across from Nat's house. It was an elegant white stucco Creole-style cottage with black window casings and door and a black wrought iron rail on the second-floor balcony. The roof was covered in deep charcoal hexagonal shingles. A thin porch ran the entire length of the house, providing a bit of shelter to the front door, set between two floor-to-ceiling windows. Bright yellow-green vines twined up the posts of the porch from the garden cozied up against its stone floor. Warm yellow light shone from every window.

Every house on Garden Drive had a carpet of mosses and creeping thyme in place of traditional lawns, forming a patchwork of greens and purple that ran down the entire length of the street, punctuated with bright beds of late-blooming flowers. It was a pleasant contrast to the whites and greys and blacks of all the homes on the street. Nat's house was almost directly in the middle of the block.

The street lights flickered on as Brenn hurried up the front walk and knocked. Nat answered so quickly Brenn suspected she had been waiting right at the door. She blinked a few times at the t-shirt Nat wore, which featured a drawing of a praying mantis holding the headless body of a smaller mantis and the words 'dinner date?' in a word bubble. She hadn't formed any solid impressions of Nat, but she wasn't exactly expecting snarky dark humor after their first meeting. Though as she thought about it, maybe she should have. Anyone who could jump in the middle of a family argument, especially when her sisters were involved, had to be unconcerned with societal expectations. Laughter floated out from deep inside the house. Oh no. Brenn grimaced a bit. "Am I late?"

"Nope, you're right in the middle." Thankfully Nat was peering down the street and missed her flinch. "I got a text from your friend Daniela that she and Walker are going to be a few minutes still. Her daughter needed to be dropped off on their way. We're gathering in the sunroom. It's in the back, through the kitchen." She waved Brenn inside and stepped onto the porch to wait for the car approaching from the west.

Brenn left her shoes on the rug at the entry and wandered slowly through Nat's house. The house felt quietly austere in manner, unconcerned at the excitement Brenn could feel in the air. She had a view into a well-appointed living room decorated in black and gold and green, luxurious and well-lived in. To her left was a room with an enormous wooden desk on which a sleek computer rested and a green velvet chair rolled neatly underneath. Brenn felt a pang of envy at the contrast to her own cluttered office. Going through the office felt like violating Nat's privacy, so she went through the living room to the kitchen.

Nat had filled her living room with elegant, artful furniture that looked slightly scary to actually use, and layered so many textures throughout that it felt as though the room was twice as big as it really was. Three gigantic photographs filled one wall, a triptych of a ghostly-looking woman among trees in a dark forest, the curves of her body faintly highlighted by an eerie golden light amidst the deep blues and purples of the night around her. Large fig trees stood sentry at both ends of the room, one stretching slightly to brush against Brenn's body as she walked past.

Maybe she should get some indoor plants, she thought. Charles Mayhew would probably love it.

Every light in the kitchen was on, highlighting a marble-topped island crowded with snacks. The deep greens and blacks of the front of the house lightened to dove grey and nearly neon lime greens, the gold accents deepening to burnished bronze. Nat had set out a charcuterie board nearly as long as the island, piled high with gourmet cheeses, figs, apricots, cherries, strawberries, and prosciutto sliced thin enough to see through. Hand-thrown ceramic bowls held different kinds of crackers, and one bowl was filled to the brim with white cheddar Cheetos. Brenn took a tiny, expensive-looking chocolate bar and a raspberry rose sparkling water.

She stepped into the sunroom, where two women were laughing at a photo on an iPhone. A black woman with impeccable eye makeup and wearing an ethereal pink dress saw her and put it on the coffee table. She smiled cheerily and said hello. Brenn waved sheepishly. "Sorry, I didn't mean to interrupt."

The blond white woman in a wheelchair flapped her hand dismissively. "No worries, come sit down."

Brenn stepped around the coffee table, settling into the corner of a trimly upholstered love seat. She put her water on a leather coaster embossed with a pattern of eyeballs. Nat had a lot of beautifully strange things in her home. She addressed the blond woman. "You're Aislynn, right? Your husband is one of my clients. Lost Seas Procurement? I'm Brenn Maren."

Aislynn snapped her fingers in recognition. "That's me. Ben was so happy when he found your business. He said you really saved his ass last year."

"He's a great client. It's certainly a challenge to find most of the things he needs." She belatedly realized that could sound like a veiled complaint, and she rushed to continue. "Not that it's a problem! I like an interesting challenge."

She turned to the woman in the chair next to her and held out her hand. "Hi, I'm Brenn. I don't think we've met before."

The woman smiled, deep dimples denting both round cheeks. "Junelle. I don't think we have met. Though...are you related to Noelle Maren-Hughes?"

Her heart sank, and Brenn shut her eyes for a few seconds longer than a blink. "Yes. She's my older sister," she said in a measured tone. "How do you know her?"

"I teach art at Briar Vale Middle. We've met at all city school staff meetings." Purposefully catching Brenn's eye, she said wryly, "She's kind of intense."

"Yes, she absolutely is. Her whole life." Brenn huffed a relieved laugh. "How do you two know each other?" She pointed between Junelle and Aislynn.

They started speaking at the same time. Junelle said, "You go."

"My daughter Nina is in one of Junelle's classes. She is adamant she loves her more than any other teacher on earth, forever and ever, the end."

"She's maybe the most talented student I've ever taught." Junelle turned back to Aislynn. "I was serious about the extra lessons. It's a joy to teach a kid that enthusiastic. Especially one at that age."

"I'm sure she would murder me if I said no." Aislynn and Junelle kept talking. Brenn let her mind wander, looking around Nat's sun porch. It was more like a straight-up conservatory rather than the humble structure the term 'sun room' suggested.

The walls and ceiling were solid glass, the large panes held in black steel framing. There were three stripes of stained glass wrapping from the ground up and over to the inner wall of the house, a cascade of tightly layered leaves rendered in dozens of different shades of green. The edges of the room were stuffed with plants, and the center held two loveseats and three armchairs arranged around a low coffee table. Strings of cafe lights crisscrossed the space overhead.

Nat walked in, three more women trailing her. Daniela, in a bright patterned skirt and a blackberry-colored T-shirt that made her golden brown skin glow, plopped down next to Brenn on the loveseat. Her leather satchel clinked as she set it on the ground next to her feet. "Hiya. You look totally fine." She motioned to Brenn's clothing. She smirked. "Completely authentic."

Brenn rolled her eyes and dryly said, "Thanks." The tall, rangy white woman that followed her in sat in the armchair closest to Dani. Her long black hair was tied up in a bun, and her eyes looked like she existed in a constant state of sleepiness. She lifted a hand and said a quiet 'hi' to the room, introducing herself as Walker Mills.

The last person to enter was a primly styled white woman with honey blond hair in a 50's style bob that framed her face with large rolled curls. She wore a creamy white fitted cashmere sweater with a high neck and short sleeves, a contrast that made her curls shine gold. Setting her drink on an end table, she warmly smiled at them with closed lips. Brenn blinked, looking closer. "Lillian? Lillian Howard?"

The woman stared back at her blankly for a split second, then recognized her. "Nice to see you, Brenn. I go by Lily now." She gracefully lowered herself into the empty chair next to Walker. "After high school, I felt like a Lily more than a Lillian."

Nat joined them, sitting on the loveseat across from Brenn. "I'm glad several of you already know each other. I'd like to open by having each of us introduce ourselves and tell a little about our abilities and our lives, and then I thought we could just chat, see how we all get along."

The air in the room suddenly seemed charged, buzzing with expectation.

NAT LOOKED AT THEM EXPECTANTLY, and they all glanced around at each other. "Uh, I'll go first. I'm Nat Hsu, as you all know. I moved to Briar Vale at the beginning of summer. For work, I'm a ghostwriter. Magic-wise, I can conjure items, and I'm a seer. Specifically, I'm clairvoyant and have some," she made a see-sawing motion with one hand, "not a lot, but some precognition."

There was a little ripple of surprise through the group. Each of Nat's abilities were rare on their own; both in the same person meant a tremendous amount of power. She waited a beat for the room to calm. She opened her mouth to speak again, but instead made a sound of pleasure as she bent towards the floor. When she rose, there was an adorable albino hognose snake cradled in her hands. "I live here, obviously, with this lovely lady whose name is Jelly."

Jelly's body was butter yellow, with creamy orange markings. Nat lifted her so she could curl around her neck. As Jelly peered out from under Nat's hair, the entire group cooed at her, telling her how gorgeous she was. Nat pointed to Aislynn, prompting her to speak. "Aislynn Palmer, I'm a GP at Briar Vale Family

Medicine. Married to a man, three kids, Nina, Wesley, and Declan. My familiar is a raccoon named Captain Twist. My abilities are why I became a doctor. I can see a person's physical health, sort of like an aura, and I can affect small manipulations within the body. Mostly mending broken bones and excising viruses, et cetera." She tapped Junelle's arm. "Your turn."

"Hello, everyone, I'm Junelle Archer. I teach middle school art, and my magic likes to express itself best in charms, in my sewing. I stitch little nudges into my sewing projects to boost the person using it. Um, I live with a very opinionated, gigantic Maine Coon named Eddie but no other humans. I stay up too late at night, I always wish on fallen eyelashes, and I have an uncontrollable obsession with strawberries." She pulled her hair back on one side to show the two different styles of strawberry earrings she was wearing. Sitting back in her chair again, Junelle gave Brenn a smile.

Brenn rushed through her own introduction, telling them briefly about Lost Seas and how her abilities made her business possible, about Charles and Mayhew, and how she was the latest in a long line of her ancestors to live in the Moon House. "...and I don't date really, I'm aro ace, and I don't have kids." Dani dug an elbow into her side. "But a couple of weeks ago, I took in a teenage girl who needs some guidance with her magic. She grew up an orphan in the normal world."

"How's that been going?" Nat asked.

"With Audrey? It's good, I think. She's settling in, enjoying school. She reads at least one book a day about magic or being a witch or magical vocation. I think she's trying to catch up on all the years she had not understanding what was going on with her."

The witches commiserated about how difficult that must have been for Audrey and spent a few minutes sharing stories of how their magic behaved when they were that age. "Oh, I have you all beat," Dani said. "I grew up in New Mexico, in a very small magical community. Like everybody knew *everybody's* business. Right after I got my first period, for two years, every time I menstruated, I left trails of nipple beehive cacti everywhere I walked. People would joke about it constantly. It was *humiliating*."

When the sympathetic groans trailed off, she continued. "I guess now that you know that remarkably embarrassing anecdote, let me balance it out. I'm Daniela Flores-McCormick. Dani. My spouse is Cameron, and we have one daughter, Lydia, who is sixteen and a truly frighteningly great kid. My familiars are moths, like this lady here." She gently petted the large moth that sat on her shirt like a brooch. "Uh, what else? I own the Phoenix Apothecary, animal not city, and potion making is my jam."

Dani started to motion to the woman who arrived with her but blurted out, "Jam like I enjoy it, not jam like fruit spread. I am a shockingly bad cook."

Watching to see if Dani was actually done, the next woman gave a succinct summary for herself. "Walker Mills. I just separated from my husband, Keith, so I'm living with Dani right now. No familiars, no kids. I can see people's desires. Looking for a job if you have any leads."

This is an interesting mix of talents, Brenn thought. She was dying to know what specialty Lillian had developed. She was two years behind Brenn in high school, but they had spent a good amount of time together as teammates on the varsity tennis team. It was clear she had relaxed from fastidious to merely prim throughout the years.

Lillian cleared her throat delicately. "My name is Lily Howard. I also grew up in Briar Vale. I am single currently, with no children. I work with two yellow canaries, who are named Lady and Liesl."

"And your ability?" Nat prompted.

"Oh yes. I occasionally paint landscape scenes, much like

automatic writing, which manifests most often as visions of windows. One can interpret answers to a specific question from what one can see out the window. I can divine information from objects as well." Lily smoothed her skirt, picking a minuscule bit of lint off it.

"So you sit down and poof! There's a painting start to finish?" Dani sat with her forearms propped on her knees, hands clasped.

"Basically, yes. I keep them all in a portfolio. A grimoire of sorts."

Junelle spoke next. "Could we see a few sometime? What an interesting way to work, both as an artist and a witch. It's nearly the opposite of my process. I have to plan every detail, or else nothing is going to work right."

"Same here," Dani chimed in. "Whenever I try to wing a potion, a disaster is never far behind."

Lily began to speak at the same time Brenn did. "Sure. Oh, you go ahead, Brenn."

"Sorry, sorry. I was going to say I understand working intuitively. I have a deck for divination that I make myself. Four times a year, I wake up from a dream that I can't remember, and then I see an image, and it won't go away until I paint it."

"How long has that been going on?" Nat watched her steadily, head tilted to the side, Jelly pressed up against her cheek. She nuzzled the snake back.

Brenn thought back. "About twenty years? I got the first one just before winter solstice the year I turned sixteen. So yeah, twenty years." Her stomach twisted. She hadn't gotten a chance to try the luck tea, and the equinox was in a week. Work took up her time while Audrey was at school, and she certainly wasn't going to try it with Audrey in the house. Maybe she should talk to Lillian after the meeting. No, Lily now. She definitely wouldn't be responsive if Brenn got her name wrong.

"So eighty cards? Eighty-four? That's an impressive deck."

Walker counted quickly on her fingers. "Eighty-four. Time math always messes with my head."

"Same here. It's annoying." Aislynn said. "But getting back to divination. I use a tarot deck myself, mostly as a way to frame an issue more than fortune telling. Does anyone else have a different method?"

Dani blushed. "I use bibliomancy sometimes."

"Oh ho, that explains the week where everything you said sounded like Charles Dickens," Brenn laughed. "Was that a bibliomancy time?"

Dani hid her eyes with her hand. "Yeah, so what? I'm very academic."

"I'm just glad to know what the hell was going on with you. It was cute but weird."

"I've had fantastic luck with *Great Expectations*." She made a face. "I don't know what that says about me." There was a beat of silence, and then the room filled with laughter.

They migrated into Nat's kitchen where, over the next couple hours, they demolished the impressive spread of snacks she had laid out and talked between bites. Or sometimes during, which was a little gross.

Brenn checked her watch. "Oh hell, it's already eleven thirty. I've got to get home, Audrey's been alone the whole night."

Among the chorus of similar sentiments, Nat raised her voice to be heard. "Before you all go, can I ask that you each tell us what goals you would have in forming a coven?"

Seeing no one else was going to speak first, Brenn started them off. "I'm interested mainly in strengthening my magic."

"I wouldn't be sad about that. I mostly want a better social life." Dani shrugged. "Sorry not sorry. Friends or bust."

Walker nodded along with her. "I want to find out who I am outside of my husband or family or work. I need accountability to not just go with the flow all the time."

Lily mentioned she was looking to gain better control of

when and how she got visions. Brenn perked up at that, though part of her was disappointed. If Lily was actively looking to improve that, it was unlikely she would have helpful advice. Junelle wanted to learn from the way other members used their magic. Aislynn sardonically admitted she was looking for a regular kid-free night with other adults.

Nat closed their meeting. "I'm going to get in touch with you individually to get your impressions, so expect a text from me in the next couple days."

❧

NAT TEXTED her the next day:

> hey, Brenn. how did you feel about last night?
>
> would you be comfortable sealing as a coven with these witches? any hesitations?

Brenn was surprised to find herself nervous. She liked all the women, but had the slightest reservation about Lillian. Lily. She was aloof, sure, and always had been prim, but Brenn sensed a coldness in her that hadn't been there in their younger years. It concerned her, but she couldn't quite figure out why.

Brenn texted back:

> I feel good about the coven. I did want to bring up Lily, though. She seems very different than when I knew her and I'm not sure if it's all a positive change.

Nat:

> Walker brought up the same concern. she felt like Lily is holding something back.
>
> said her desires felt a little muddy?

Strangely, Brenn found this reassuring. Maybe she was just sensing ambivalence in Lily, if Walker couldn't get a read on her desires. If a person doesn't have a clear idea of what they want, or don't want, Brenn wouldn't be able to find an easy way to persuade them of anything. That always felt discomfiting to her.

Brenn:

> To be fair, I haven't talked to her in nearly twenty years. I'm sure that's all it is. She was very accomplished when we were in school. I'm sure she'll be a great member.

Nat:

> so, not enough of a concern for us to regroup?

Brenn:

> No, no. I'm sure it's nothing major. It's been a long time, I'm just overthinking.

"BRENN! ARE YOU HOME?" Audrey bounced into the house with a clatter. Charles loped in from the kitchen to greet her, chirping the entire way. "Hi, Charles."

Brenn leaned around her office door. "I'm home. What's up?"

"We had a Sorcery Circle meeting at lunch, and the kids taught me a new thing. Look." She shook some M&Ms from a bag into her palm. With the fingers of her other hand, she made a swirling motion over the candy, chanting, 'sweet little treat, hop on the beat'. The candy danced in the air a few inches above her hand. Brenn didn't think Audrey's grin could get bigger.

"Nice! Your control is getting much more precise. I'm impressed you've progressed so fast." She snagged an M&M and popped it in her mouth.

Audrey caught a piece of candy from the air with her mouth. "I think I might join the Charms and Chums Club also. It sounds like fun. And I'll meet more people."

"The Charms and what club?" Brenn snorted.

"Chums? Like, chum. It means friends." Audrey ate another handful of M&Ms.

"No, I know what it means. I just didn't think anyone under the age of eighty used that word anymore." Brenn repeated to herself, "chums."

"Whatever, grandma." Audrey rolled her eyes. "The whole club is going to some diner by the fairgrounds tomorrow. We have a test next week that we're studying for." The candy fell back onto her palm, which was a little sweaty from the effort of keeping the spell going. "Can I go? I have a ride there, but I might need a ride back. My books and stuff are too heavy to bike."

"Sure, that should be fine. I have a meeting tomorrow afternoon anyway. Cherry On Top?"

"Huh? For what?"

"That's the diner up by the fairgrounds. Unless you are on the motel side, then it might be Darla's."

"I think it's the Cherry one. It's on East Pleasant." She licked the last of the red and blue food dye from her palm. "What?" she asked innocently when she noticed Brenn's amused disgust.

SATURDAY AFTERNOON SAW Brenn on the far east side of downtown to meet with the rest of her potential coven to prepare for their sealing ritual. Dani had mentioned in their group chat she had been craving bubble tea, especially now that all the fall flavors were out, and no one had objected.

Brenn liked how Bubble Babes Boba went full tilt on the autumn decor. Toddler-sized cups lined their windows, filled with tiny, light-up jack-o-lanterns, colorful leaves, and miniature pointy witches' hats. Each cup had a broom sticking out of it in place of a straw. Strands of ghost-shaped garland swung over them. Brenn swerved around two kids admiring the decorations and a sandwich sign asking her to 'pop in for our pumpkin spice!'.

Walker had her chair tilted on two legs so she could watch the door. When she saw Brenn notice her wave, she thumped her chair back flat on the floor, disappearing behind the wall of the little alcove where the rest of the coven sat. They had shoved two small tables together, the tops of which were littered with fresh cups of bubble tea and drifts of paper. Brenn swung her bag onto the empty chair, assuming it was hers. "I'm going to get a tea. Need anything?"

"Yeah, babe, would you please get me an order of pandan mochi waffles?" Dani stretched over the table to hand Brenn her card.

Juggling two plates of waffles and her tumbler of tea, Brenn wove around the other tables, nodding hello at the people she was acquainted with. As she rounded the corner into the alcove, Aislynn moved her bag so she could sit.

"Thanks. Have you all been here long?" Brenn asked as she passed Dani her plate.

"Nah, maybe ten minutes. Enough time to get our drinks and make a mess." Aislynn said, gesturing to the tables. "You aren't late."

Brenn dropped into her chair with a noisy exhale. "Whew, good. I hate being the last one to show up." She counted to ten in her head as she fiddled with her straw wrapper, trying to calm herself.

Nat cleared her throat. "So, let's talk about the ritual. This is what I'm thinking so far." She unfolded a piece of paper from her pocket. "A traditional casting circle, out in the woods, by the river. Several personal components from each of us, and bound with fire and released to air. Ideally, we'd seal next Friday, on the equinox."

"Are you thinking off Kestrel or Riverside?" Walker swirled her straw around in her cup.

"Kestrel. I'll reserve the meeting room, so it's less likely people will be wandering around."

Dani raised her hand. "Maybe we should take a quick check to make sure everyone has the equinox open?"

"I have no commitments next weekend yet, so I will be there." Lily leafed through her datebook and made a notation.

Aislynn was scrolling on her phone. "I'm not on call next week, so that works for me. I'm sure Ben and the kids can find something fun to do without me."

"Yep, good for me too!" Junelle motioned to Dani for her pen. She tore a strip off a sheet of paper, wrote the date down, and stuck it in her wallet.

Brenn said, "I'm free. I'd like to arrange someone to hang out with Audrey." She asked Dani. "Is Lydia around?"

"She and Cameron are going out of town that weekend. There's some convention thing for enamel artists in Saugatuck. Lyd's started charm work, and she's 'exploring transformative mediums'. I'm staying here since Phoenix does good business on the equinoxes. So I am free, but Lydia is not."

"My schedule is basically the same as Dani's as long as I'm sleeping at her house, so I'm available also." Walker rested her elbows on the table as she took a long sip from her tea. She chewed her boba thoughtfully. Addressing Nat, she asked, "You've got earth, fire, air, water. Personal components for spirit? What are you looking for?"

"We'll need a strand of hair from everyone's bodies, and—"

"Why not say 'our heads'?" Lily interrupted.

"Because I don't know if any of you wear a wig? I did check at our first meeting, and all of you at least have arm hair, so that's why I designed the ritual this way. It doesn't have to be a long piece of hair, we just need something from our corporeal forms." Seeing Lily's mouth open, Nat held a hand up. "We could have done fingernails, but you and Junelle both have nicely painted nails, and, besides, that's a little gross."

There was a beat of silence while they all thought about that.

Nat continued. "And I definitely don't mess around with blood magic. Actually let's add that to the bylaws."

"No blood magic?" Dani added a note to the long list she had been writing.

"Yeah, and negative magic only by unanimous vote." Nat tapped the table with her fingertip.

"Why not say no negative magic period?" Lily examined her nail polish, smoothing the edge of one nail.

"I think it's smart to do it that way. Sometimes you have to get down in the dirt." Brenn bristled a little at Lily's continued interruptions, and her response came out a little ruder than she intended.

Nat nodded at her. "I agree. Leaving ourselves a very limited window is better than blindly assuming we won't ever need it. But back to the ritual, each of us needs to contribute a single tear."

"How should we collect that? Does it need to stay liquid?" There was nothing in Lily's voice to indicate she noticed how short Brenn had been with her.

"Nope, use a clean piece of cloth that's made of natural materials. Cotton, linen, that sort of thing. And we need candles. Whatever color each of you wants."

Junelle piped up. "Will beeswax work? I live down the street from the Bee Valet, and I can pick them up if you want."

"Oh, I love that place. I don't know how they manage to do eucalyptus honey in Michigan, but it's so good." Aislynn slurped her tea loudly.

Brenn leaned closer to her. "There's a small grove of eucalyptus at one of the farms. I tracked down some plants that had been bred for zone 5 for a client."

Aislynn focused on her. "I'd love to hear more about your business. It sounds exciting, like a constant treasure hunt." Brenn started telling her about Lost Seas, and they passed the rest of the afternoon in conversation and multiple rounds of tea.

The sun was low in the sky by the time they packed up and left Bubble Babes. "Oh damn. Damnit." Brenn winced as she looked at her watch. "I am so late to pick up Audrey."

She waved at their chorus of goodbyes, and let loose with a steady stream of cursing once she was alone in her truck, banging her forehead softly against the steering wheel. Great way to let the kid know you care, you idiot, she admonished herself.

BRENN RUSHED from her truck into the diner. She spotted Audrey in the end booth, her head laying on her arms on the table. "Audrey, I'm so sorry. I lost track of time." She slid onto the other bench. "Hey, you awake?"

A muffled 'yes' came from Audrey's folded arms.

"Can you look at me please?" Brenn asked. Audrey lifted her head, a blank look on her face.

Brenn's heart clenched at that. She absently rubbed her sternum as she apologized again. "I'm sorry. Is there a reason you didn't text me?"

"My phone died. I don't have a way to charge it."

Brenn realized what the issue was. "And you don't have my number out of your phone."

"No. Can we go home now?" Her voice was tired.

"Next time, ask at the counter. Someone almost certainly knows me." Brenn took her backpack from her, heaving it over her own shoulder. "Not that I'm expecting there will be a next time. I'm really sorry, Audrey."

Audrey lagged behind, not reaching the truck until Brenn had slung her backpack in the back. Brenn leaned against the rear door for a few seconds, looking miserably off into the distance as she swallowed hard a couple times. She hated, hated the feeling of screwing up.

Brenn was going to ask her how the afternoon went, but

Audrey was slumped against the window, eyes closed, so she just squeezed her lips between her teeth and started the truck.

The ride home was uncomfortably quiet.

BRENN SPENT the next week trying to make amends for forgetting Audrey. She took her to her Spell Development meeting, which delighted Audrey, who mastered two of the spells that were shared that night and beamed as the adult witches of the group praised her efforts. They went shopping for scented candles for Audrey's bathroom, and to an open mic night at The Minnow, and tried a different restaurant for dinner each night. Audrey gave her several young adult novels to read and report back on.

On Thursday, the weather finally got properly autumnal. Brenn taught her how to knit while they sat in a coffee shop after school got out and drank themselves silly on pumpkin spice lattes.

Audrey groaned as she had to pull several stitches out of her scarf. "Hey, Brenn?" She stuck the tip of her tongue out while she concentrated on transferring loops of yarn onto her other needle. "Thanks for this week."

"What do you mean?" Brenn's needles flashed as she purled a row of the golden yellow knee socks she was knitting for her father's birthday. Normally she'd spell her needles to move even faster, but she tried last week and ended up having to rip out fifteen entire rows and a heel.

"Taking me to Spell Dev, the dinners, everything. It's been really nice." Audrey whispered a triumphant 'yes!' as she successfully finished a row. She carefully laid her knitting down and took a long drink of her latte.

Brenn mirrored her. "It's no trouble. Hey, I did want to ask you—tomorrow night I'm going to be out with the coven. Do you want me to see if Cleo wants to come over for dinner and then hang out with you while I'm gone?"

Audrey's eyes lit up. "Yes! Can we? Would she come?"

"Well, I already kind of did, so yes." From the way Audrey had gushed about Witchery Aesthetica and Cleo's social media prowess, Brenn had hoped she would be enthusiastic. And that she wouldn't see it as babysitting. Which it wasn't. Entirely.

BRENN PACKED a satchel for the sealing. Her tear had been caught on a scrap of silk, a strand from one of her curls was coiled in a tiny envelope, and she tossed in a box of matches just in case. She spent a minute considering, then took her bag into the kitchen and stuffed a few bottles of water and assorted snacks in as well.

Rummaging through the foyer closet for a sweater, she jumped and bumped her head as her phone buzzed in her pocket. She answered it before checking the caller ID, a move she regretted as soon as her mother's voice rang out from the receiver.

"Brenn darling, what's this I hear about you housing an orphan child?"

"Hi, Mama. How are you and Poppy?" It took everything Brenn had to contain the snarky response she had at the ready. "I am helping a teenage girl. Her name is Audrey, she's fifteen, and she was raised in the normal world. I suppose Noelle has at least told you that much?"

Her mother sniffed disdainfully. "Well, of course she did. I don't know why you never want to let your father and me into your life. Noelle calls us every day after dinner. Would it be so hard for you to make an effort like that?"

"Mama, Noelle and I are very different. Plus, what would we even have to talk about that often?" Her mother needed to air her grievances for at least five full minutes before she could even entertain listening to reason. Brenn settled into the foyer chair to let her mother talk at her. She had spent more time in this chair in the past three weeks than she had in the last three years. The cushions could stand to be re-stuffed. Maybe The Napping Cat made house calls. That would be convenient. She guessed she could talk to her mother about reupholstering her furniture if she insisted on daily phone calls.

"We are interesting people, darling. Interesting people have no lack of subjects to discuss." Right, like their furniture. "Now, tell me more about this child."

"She's a nice girl who needs help. I have the room and a flexible schedule so it makes sense I help her." Brenn tugged a curl out of her ponytail. "If you want to meet her, we can—"

"Of course we want to meet her. I don't feel comfortable with you living with a stranger. We are going to have your birthday party on Sunday afternoon, so bring her along then. It will be our family, your Auntie Violet, the Isaacs, and a few of Noelle's neighbors."

"Did anyone want to ask me if I was available on Sunday first?"

"You are always available on the weekends, dear. We know your life isn't as...full as Noelle's or Cleo's."

"Thanks, Ma." Brenn said dryly.

"Now darling, don't get upset. There's no reason to. I simply meant you have no children, and your business doesn't require you to keep regular hours for your customers. Your schedule is more fluid than either of your sisters. That's simple logic, Brenn."

"No, you're right. So it's at Noelle's house? What time?" The sooner she acquiesced, the sooner she could hang up. The sooner she could hang up, the happier she'd be. Her mother rattled out more detail than Brenn could ever need. The doorbell rang then, and Brenn mouthed a 'thank you' in the air. "Mama,

I have to go now, that's the door. Cleo's coming over for dinner tonight."

"It is so nice to see you girls spending time together. I trust you prepared your guests a proper and healthful meal. Give her a kiss from me and your father. We will see you on Sunday. Do not be late, and please make sure Audrey is dressed presentably."

Brenn sighed again. "Yes, Mama, we will arrive on time and be dressed appropriately. Goodbye, Mama."

The delivery boy was leaning against the porch rail, idly scrolling through his phone. He held out the bag and the receipt without looking up. "Have a good night, ma'am," he mumbled. Spinning on his heel, he slouched back to his car, never once meeting Brenn's eyes. She was slightly impressed at his commitment to apathy.

Cleo neatly sidestepped the delivery boy as she strode up the front walk, sharing with Brenn a mutual 'what the hell' look. Brenn pushed the door open further for Cleo to walk inside. "Yeah, I have no idea," she said, waving her hand in the direction of the kid.

"Hiya, house," Cleo said as she stroked the door frame. The house trembled ever so slightly in response. She made kissing noises at it. "What's for dinner?"

Brenn held up the bag. "Dolly's. Hope you feel like southern."

"I always feel like Dolly's. Where's Audrey?"

"Upstairs. She is very excited to hang with you tonight." Brenn kicked the door shut while yelling up the stairs again. "Audrey! Cleo's here!"

"You guys are getting along well?" Cleo half-whispered as Audrey clattered down the stairs.

Brenn couldn't contain a goofy smile as she replied sotto voce. "I think so. It's kind of fun to be around someone that excited about magic." She thought about Audrey's proud grin every time she mastered a new spell, her puttering around on the weekends and keeping up a steady stream of chatter with Charle Mayhew, her teenage accoutrements littering the house, and Brenn's shoulders relaxed.

"Honestly, that's a big part of why I started the store. Even though a lot of my customers are normies, they still get all fired up about it." Cleo dropped her bag on the foyer chair, kicking her shoes under it.

Audrey bounced up between them. "Cleo, hi! Nice to see you again!"

"Hey, sweetheart. I'm glad we're getting some time to hang out together." Cleo took the bag from Brenn and followed Audrey into the kitchen. "Did you guys get fried green tomatoes?"

Dinner went smoothly, if Brenn hadn't wanted to be an active participant in the cozy little conversation between Cleo and Audrey. The two of them barely took a breath the entire meal, dishing on just about every topic under the sun. Brenn wasn't sure what half the things they talked about even were. Audrey seemed more bubbly than she ever had been around Brenn, and that tiny irritation was like a burr in her sock, pricking her every time she took a step.

She did the dishes on her own, sending Audrey and Cleo to the living room so she could stew in privacy before she had to leave. There was no reason she shouldn't be happy that Audrey was happy and that her sister was helping her for a change, but, well, here she was. Jealous because two people she genuinely liked and cared about were having a good time together.

She stuffed a few extra spellcasting supplies into her bag, feeling small and petty for being upset at how well Audrey and Cleo got along. Cleo never had trouble finding a way to talk to people, a skill Brenn had to constantly work on. Brenn wordlessly grumped around for a few seconds, making faces and shaking her arms about, trying to dispel her terrible mood, calling out a goodbye to Audrey and Cleo as she left.

Nine

BRENN WOUND DOWN the narrow road through the woods in the September twilight, her windows rolled all the way down to let the chilly air tease the ends of her hair. She made an active effort to not be annoyed that Cleo was so much more outgoing and fun than her.

The further she drove down Kestrel, the closer the trees bent toward the road. She found herself singing along loudly to her 'hey I'm actually a witch' playlist, startling a group of goldfinches and sparrows.

The scent of wood smoke and pennies, the bright tang of falling leaves, the whispered promise of cold evenings, all the delicious scents of autumn swirled around the cab of her truck. She drew the deepest breath she could, luxuriating in the richness of the night air. Fireflies lit up among the undergrowth. It would be too late in the year for them anywhere else in Michigan but not in the magic of Briar Vale.

When she pulled up, Nat, Junelle, Dani, and Walker were already waiting on the benches next to the diminutive brick building that housed the Kestrel Woods Meeting Center. A shiver of electric thrill ran through her bones, pebbling her skin with goosebumps. Nat stood as she walked towards them, a half-smile on her face. "Hey, Brenn. Feeling good?"

"Electric, actually." She showed her goosebumps to Nat, who laughed as she ran a finger down Brenn's arm. Squeezing her hand, Nat lowered her voice to say, "I'm very glad you made it. I think you are going to be a real asset to our coven." They both turned as they heard the sound of a car crunching through a spot of gravel that littered the entrance of the parking lot.

Aislynn waved at them as she stood carefully, holding the driver's side door of her SUV. Lily slammed the trunk shut and brought Aislynn's wheelchair around to her. She settled into it and wheeled herself to the benches. Nat sucked air through her teeth. "Shit. I forgot how rocky the path to the river spot is here. Will you be okay to get down there?"

"I've been down there before, so yes, but this is also my outdoor chair. Ben modified it and sigiled the wheels so they can handle rougher terrain." She pointed to the rims of her wheels, where teeny sigils glowed silver in the dimming light.

"I'm such a jackass. I should have asked before choosing the spot."

"Hey, I will appreciate if you make the effort, but I don't have a problem advocating for myself. Comes with the territory." Aislynn shrugged, and then rolled herself off the sidewalk and onto the grass.

"Noted. I'll do better in the future." Nat gathered them around her. "This is as good a time as any to bring this up. After tonight, I don't want our structure to have a leader. I designed our sealing ritual so I'll lead us tonight, but I wanted to mention it. Any of us should feel free to speak on whatever we want, and we'll take a vote for decisions?"

Dani clapped her hands together. "Let's take our first vote now. No leader?" She raised her hand, along with the rest of the group, moving almost at the exact same time. "Great! All agreed. Shall we?"

They filed down the path behind the center. Junelle flicked her fingers, and five glowing globes flew into the air above their heads, lighting their way. An owl hooted in the distance, and bats swooped through the branches, hunting for bugs.

A sealing is the most important ritual a coven performs. It sets the intentions of each witch in the circle to be bound to her fellow witches for as long as they are alive and sometimes beyond. The seal can be broken in certain circumstances, but generally can only be done under the supervision of a guardian. With only thirteen guardians in the world active at any given time, sealing is a commitment that is nearly permanent.

Nat led them to a clearing on the north bank of the Thorn River. Stone benches covered in moss ringed a circular platform holding luminous white sand. Light from the moon filtered through the trees, creating lacy patterns of light and shadow on the ground and the mossy benches and their bodies.

Taking out a driftwood wand, Nat drew a circle in the sand. She etched seven sigils on the inside edge, one in front of each of them. She prodded the tip of her wand into the sand, making little divots. Junelle followed after her, setting slender candles in each hole with a screwing motion. Nat put a shallow ceramic bowl in the center of the sand.

"Write your signature on a slip of this paper, then fold it around your tear and a strand of your hair. Drop it in the bowl when you're ready." She handed a half-size clipboard with seven strips of handmade paper to Lily, along with a pen. While Lily was signing her slip, the other women produced coiled strands of hair and scraps of cloth from pockets and bags and purses. As they finished putting their components in the bowl, they each took a place around the platform. Dani held her arm out for Aislynn to steady herself as she stepped from her chair to sit on a bench.

Nat was the last one to carefully fold her paper and drop it into the bowl. She took slender sticks of seven woods—aspen, paper birch, hawthorn, sugar maple, redbud, sycamore, and tuliptree—and laid them atop the little packets, securing them from the breeze.

"Now follow what I do, from my left." She looked at Walker sitting on her left, who nodded back. Nat took three deep breaths in and out, held her casting hand palm out towards the circle, and recited the spell. "I, Natalie Hsu, perform my intention to be bound to these witches as a coven, this night to the end of all things." She flipped her hand palm up and snapped her fingers, lighting her candle.

Walker glanced over to make sure she was finished, then took her breaths, held her hand out, recited the spell, lit her candle. Aislynn, then Dani, Junelle, and Lily followed in succession. Brenn finished, "...the end of all things," turned her palm up and snapped. And her candle stayed appallingly dark.

Fiercely thanking the universe that the evening dark and her brown skin hid the ferocious blush climbing up her face, Brenn straightened her spine. She scowled in concentration, furious with herself. Drawing in a deep breath, she slowly blew her exhale towards the wick of her candle, snapping her fingers sharply in an upward motion. The flame sparked and caught. Out of the corner of her eye, she saw Nat nod once in her direction.

Nat held her left hand out to Walker, who took it in her right, and in turn held her own left hand to Aislynn, each witch repeating the action until Nat took Brenn's hand, completing the circle. The candles dimmed. All noise in the clearing quieted, leaving only the sound of their breathing.

Suddenly the flames from each candle shot up in the air and met in the middle of the circle, looking like the spokes of a wheel. With a fizzy crackling sound, the fire zipped from the wicks down into the bowl of their essence packets. Those burst into flame with a flash, and in an instant, burnt entirely, leaving a plume of green-colored smoke hovering over a small pile of ash.

Dropping Brenn and Walker's hands, Nat cocked her head to the side. "Green?" she asked, mostly to herself. She stared blankly into the distance, fingers twitching as though she were counting.

Lily leaned over Brenn. "Is it not supposed to be?"

Nat's gaze snapped to her. "It's not what I was expecting. Though green is my favorite color, so there's a chance I worked an accidental intention into the ritual."

She stared hard at the center of the circle for a long minute and then shrugged it off. The smoke floated up into the sky. As the last wisp of it disappeared, the air sparked with electricity.

Brenn felt power throbbing through her body. Her joints buzzed, the insides of her teeth vibrated with it. She threw her arms out to the sides, stretching as far as she could.

Aislynn started laughing. "This is incredible. I can feel every nerve in my body right now."

Brenn *listened* to the coven and sensed their connection like a thick, velvety rope. She thought about tugging it, and everyone stopped to look at her. "What was that?" Walker asked in a fascinated voice.

"I thought about pulling on our connection, and, uh, I guess I did?" She closed her eyes, prodding their connection in different directions. She felt it like her every nerve extended out into their connection.

"Brenn?" Dani said in a wavering voice. "Could you please not do that right now? It's making me dizzy."

Brenn's eyes flew open. "Sorry! Sorry! It feels so weird." She forced her conscious mind back to the real world.

"It does feel quite strange." Lily agreed. "It's almost as though you each have a flavor, but not a flavor? I can taste it with my mind."

Junelle gave her a skeptical look. "That sounds really unpleasant."

"Oh, no, it's not. I'm just more aware of each of you than I thought I would be." Lily tilted her head to one side. "It's not a bad feeling. Perhaps slightly overwhelming."

Nat stepped to the platform, tossing the candle stubs into the bowl of ash and smoothing the sand back to a flat plane. She flexed her fingers. "Do you want to try casting a spell together?" she asked as she set the bowl on the bench behind her.

"I actually prepared one that we could do to test the power boost of casting together." Lily slipped a hand into her purse, pulling out a seed and a miniature rose bush with three small buds. "I grew this bush from seed this morning, with a sixty-second concentration time. I'd like us to do the same with this seed, from the same hip, and compare the differences. If you are all amenable."

"That's a great idea. I am all for testable results. Is there an incantation or something?" Dani rubbed her hands together eagerly.

"Nothing formal. I used 'sprout and grow, branch and leaf', but it didn't feel as if it needed to be specific." Lily placed the seed in the middle of the sand and the bush on her bench. She laid her phone on the edge of the platform, the timer app open and set for one minute. "Ready?" At their nods, she tapped the start button.

A pleasant hum filled the clearing as the coven murmured their individual incantations. Brenn had a difficult time not submerging herself fully in the magic as she chanted 'sprout, grow, flourish'. The feeling of power in her body made her want to cry, or maybe roll around in the grass, or leap around like a small child in a swimming pool. She squeezed her eyes shut.

"Oh holy shit," she heard Junelle say as Lily's alarm rang. She opened her eyes, and her jaw dropped. The seed had become a nearly five-foot-tall rose bush with dozens of fully bloomed roses in a rainbow of colors. As she stroked the petals of a blossom, she started laughing helplessly.

Nat rubbed a glossy green leaf between her thumb and forefinger with reverence. "I think the sealing was successful."

Walker dug a bottle of water out of her tote and took a long drag. "Oh, you think? For fuck's sake." She pulled a bag of soft licorice chews from a pocket and stuffed a few in her mouth, talking around them. "Also, you all are going to have to learn to tone down your desires around me, holy cow. I barely have to think your name and I've got your wishes clear as a bell."

Nat, Dani, and Aislynn began discussing ways to meet Walker's request immediately. Junelle came over to sit next to Brenn on her bench, and Lily hurriedly wrote notes in a pristine leather-covered journal. Brenn leaned into Junelle and couldn't remember the last time she'd felt so happy.

Ten

BRENN TURNED TO AUDREY, her face serious. "Ready?" she asked.

"Ready," Audrey said, taking a deep fortifying breath. "I mean, I'll have to meet them sometime, right?"

Brenn had spent the day before preparing Audrey for her family's party. Her parents, Sasha and Carl Maren, had been social butterflies as long as she could remember, throwing elaborate parties for every occasion they came across. Since they had moved to the condo, they had been contenting themselves with the odd dinner party and receptions at the conferences they gave around the country. Brenn hoped Noelle, or at least her wife Jasmine, had been able to curb their parents' tendency towards extravagance. She knew firsthand how difficult it could be to say no to their parents.

She and Audrey slid out of the truck. Her eldest niece, Isadora, threw the front doors open wide. "Auntie Brenn! Happy birthday!" she shouted, loud enough that a man walking his dog startled a step on the sidewalk.

Brenn held her arms out for a hug. "Thanks, Isa. This is

Audrey. Audrey, Isadora." She held Isa out at arm's length. "I swear you've grown five inches since the last time I saw you."

"Probably six." Isadora rolled her eyes and took Audrey by the hand to tug her into the house. "Come meet everyone. They're *dying* to meet you."

Audrey tossed a glance over her shoulder at Brenn, who shrugged back. She followed the girls through the house into the backyard, snagging a strawberry off the platter on the kitchen counter. Brenn took a deep breath as she heard Noelle's voice rise above everyone else's.

She straightened her shoulders and walked out onto the patio.

There was a homemade banner tied along the fence that said 'happy birthday auntie brenn and welcome audrey' in charmingly drippy painted letters. The rest of her nieces and nephews crashed into her for an enthusiastic hug as soon as Brenn set foot in the backyard. Laughing, she rocked back on her heels. "Hey, best-kids-in-the-world! I love the banner you made." She waded through the mass of kids to her parents. "Hello, Mama, Poppy. This is Audrey." She turned to Audrey. "These are my parents, Sasha and Carl Maren."

After her parents greeted Audrey, Brenn ushered her around the party, introducing her to Noelle's kids and neighbors. Her polite smile turned real when they got to an elegant dark-skinned woman with close-cropped silver hair. "Auntie Violet! You're back!"

"Hello Bunny, happy birthday! This must be Audrey. Hello to you, dearheart." She clasped one of Audrey's hands between both of her own. "I hope once you are more settled you and Brenn and I can spend some quality time together."

"Hello, Ms. Maren," Audrey started.

Violet wagged a finger at her. "No, no, you call me Auntie Violet. You're living with Brenn, you count as an honorary niece."

Audrey flushed, looking pleased. "Okay, Auntie Violet. It's very nice to meet you, Brenn has told me a lot about you."

Brenn stood off on the side of the yard as Violet warmly talked to Audrey about how she was enjoying Briar Vale. Her nerves felt less buzzy now that they were here and Audrey's introduction appeared to be going well. She smoothed an imaginary wrinkle from her shirt to have something to do with her hands. Someone squeezed her arm, and she nearly jumped a mile.

Arlo handed her a drink. She punched him lightly in the arm, then took the glass and smiled. "You are a lifesaver."

"I've been to enough of your family's parties to know the schedule. Hello to your parents, stand by yourself awkwardly, immediate stiff drink."

She laughed as he pulled a bottle of beer out of his jeans pocket. "You know, pocket size is one of my passions. I won't rest until every pair of women's pants has adequately sized pockets."

"That's an excellent quest." He held out a small box wrapped in black paper tied with a bright magenta silk ribbon. "Happy birthday. Don't get too excited."

"Way to manage expectations." Brenn gave him her drink so she could unwrap the gift. She held a miniature crystal ball. When she rubbed the top of the ball, sparkling stars swirled around, parting to reveal her fortune. 'Congratulations, you can read,' it said. She snorted. "Well, it only speaks the truth. Thanks, Arlo."

"I spelled it to have thirty-seven different fortunes." He looked pleased with himself. "Though fair warning, a few came from Vivica and Terry, and I'm not sure if it's that they don't really get human humor, or if they understand it *too* well."

Brenn radiated pure delight. "I *cannot* wait to get those." She carefully boxed the crystal ball again, tying the ribbon into a handle.

They drifted across the yard closer to her family as they spoke. She was about to take a sip of her drink but had to lift it above the heads of a group of kids as they ran by. One girl tripped, and the rest ran away shrieking.

Brenn started to reach for her niece, but Noelle got to Savannah first, brushing bits of grass off her dress. "This one is having some issues with uncontrolled speed. We had to go to Mars Estrella for a charm to keep her grounded." She held up her daughter's arm to show a light metal cuff. "She's obsessed with those warrior princess books Jasmine is recording right now, so we had Mars do a battle cuff style. We let Savvy make up some sigils, strength, endurance, and courage."

One of her neighbors asked, with alarm, if Mars had spelled the sigils on.

Noelle laughed dismissively. "No, of course they aren't activated. I do not need to run after a nine-year-old with super strength. Can you imagine?"

Savannah squirmed out of her grip and ran across the yard to rejoin the boisterous group of children playing some kind of playground game under the treehouse in the corner. Brenn watched wistfully, wanting to join them instead of making awkward small talk.

Noelle turned to her. "Happy birthday, Brenn. We left gifts inside," she said, glancing at the box Brenn held. "We all hope you are having a great day."

Brenn gave her a tight smile, thanking her for hosting the party. She overheard her mother say 'dragon scale' and excused herself to wander over to join that conversation. Cleo nodded and made a note in her phone as Sasha opined about crystals. "... my darling, you should start carrying them in your shop. Black-bone opals. They are rare, but the refraction produces spectacular results. We procure ours from Glass Moon. I can..." she trailed off as she noticed Brenn. "Hello darling."

Brenn gestured to Cleo's phone. "You know that Ken gets those from me, right?"

"What was that dear?" Sasha asked as she fussed with Cleo's hair.

"I supply Glass Moon with blackbone opals. Ken asked me to find a stone that could amplify starlight for collection, and I tracked those down, and now I am the only supplier in all of North America."

Sasha looked at her blankly. "That's nice, darling, what an accomplishment."

Brenn gritted her teeth. "I'm saying, I procure them, take them to Ken, and then you buy them from him. You could cut out the extra steps and just come to me. I can find anything you need."

"Oh darling, don't worry about all that. We don't want to put anything extra on your plate." Glancing around the yard, she added, "Especially now since your responsibilities have increased, with young Audrey there."

Brenn held in a sigh. "Okay, Ma. Well, you know where to find me if you ever need my help." She shook her empty glass. "I'm going inside for a refill."

ONCE INSIDE NOELLE'S KITCHEN, Brenn slumped on a bar stool at their lunch counter. She rested her head on her arms. She heard the back door close again.

"Partied out?"

She peered out of one eye. Noelle's wife, Jasmine, was on the other side of the counter, cutting a block of cheddar into cubes.

"How did you guess?" Brenn lifted her head.

Jasmine snorted. "I've been married to your sister for sixteen years. I know how it goes."

"Yeah, you chose to bring this on yourself." Brenn forced herself to change the subject. It was a little too depressing to talk about her family when she was supposed to be enjoying herself. "I heard you are doing the audiobook for that warrior princess series now?"

"Yes indeed. Savvy is obsessed. The kids figured out a listening spell to eavesdrop while I work. They call it the 'Tin Can Talker'." She offered Brenn a cheese cube speared on the tip of her knife. "They took the hammers out of a couple of bells and tied a string between them, and shoved one under my door. It doesn't seem to affect the recording, so I let them believe they've pulled one over on me."

Brenn delicately took it. "That's pretty ingenious, honestly."

"It is, but I am dreading when Sav and the twins are teenagers at the same time if their spellcasting together is already this good. Lucky for all of us that Jean Dora doesn't mind if the kids eavesdrop as I'm recording." She whistled a short tune, and the cheese and fruit she cut rose into the air and arranged themselves neatly on the plate.

"I can't blame them, those books are pretty charming. I listened to the first one when they read it on the radio station, and I was hooked," Brenn said.

"I'll text you when I'm recording next." She wiggled her eyebrows at Brenn. "You can come sit around the tin can with the kids if you want," Jasmine offered in a singsong voice as she went back outside with her tray of cheese. She held the door for Violet.

"Be careful, I just might." Brenn smiled genuinely at her sister-in-law and her aunt. She leaned across the counter to grab the pitcher of sangria and filled her glass to the brim. "Auntie Violet?" She held the pitcher out in invitation.

"Thank you, but no thank you, Bunny. I am abstaining in preparation for a ritual I am doing with the girls next week." Violet went to the refrigerator for iced tea. "Your Audrey is a delightful child, sweetling. I can see how the two of you get along so well."

"I think you're the only one. Nobody thinks I can actually help her." Brenn blinked back a tear. "I know I can, though."

"Well. If you think you can make a positive difference in that girl's life, then I have no choice but to believe you." Violet tipped Brenn's chin up with a couple fingers. "If your heart and your mind are telling you the same thing, that's the path you should follow."

Brenn swallowed hard. "It is, but then there's that tiny voice telling me that Noelle and my mom are right, and I don't have the right experience, or enough experience, to provide what Audrey actually needs."

Violet pulled the long-handled tea spoon she was using out of her tea, shaking a few drops off it, and held it as a makeshift wand. She drew in the air, then tapped the spoon on the back of Brenn's hand. An elaborate gold-colored line drawing of peonies and twisting vines bloomed up Brenn's arm like a filigree tattoo. "You are very capable. I've known you your entire life. If you ever need anything, you come and call on me. I am always available for you." They both watched the peonies bloom and blossom across Brenn's arm. Violet briskly brushed her hands together and gestured to the door. "Now, let's go back to the party so we can have some cake and presents and then go the hell home."

Eleven

WHEN THEY GOT BACK to the Moon House after the party, Brenn greeted the house and Charles and Mayhew and continued silently into her lying room. She flopped onto the cushions, too exhausted to turn on the aurora machine or a playlist. There were some shuffling noises, and she opened one eye to see Audrey dragging the big cushion from the living room sofa into the room. Audrey flipped the switch on the aurora, plugged Brenn's phone into the speaker, and laid down on her own cushion as her "maybe I'll die of ennui" playlist started playing softly.

A smile fluttered at the edges of Brenn's mouth. She gazed up at the ceiling as her muscles finally relaxed.

EACH NIGHT THAT WEEK, once Audrey got home from school, she and Brenn tested her magic to see what she responded to best. Brenn spent a few minutes jotting down all the ways to do magic and items they could try to focus her energy. "Well, we've had some success with simple gestures, concentration, and free-form incantations. How is your wand class going?"

"Enh. Okay, but it feels fake." Audrey grimaced.

Brenn looked up from her notebook. "Huh. Like the motions or the wand itself feels wrong?"

"Both, I guess? It feels cheesy? To wave a wand around. Like I'm a five-year-old playing fairies."

Brenn nodded with a thoughtful frown. She slashed through a few words. "Let's start with crystals then, and maybe some naming."

The crystals went okay, and the naming did nothing for Audrey. Tuesday, they figured out telling worked better for her than asking, and her hand gestures took ten to fifteen iterations before they had any effect. Brenn decided to hold off on potion-making until Audrey had taken a regular chemistry class too. She didn't seem to be able to brew tea strong enough to produce any outcome besides a pleasant-ish beverage.

Cooking was a bit more successful. She did manage a batch of brownies that gave the consumer the ability to fully quote any film they had ever seen. Audrey and Brenn went through three full pans and a couple of stomachaches before they managed to quote the same movie at the same time. When they finally synced, Audrey was so excited she rushed around to set up her phone to record them. She insisted on transferring the video to Brenn's laptop as a backup.

Brenn gave her a crash course in runes, sigils, and wards, which Audrey found so boring she nodded off while Brenn was still talking. She had to acknowledge it wasn't the most scintil-lating subject to address at nine-thirty at night. She nudged Audrey slightly awake and sent her up to bed.

"TODAY, I think let's do some divination. I use my deck mostly for focus, though the cards do often tell me if something is coming that I should pay attention to." She fanned her deck out so Audrey could look at the images, careful not to flip any. She still was drawing blank cards every time she read them, and she wasn't sure if it was the motion or the intention that caused them to show blank faces. Just spreading them out seemed safe enough.

"I'm going to start you with a traditional tarot deck," Brenn said as she rummaged through a side table drawer. "I thought there was one in here that my sisters and I all used when we were your age."

Brenn got on her knees and shoved her arm into the drawer up to her shoulder. Audrey watched her straining for the recesses of the drawer, then got to walk to the back side of the table. It was small enough that an adult shouldn't be able to fit more than their hand inside. She was about to ask when Brenn shouted.

"Ha!" Brenn triumphantly held a dusty black velvet bag over her head. "Found it!"

Audrey took the bag from her, fingers bumping over the embroidery on the front. The cards inside were rendered in blues and greens and purples, the edges feathered from use. She flipped through.

"That deck is based on the Rider-Waite tarot deck. There are four? five? books in our library about reading tarot. If you can't find one, ask Charles Mayhew. They know where everything is."

Slowly thumbing through the deck, Audrey nodded absently in her direction.

Brenn watched her flip through the cards, taking note of the images Audrey paused at. She grabbed a pen and a notebook from the drawer and scribbled a few questions down. "So, when you start using a deck, it's a good idea to get to know that specific deck. I want you to think about these questions as you shuffle the deck, and then when it feels ready, lay one card down for each question."

Audrey read the paper Brenn handed her. "Should I do this now?"

"Nah, do it on your own when you feel ready." Brenn motioned her over to the coffee table. "You can also use reflective surfaces for scrying. Have your teachers gone over that yet?"

"Not really. I've heard the word before. Is it like looking in a crystal ball to see the future?"

"Technically, yes. It's more like looking for clues so you can make an educated guess at what's to come. True time magic, like precognition, is really rare and really difficult. Most people can't manage more than vague hints from things like oracle cards or crystals. Scrying for clairvoyance is a serious skill that takes practice before you can rely on your results." Uncapping a bottle of water on the table, she filled a saucer she had left on the table. "Usually, scrying is better suited to finding information your unconscious mind knows." She lit a candle and placed it next to the saucer. "Look into the water and let your mind wander. Just always keep your eyes on the water. If you see something, let me know."

Audrey cleared her throat and stared intently into the water. A couple of minutes later, she made a surprised noise. "A lake! There's a lake with tons of orange and yellow roses and a little beach."

Brenn blinked. Huh. "Can you tell what time of day it is?"

"Right before sunset? The light is really golden colored." Audrey looked up. "Is that right?"

"Yeah, actually. I was planning to take you up by Thorn Lake and try some elemental magic. Maybe some weather stuff. You want to go after dinner?"

"Cool! Yes, please."

Brenn was a little unsettled at how quickly Audrey took to scrying. Though maybe Brenn was just bad at it. She made a mental note to call Audrey's school and see if they had more in-depth instruction for her.

As well as she had done with the scrying, Audrey really shone once they went outside and tried using the weather to enhance her casting. The north beach of Thorn Lake was deserted, which suited Brenn nicely. She coached Audrey in ways to call the wind, to move water, and heat and cool the air. Audrey managed to get a fine spray to lift off the surface of the lake and angled it until the sun made a rainbow in the mist. She threw her head back and laughed and laughed.

THE NEXT DAY, Audrey was dragging. Brenn expected she would be more tired than usual, but not to this degree. She racked her brain for low-key activities they could do without magic that didn't involve just staring at the television. "Do you want to help me make some miniatures?"

Audrey bit the edge of her fingernail. "I don't want to ruin any of your stuff."

"There is no perfection without practice, friend. Come on, we'll use things from my box of scraps, so you don't have to worry." Brenn ran up the stairs, waiting at the landing on the third floor for Audrey to plod the rest of the way up. "What's going on with you?"

Audrey shrugged. Brenn opened the door to the tower room. "Audrey, I'm getting a little concerned. Is it school? Your magic? Are you ill? Is it something I'm doing?"

Audrey melted onto the dining chair next to the work table. "School's okay. Magic's okay. You're okay."

"Are you feeling sick?"

"No, just tired." She visibly shook herself. "I'll go to bed early tonight. Maybe we practiced too much this week."

"Alright, well, we don't need to use magic to make a mini."

Brenn dumped a worn cardboard box out on the table. A storm of wildly colored materials flooded the tabletop. She chopped her arm down the middle, shoving half towards Audrey. They started sifting through in silence. After ten minutes of quiet, Brenn couldn't hold it in anymore. "This is ridiculous."

Audrey looked up from the tiny clay creatures she was standing in a row. "I'm sorry. I can leave if you want."

"No, I don't want. I meant the silence in here, not you." Brenn plugged her phone into a speaker hanging from a shelf. A sudden cacophony blared out. "This is my 'songs to listen to when I want to punch the universe in the face' playlist." She shouted over the music, doing an exaggerated shimmy in Audrey's direction.

She saw a quiver on Audrey's lips. Grabbing two tiny Mothmen figures from her pile, Brenn used them to make a ridiculous flourish motion that propped two pieces of textured paper up to act as theater curtains. On her makeshift stage, she danced her figures around while howling out the lyrics of the song in a different voice for each Mothman. Audrey pulled her lips in, biting them from the inside. "You can laugh, Audrey, it's a good time, don't be a dork, have some fun," she sang at her in the melody of the song.

Audrey tossed a handful of sequins at her. "You are the only dork here."

But she did seem less tired.

~

"THANKS FOR LETTING ME BORROW THIS," Brenn said, tapping the *Hocus Pocus* DVD case on her palm. "My parents never let us have this one when we were kids."

"No?" Aislynn backed out of the walk-in closet that held her family's collection of board games, movies, and craft supplies. "Why on earth not? They hate joy?"

Brenn snorted. "Kind of? My suspicion is that it wasn't 'arty' enough. Although, my mother hated that *Wind Beneath My Wings* song, so it may have been the mere presence of Bette Midler."

"Not a *Beaches* kinda gal?" Aislynn gave her a sly look. She lifted her eyebrows suggestively. "I have that one on DVD *and* VHS. We also have the complete series of Buffy if you want."

"Oh, the idea of my mother liking *Beaches*, oh boy." Brenn laughed. "And I'll pass on Buffy for right now. I've drawn the line at movies only this time."

Aislynn's raccoon familiar scampered out of the closet after her. He wore a little fanny pack around his furry waist, silkscreened with the logo for Camp Curiosity '96. Aislynn handed him a multi-tool. "Here, Cap, I found this behind the movie boxes."

He took it from her and casually stuck it in his fanny pack before running off. Brenn watched him with a half-smile on her face. She asked, "So, you were a Curiosity kid?"

"Me and Ben both, in '96. My sister went in '95." Aislynn went to their kitchen. "You want a drink? I have an open bottle of white that should get finished tonight."

Brenn glanced at her watch. "Sure, I could have one glass." She accepted the wine Aislynn held out to her and sat on the bench in the breakfast nook. "I was a '98 camper. It's a shame Audrey is too old to go now. I think she would love it."

"Nina went last year and won't shut up about it. The boys seethe with jealousy every time she brings it up. I've told them a million times that we are definitely sending them when they turn twelve..."

Brenn let her mind drift as she listened to Aislynn. She wondered if hauling out her old photos from camp would be interesting for Audrey, or if it would be too much like rubbing her face in yet another magical milestone she'd missed.

~

"SO, *Hocus Pocus, Practical Magic, Stardust, Teen Witch, The Witches, The Craft,* and *Bedknobs and Broomsticks.* Plus *The Addams Family* and *Addams Family Values* if we have time." Brenn slapped each DVD on the pile. "Anything you want to add? We'll pass the video store on the way to get food."

"Uh, no. Do you think we'll need more than nine movies?" Audrey tossed four more pillows on the giant pile on the living room floor. "Is that enough pillows? I can go get the ones from the porch too."

Brenn surveyed the makeshift pillow cloud with a critical eye. "We'll start with that. It's not like we can't get them later."

Audrey asked that they have a day just at home, relaxing. Brenn declared a movie marathon day. When she was young, on the rare weekends when her parents were both at home with free time, the Maren family would throw every pillow and cushion in the house on the living room floor and have a movie marathon that lasted the entire day. It was one of the few times she felt fully a member of her own family.

Brenn had occasionally binged several movies in a row by herself as an adult, but it wasn't the same without someone to watch with. She drew in a deep breath, trying to dislodge the lonely feeling deep in her chest.

"Brenn?" Audrey called from the foyer. "We should go if you want to be back by ten."

"Coming," she shouted back. She addressed Charles Mayhew, sitting primly on the back cushions of the sofa. "We'll be back shortly fellas, hold down the fort. Ha, literally." Brenn would swear, if corvids could roll their eyes, Mayhew would have right then. Brenn pointed at him. "I can read your attitude, sir."

"Bye-bye," he croaked at her.

She threw up her hands and went to meet Audrey in the foyer.

FORTY-FIVE MINUTES LATER, they staggered into the Moon House laden with grocery bags. Brenn managed to greet the house by stroking the door frame with the back of her hand. Audrey stopped to nuzzle her cheek against it, and the house creaked in response. "I love this house," Audrey told Brenn.

Unpacking their snacks took another half hour. "Do you think we got enough?" Brenn asked, hands on her hips.

"We aren't going to be able to eat this all ourselves. We'd need like four marathons to finish it all." Audrey brought out plates for their lunches.

"You serve up our lunches and bring them in. I'm going to light the fire." Brenn went to the screened porch and grabbed a grey waxed canvas carrier filled with logs. She hauled it into the living room, setting it by the fireplace. Audrey came into the room balancing plates on top of a couple of bowls, with a bag of chips and a giant bag of M&M's clutched in her teeth. She opened her mouth to drop the bags on the couch and managed to transfer the bowls and the plates to the coffee table without spilling a single drop. "Gonna get our drinks!" she trilled as she bounced back out of the room.

Brenn waited until she heard her all the way down the hall and then snapped her fingers at the pile of logs and kindling in the fireplace. She couldn't get any fire to appear, much less catch. Mayhew flew over, dropping a book of matches in her lap. "Thanks, Mayhew," she said, defeated. She hurriedly struck several matches at once, tossing them into the fireplace.

When Audrey bounced back into the room, Brenn was perched on the pillow pile, plate in her lap, fire roaring.

"I am into this," Audrey said, handing her a bottle of sparkling water. "What's first?"

"Depends. Are there any you haven't seen yet?" Brenn set her plate aside to grab the stack of movies. She fanned them out.

Audrey picked up *Bedknobs and Broomsticks*, studying the back cover copy. "I don't know what this one is."

"Oh ho ho, Angela Lansbury is an apprentice witch who flies a bed under the sea to enter a dance contest and ends up fighting Nazis. It's utter madness."

Audrey crawled over to the TV stand on her knees and put the DVD in. "I'll take your word for it."

"My friend, you do not have to. In two hours, you yourself will possess the arcane knowledge."

Two hours later, Audrey sat cross-legged on a sofa cushion, leaning forward on her elbows. "I was not ready for whatever that was." She started laughing hysterically.

"I told you." Brenn slid the DVD out of the player and held up two more cases. "*Hocus Pocus* or *Teen Witch*? Those are the best follow-ups, energetically."

Audrey pointed at *Hocus Pocus*, her cheeks stuffed full of snacks. They managed two and a half more movies before they were ready to order in dinner. Brenn watched Audrey with half an eye during each movie, a little buzz of happiness hitting her every time Audrey reacted to the films with delight. She thought about Ms. Price from *Bedknobs* and her relationship with her orphan wards, and that made Brenn think about her own relationship with Audrey. She was feeling increasingly worse about keeping such a huge secret, especially from someone depending on her and living in her house. Picking at her food, she decided to come clean with Audrey.

When they finished dinner, Brenn paused *Stardust*. Her stomach swooped unpleasantly and her palms were clammy, but she pressed on. "So, there's something I need to tell you." She took a shaky breath. "A few days before you showed up in town, my magic started getting weird."

"Weird?" Audrey asked.

"Like, not as strong, and not as precise. I've been trying to fix it. I got a book from Arlo, and joining the coven gave me a boost. It's not gone, I just don't know what is going on with it. I thought you should know."

Audrey looked perplexed. "But I've seen you do magic."

"Yes, but it's not normal. And no one else knows that I'm struggling right now. I really want to keep it that way. And you definitely cannot tell Noelle. She would lose her shit." Brenn made a face. "I probably shouldn't have told you, but I want to be honest with you."

"But. Am I going to have to leave?" Audrey's voice was small, and it twisted Brenn's heart.

"No, I don't want you to. We are doing fine so far, yeah?" At Audrey's nod, she kept going. "And I am working on fixing it, I think it will be fine in a couple weeks. It's just a little weird right now."

"Oh-kay" Audrey sounded unsure. "You will be alright?"

"Of course. This happens sometimes. It's nothing you need to worry about." She picked the remote up again. "Have you ever felt unsafe here?"

"Oh. No, I haven't. Is there any way for me to help?" Audrey brightened a bit as she thought about that.

"Nope, just don't make fun of me if you see me doing some strange rituals from the book I got."

Audrey snuggled back down into the pillows. "If you're going to be fine, and your magic will be okay soon, then we don't have to worry?"

"I'm not worried." Brenn admonished herself silently for being a filthy liar.

"Okay. Can we watch *The Craft* next?"

Brenn unpaused the movie. As they watched together, Brenn scolded herself for bringing it up. She wasn't being honest with her half-truths and deflection, and now she went and shoveled some of her own worry onto Audrey. And, even worse, if

Noelle somehow found out, they'd be sunk. Brenn pressed her lips together, unable to concentrate on the television as she tried to figure out what to do. The next time the coven was together, she would try to gauge if she could tell them without being kicked out. Her breath caught as she started to panic at the thought of losing the coven so soon. She rubbed her chest, trying to dispel the tightness.

Mayhew noticed her agitation and sat behind her, his head on her shoulder. She nuzzled the top of his head, forcing herself to concentrate on Michelle Pfeiffer's gleefully evil witch creating havoc throughout Stormhold. She tried not to think about where the line between good witch and evil witch lay, or how close she might be edging to that line.

Twelve

ON MONDAY, the coven met again.

"This is such a weird place to meet." Nat roamed around Junelle's classroom, opening cupboards, reading posters on the wall. "I can't remember the last time I was in an elementary school classroom."

Junelle was bent over her planner. "Middle school."

"Huh?" Nat asked.

"It's actually middle school. Pre-teens. Less innocence, waaaay more hormones. Not enough deodorant." She slid her planner into her messenger bag hanging on the back of her chair. "Kids this age are funny as hell, but also little shits in the same breath."

Aislynn called out a homework reminder to her daughter down the hallway outside the door. Coming into the room, she rolled her eyes. "You'd think I asked her to read the entire Library of Congress by herself walking uphill in the snow barefoot. Do they get any easier as they get older?"

"Maybe when they can drive? At least then they won't be in the house as much." Junelle spun her chair back and forth.

Dani chimed in. "This is true. Though maybe I shouldn't talk, Lydia has always been pretty easy to deal with."

Lily asked Junelle for cleaning wipes and scrubbed at a desk and plastic chair vigorously. She held them out. "Anyone else?"

Walker grabbed them and quickly wiped down the rest of the desks and chairs in the group Lily sat at. She washed her hands in the sink.

"Have a lot of experience with children?" Junelle asked.

Walker looked perplexed for a second. "Oh, no, just my cousin's kids. Who have given me strep throat enough times that I don't take chances with stuff kids even *might* have germed up."

"Next time, come see me right away. I'm pretty good with strep." Aislynn passed her a business card. "That goes for all of you. Especially you, teach." She pointed at Junelle.

"Yeah, yeah. I do okay. I think I've been exposed to enough stuff that a twenty-minute nap and a pot of licorice root tea has me up and running in no time." She held out a pack of dry erase markers. "Should we use the board if we are doing bylaws and such today?"

"I can take the notes if no one minds." Nat took the markers from her. "I plot all my books on a giant whiteboard, so I've developed pretty decent sideways-wall handwriting."

Junelle rolled her chair to the pod of desks the other women sat at. "Please, knock yourself out. I hate writing on the board. Dry erase squicks me out."

Brenn laughed. "That's bad luck. At least it's not chalk?"

Junelle shuddered and made a hairball noise. Dani said, "At least with whiteboards no one can run their fingernails down it."

"Why would you bring that up? I can hear it in my mind now!" Aislynn wiggled her shoulders like she was trying to dislodge the memory physically.

Nat wrote in large capital letters 'BYLAWS'. Under that, she added a dash and 'no chalkboards'. 'Negative magic by unanimous vote only' and 'no blood magic' followed. She took a step to the right and started another list labeled 'CONSIDERA-TIONS'. There she wrote 'snacks at all meetings?' and 'coven name'. She turned back to the room. "What else?"

"I think it would be a good idea to start keeping a grimoire of sorts, to keep track of what we cast and any development notes," Dani said.

Lily nodded approvingly. "I concur. I propose we add a goals list for spells we'd like to attempt and a desires list for castings that we have not yet developed."

Nat added both to the board. "It would be nice to have some sort of charm that allows us to access the grimoire even if we are not physically with it."

"I mean, the internet exists." Brenn added. At the quizzical and/or concerned looks sent at her, she made a face. "That was a joke."

"Oh, thank fuck," Dani said. "I didn't know how to tactfully say 'the internet is not secure, you dingdong' in a diplomatic way."

"A physical record allows us to better restrict unwanted access to our proprietary materials," Lily responded primly. A pause. "You dingdong."

Unfortunately, as Lily spoke, Dani had just taken a large sip of her tea, which reappeared forcefully through her nostrils. Brenn snorted, and there were a few giggles that turned into full laughter. Lily smiled smugly as she handed a tissue over to Dani.

A COUPLE OF HOURS LATER, the entire board was covered in bylaws and customs the coven had agreed on. The only 'considerations' item that was not stricken through was 'coven name'.

"We can't register as an official coven until we have a name." Nat's voice was tired.

"What's the point of registering? Who cares?" Dani squirmed in her chair. "I don't really see us going to those competitions, so why would we need a name?"

"There are some benefits, and we do have a duty to the larger community. Once we're registered, we'll be on the relief list to provide aid if there's ever a need. And yeah, the competitions don't seem like our thing, but there are various conferences you can only attend as an officially registered coven. Plus, it will give us certain status as far as distribution of resources from the state."

"Resources from the state?" Lily arched an eyebrow.

"We can request use of rare materials, get access to research materials only available to sealed covens, that sort of thing." Nat picked up her phone. "I'm going to start a running list of names that we can all contribute to. If you have an idea, write it down."

Walker raised her hand. "What was the name of your last coven, Nat?"

"Oh, right. You were in a coven before," Aislynn said thoughtfully. "How did you leave that sealing? Or is that an invasive question?"

Nat set her phone down. "No, it's not invasive. There was a guardian in my last town right around the time I was leaving, and another witch had arrived in town so the guardian did a ritual that essentially just swapped us." She made a crossing motion with her hands. "And our official name was the Sisters of the Luminescent Bond."

"Wow," Walker managed in a strained voice.

Nat laughed ruefully. "It's a lot, I know. But they were great. Very earnest. And there were twelve of us in that coven, so we had more success with majority rule than full consensus. I can't lie; that name is the reason I am pushing so hard for each of us to agree."

"That makes sense. Um, if we are wrapping up the business part of the meeting, I have a spell request." Junelle got up. From the closet in the corner of the room, she pulled out stacks of paper in shades of pink, orange, purple, and green. "The high school is doing *Into The Woods*, and my classses got voluntold to make the trees for the sets. I'd like to cut all these leaves by magic, and I think we could get them all cut pretty quickly if we worked together."

"Sure," Brenn said, cuffing her shirt sleeves. "Voluntold. That's a genius portmanteau."

"Right? Depressingly perfect." Junelle stacked the paper on her large table. The other women gathered in a circle. "I have no idea why the director thought middle schoolers would have enough focus to cut hundreds of leaves."

Aislynn tipped her head to the side, studying the paper. "Do you have templates for the leaf shapes you want? I have a snipping spell I use to cut my kids' hair, and I think we could use it for this."

Junelle grabbed a pair of scissors and cut a few different shapes. "We can do each color with the same shape. Then I can have my kids put the folds in and practice sticking incantations to put them on branches."

Aislynn had Walker pass scissors out to everyone while she practiced with a scrap sheet of paper. A few adjustments later, she had the process down and taught the rest of them how to do her spell. Nat sat down next to Brenn, and as they cut, Brenn could have sworn she felt Nat push some magic at her through the weird cord-like connection she felt at the sealing. The edges of her leaves got much neater so she wasn't about to complain.

About fifteen minutes later, Junelle had a mound of hundreds of paper leaves.

"Oh, my little strawberries, I love you with all my heart. This would have taken me forever on my own. I'm definitely in charge of snacks for our next meeting." She made a shooing motion, and the stacks of paper whooshed across the room into several empty bins she had set by the windows.

They cleaned up the scraps of colored paper, and Dani transferred the notes on the board into a sticker-covered notebook.

As they worked, Brenn caught them up on Audrey's progress. "I keep trying to get Noelle off my back, but my sisters are annoyingly resistant to my suggestion abilities."

Walker had her stockinged feet propped up on a desk, legs crossed at the ankles. "Brenn. How does that work exactly?"

"Persuasion?" Walker nodded. Brenn thought for a second. "So everyone has a resonance, right? You move along at a certain frequency, and once you're moving that way, you stay on that path unless something affects it."

"An object in motion?" Lily asked.

"Sort of? Path probably isn't the right word. It's more like an aura. Anyway, I can sense that resonance, and I can push it, shape it. And then the rest of the process is just the Speech and Debate stuff we learned in high school, using words to get people where you want them. But people have free will; I can't make anyone do anything they don't want to do or aren't at least open to doing." She absently folded and unfolded a bit of leftover paper.

Nat looked thoughtful. "What happens if you put a lot of force in it?"

"Well. I can exert a tremendous amount of pressure, but I don't generally. Because, one, I feel gross about superseding someone's autonomy, and two, it wipes me the hell out. I can train if I know it's something I'll be doing beforehand, like conditioning for a marathon, but mostly I'll be laid out. Exhaustion, headache, nausea. Fever and chills sometimes. I don't know if it would be different with you all casting with me, but I also don't want to risk blowback running through the entire coven."

"That sounds awful to test." Walker put her feet back on the floor. "How did you figure it out?"

"I've done really intense persuasion only twice. Once when I was in college, and this complete asshole was stalking a girl in one of my classes and escalating to an extremely scary degree. No one would help her because he hadn't gotten violent yet, but come on. So I pushed him into forgetting he cared she existed and got him to relocate to rural Alaska. That was when I was eighteen and in prime health. I was in bed for ten days, failed one class, and lost thirty pounds." She nodded along with everyone's horrified gasps and chewed her lip. "The second time was in my late twenties, and I woke up in the hospital. So if I need to be functional, I have to find other ways."

"Is that what your family wanted you to do at Witchery Aesthetica?" Nat asked.

"My sisters wanted me to brute force the information from Audrey, so kinda? With her age and emotional state, I probably would have just ended up with a migraine. But I also don't like to force people into things, so..." Brenn shrugged.

"You're a good egg, Brenn Maren." Dani smiled at her. "Does anyone have any magic they want to do next time?"

Walker raised her hand. "I've been working on an umbrella spell that uses whatever natural materials you have on hand if you want to try that."

"Is that what you've been doing in the backyard?" Dani asked. "We all might want to bring hats. She's come in with leaves in her hair for the past week."

Walker tossed a wad of paper at her. "Bite me. It's going to be cool. When I figure it out."

Dani stuck her tongue out.

Lily ignored their antics as she spoke. "I was thinking we could develop a searching spell with wind as the base. We'd have to gather some ingredients outdoors. Is anyone available on Wednesday? The weather forecast looks optimal then."

There was a flurry of movement as calendars were checked, and a chorus of assents followed. Junelle stood up. "Great. Let's meet at the Wonder Mug in Summit Park. If I'm going to be traipsing around in the cold, I need a hot chocolate. Seven? Seven thirty?"

Nat shoved her hair up under a striped knit hat with a large pompon on top. "Seven-thirty is better for me."

Dani waggled her eyebrows up and down. "Hot dinner date?"

"Ooohooo," Junelle teased.

Nat fake-glared at her. "Are *you* a middle schooler?"

Junelle wrinkled her nose in response. "Yeah, yeah. But seriously, date?"

"Actually, I do," Nat said, dignified. "I'm taking the woman who runs the observatory out for an early dinner. First date."

"Oh, she's super nice. I dated her roommate when we were in college." Junelle heaved a bulging tote over her shoulder. "Do we need to push our time back?" Nat told her no, and she escorted them out of her room, locking the door with a jingle of her keys. "See you all on Wednesday!" she chirped.

Thirteen

BRENN HAULED an old free-standing mirror up from the basement. Panting, she dragged it to the middle of the foyer, unwilling to take it any farther. "What the hell did they make old furniture out of?" she wheezed to Mayhew. "This thing weighs a ton."

She pushed the foyer chair in front of the mirror, and flopped into it. Talking to the coven about her abilities last night had given her an idea—she knew her persuasion didn't work on her family members, but she had never tried it on herself. She was aiming for a—she hoped—sweet spot between reciting affirmations in a mirror and self-hypnosis.

Brenn had three hours before Audrey was due home from school, so time enough to try a few different approaches. She angled the mirror so she could see herself fully, but that caught a glare from the window and reflected it into her eyes. She got up and drew the curtain closed, but then the room was too dark so she got some candles out and lit them. A little ambiance couldn't hurt. She wasted another ten minutes trying to find the perfect position in the chair but had to admit she was procrastinating because she was nervous.

"Here we go," she said, rubbing her hands together. She turned to Mayhew. "Stick around while I try this, yeah?"

He clacked his beak at her. "Hurry up," he said.

Brenn scowled at him. Breathing deeply, she stared at her reflection. Listening for her personal resonance felt strange, like trying to cut her own hair in the mirror. Everything felt backwards. She shut her eyes.

That helped. With her eyes closed she was able to grasp the edge of her own aura. Once she had a firm hold, she looked back into the mirror. Her reflection sparkled and she breathed out a tiny 'a-ha' as she started to shape herself. "Your magic is fine," she whispered. "Better than ever. You are strong, you are enough, you are capable."

She felt a ripple of muscle twitches down her body and hesitated. When nothing else happened, she continued to whisper the result she wanted. "Your magic is fine. Your cards aren't blank. Your spells won't backfire."

She *pushed*. And then there was a painful clapping noise as the air pressure in the room dropped rapidly. The mirror seesawed in its frame.

Brenn felt an immense pressure in her ears and sinuses. She stretched her jaw, then held her nose and swallowed hard, trying to get her ears to pop. A sudden high-pitched squealing made her clap her hands over her ears which only amplified the sound and made her dizzy. She leaned over the arm of the chair and retched.

At least she knew now her powers didn't work on herself, either.

BRENN SAT in her darkened office, attempting valiantly to get work done. Her body throbbed everywhere. Using a rose quartz tumble she kept on her desk, she massaged her eyebrows, rolling it back and forth, trying to ease her headache. A crashing sound echoed from the foyer as Audrey got home from school.

"Hey, Brenn, what is that mirror doing there? I ran into it. It didn't break or anything but you should probably move it." Audrey swung her upper body into the room, hanging onto the door frame. "Are you busy this week? I have a thing to do for Sorcery Circle, and maybe you can tell me if it's good? And I need a few things from a craft store."

Brenn set her crystal down. She flipped through her planner. "Sorry, Audrey, I still have a lot of work to do tonight. And I've got a terrible headache. Tomorrow night I have a coven thing, so probably not tomorrow either. Could we do it Thursday after school?"

"I have a meeting for the yearbook committee on Thursday. And I'm going home with Lydia after school on Friday."

"How about this weekend? I have a pick up on Saturday morning, but otherwise, I'm free."

Audrey seemed a little subdued but nodded. "Oh. It's fine. I can ask someone else tomorrow too. It's not a big deal."

THE NEXT MORNING, while she was waiting for her second pot of coffee to brew, Brenn flipped through more of *Middle-Aged*. Chapter eleven was all about using hallucinogenic drugs to step out of the false restrictions her mind imposed on her. Supposedly this would allow her to access a higher consciousness which would facilitate a dialogue with her magic. She did still have that tin of Mina's tea.

She texted the coven group chat.

Brenn:

> How bad an idea is it to do psychotropic
> drugs with a teen in the house?

Dani replied immediately:

> do you want me to have Lydia ask Audrey to
> sleep over on Friday instead of just dinner?

Walker:

> Is that really what you want to do?

Junelle:

> As a professional, I'm gonna say not great.

She bit the skin by her thumbnail, trying to decide if it was irresponsible to pawn Audrey off all night on Friday so she could do drugs. She really did have to work early on Saturday. Her phone pinged several more times.
Aislynn:

> I can recommend some safety precautions.
>
> Come by my office.

Lily:

> Brenn, do you not remember what happened
> that time the whole tennis team smoked
> weed after the tournament in Mackinac City?

Nat:

> uh, if you want to experiment I guess we
> could at our next meeting.
>
> but you are a grown-up so...
>
> make your own choices?

Dani:

> wait, we are going to get high at our next
> meeting? i'm going to make a little something
> special then.

Junelle:

> Oh boy.

Brenn:

> Never mind, this got a little out of hand. We
> definitely do not need to get high tonight.

BRENN WAS STILL THINKING about ways to fix her magic as she finished her morning deliveries. She wasn't sure drugs were the answer. Well, hallucinogens. She was downing painkillers like nobody's business after her disastrous experiment yesterday.

Her stomach growled loudly, derailing her train of thought. She decided to stop at Kim's Lunch Spot to pick up some bulgogi and bao. It had been her favorite lunch spot since they opened several years ago. April Kim was Korean American, and Kim Liang was Chinese American. They had each had a food stall at the farmer's market that ran all summer in Briar Vale. One summer, their booths had been right next to each other, and they had been busier than they ever had been before. They decided to combine forces, and one of the Vale's most popular lunch restaurants was born.

The line snaked around the building when Brenn joined it. She scrolled through her phone while she waited, reading about all the ways Sabrina and her aunts fixed their malfunctioning magic on the original *Sabrina the Teenage Witch* television series. If only TV logic applied to real life.

Still reading on her phone, she shuffled around the corner and into the restaurant. As she looked up at the menu on the back wall, a familiar bossy voice caught her attention. Noelle and Audrey were at a table a couple rows over. She suddenly had no appetite.

April waved at her from the open kitchen. "Hey, Brenn. The usual?"

She nodded and gave her a thumbs up. April called her order and name to the kid working the register.

Brenn wove through the tables and pulled an empty chair up to the table Noelle and Audrey were at. "I didn't know you two had plans today."

Noelle daintily patted her lips with her napkin. "The district has a half day today. Didn't you read the schedule? It should have been on your school calendar."

"Must have slipped my mind." Brenn valiantly tried to hide her surprise and hurt. "Are you doing anything else after this?" she asked Audrey.

"Yeah, Noelle is taking me down to the craft store by Teeny's. I need to get some supplies for charms club." Audrey offered Brenn some kimchi.

Brenn waved it off. "I could have taken you. You just have to ask."

"I did, but you're busy, and I need to get it before Friday." Audrey refilled her teacup from the pot on the table, taking a deep sniff of the steam curling up from her green tea.

Noelle looked up from her phone. "I needed to stop by the computer repair place down there anyway, so it's no trouble." Her phone dinged, and she made an irritated noise as she started typing fiercely. "I'd like to spend a little time with Audrey anyways."

Brenn watched her, biting back a sigh. She grabbed a slice of cucumber from one of the tiny bowls in front of Audrey. "Remember, I have my meeting tonight. Will I see you before I have to leave for that?"

"If you aren't going to be home, why doesn't Audrey come home with me for dinner tonight? Jasmine is making tacos, so we'll have plenty of food. I can give her a ride after so she doesn't have to walk home in the dark," Noelle said.

"Oh, can I? I wanted to ask Jasmine if she would help me with a thing for school too," Audrey asked, her eyes bright.

Brenn wanted to say no but knew that was unfair. She should be happy that Audrey had a good circle of support. "Sure. Tacos sound better than leftovers anyway, which is what I had planned for tonight."

The kid at the counter called her name. Brenn stood up and returned the chair she'd borrowed. "That's my food. Audrey, have fun and be safe. Noelle, thanks. I'll see you around."

Brenn managed to keep her expression even and pleasant until she was the next block over. She wordlessly growled in frustration, making a woman crossing the street jump. "Shit," she muttered. She chastised herself for expecting that she would be the only one Audrey would turn to for help or company. She didn't even want to limit Audrey that way. Noelle obviously was filling a need that Brenn couldn't, so what right did Brenn have to get so bent out of shape?

Fourteen

THE WIND HAD COOLED CONSIDERABLY by the time Brenn had to leave. She dug around in her closet until she found her thick burnt orange cable knit sweater. It used to be her father's, and she'd managed to acquire it surreptitiously her senior year of college. She suspected he had been fully aware she'd absconded with it and had let her without comment. That made her feel doubly warm whenever she wore it.

"Hey, fellas, you want to come with to Summit?" she shouted as she laced up her boots. Charles came loping into the foyer, chittering a question at her. "Hmm?" She tossed a pair of gloves into her bag. "Oh, I think a few hours? You'll have time to do your regular thing, regardless." He climbed up onto the seat of the chair, peered into her bag, and stared at her until she rearranged her things to make him a cozy nest to curl up in. Brenn jingled her keys impatiently. "Mayhew, we're leaving!"

An annoyed caw came from the direction of the library. "Good bird ready," he croaked as he flew onto her shoulder, his talons tangling in her sweater. She poked her fingertip into his feathers.

"Yeah, yeah, good bird," she said with affection.

Summit Park created the far eastern border of downtown Briar Vale, a wedge-shaped expanse of green tucked between the Thorn and Bramble Rivers. Copses of birch and maple and aspen trees dotted the large park with splotches of fall color in reds, oranges, and yellows. Usually, once a month or so, all the familiars living in town held a meeting of their own at the circle of rowan trees next to the Bramble River. Charles Mayhew had friends that permanently lived there, and so Brenn liked to make sure she brought them over at least once a week so they could socialize.

The street lamps in the park glowed orange under the canopy of trees. The overcast sky had been a thin, watery grey the entire day, making it feel colder than it actually was. Junelle, Dani, and Walker were huddled together next to the Wonder Mug cart as she strode across the grass. Walker had an enormous plaid scarf wrapped around her neck. Junelle and Dani clutched steaming cups of hot chocolate. Brenn ordered her own hot chocolate and joined the group. Once she was around the other members of her coven, her shoulders relaxed and her headache eased. The cord of connection she felt every time they were together pulsed pleasantly through her.

"Is that Mayhew?" Walker asked, nodding to the crow sitting on Brenn's shoulder.

"Yep. And this..." she rooted around in her bag and pulled out a very snuggly ermine. "...is Charles."

Walker offered her hand for them to smell and said hellos. Nat strolled over from the north side of the park and greeted each of them, including Brenn's familiars. "Are these fine fellows coming with us tonight?"

"Nah, I bring them over here once a week or so, so they can meet with their peers. I figured I'd get a two-in-one tonight since we're here anyways."

"Who's this?" Aislynn asked with delight as she came down

the sidewalk. Brenn introduced Charles Mayhew to her and then Lily, who joined them a minute later.

Brenn lowered Charles to the ground. "I'll whistle for you when we're done, k? Don't go too far, or else you both are walking home." She noticed Mayhew's pointed look. "Okay, okay, or flying home. For crying out loud."

Lily sipped her hot chocolate. "Hello, everyone. Tonight I'd like to gather fallen leaves, especially those the wind has moved far from their origin, and feathers. The lighter, the better for the feathers. This is going to be a clarity-seeking spell, so I'd like as much light as possible." She handed them each a brown paper lunch bag. "Also, if you see any eyebright, please pick a few stems."

"Color or mass?" Walker asked over the rim of her cup.

"Pardon?" Lily asked.

"The feathers. Light as in color or as in mass? Or size, I guess?"

Lily squinted into the distance, brow furrowed as she considered. "Either. Or both. I'm not sure which would be most effective, actually."

Walker saluted her and wandered further into the trees.

Nat caught up with Brenn as she headed towards the east end of the park, where the Thorn River diverged into the Bramble to the south. "Brenn. How have you been?"

Brenn tripped over a branch. "I'm fine. Why?"

"Your text yesterday sounded like you were trying to figure something out." Nat bent abruptly. She straightened and held up a tiny downy feather. "You know I am always around if you want to chat about things."

"Oh, no, I'm fine. I was reading a book about expanding consciousness. I never did drugs in college. Or ever."

"Gotcha. I do know someone who makes a certain kind of tea if you ever want any..." she waggled her eyebrows.

Brenn smirked. "I have some of my own."

Aislynn joined them then. "Is this the drug conversation? Because I have professional knowledge. Use me!" She plucked a red-orange leaf blowing past. "Plus, I had a wild phase when I was younger."

"Seriously?" Brenn laughed. "I wasn't really planning to do drugs any time soon, but I'll definitely call you if I do." She grabbed several yellow and orange oak leaves that were piled at the base of a sugar maple. Carefully picking her way down to the bank of the river, she ran her hand through the long grass on the water's edge. Holding the dry pieces of grass that had come loose, she asked, "Do you think these would be useful?"

"If not for Lily's spell, I bet it would be useful for a future casting." Nat took an abandoned bird's nest from a low branch and put it in her bag. "I think grab anything that might be practical."

They spent an hour gathering natural materials in the quiet dark. Lily cast a beacon over her head. She peered into each bag, a satisfied look on her face. "This is wonderful. I will take these with me and sort them. We should think about where to store our repository of ingredients for future spells."

"We could rent a locker in the Kestrel Meeting Center," Nat suggested. "I'll call in the morning."

"I could shift some stuff around in my storeroom if we need to," Brenn offered. "I can also get us proper storage containers if you let me know what you want."

Dani clapped her hands. "Great! Can we do some fun stuff now? Not that it wasn't fun to spend time with you, of course. I had a nice time. Yay, autumn!"

Walker shook her head with affection. "My umbrella spell is ready enough to test if you want."

Aislynn, Lily, and Brenn broke into spontaneous applause. Walker herded them to the far end of the park, where there was an open place under the tree cover. She made sure they could see her in the moonlight.

"Yeah, so you need enough material for a framework. I've been using fallen leaves because, duh, it's autumn, and they have a lot of surface area, but you could make twigs or grass work. So gather whatever you're using up." She kicked some leaves into a rough mound. "Then you need to coat them in magic," she made a sweeping motion over the pile, fingers spread and palm facing down, "and float them up and form the canopy." The leaves followed her hand as she flung her arm over her head, palm facing the sky this time. She touched each fingertip to her thumb in turn. "Keep an idea of the ribs of an umbrella in your head the entire time the stuff is in the air." Walker sketched a rough shape in the air to indicate ribs but stopped as her leaves listed sloppily to one side. "The incantation is 'umbrella to compel, rain to repel'. Sorry about that, rhyming works best for this one, but I'm not great at making them up."

The leaves shuddered then snapped into a loose spiral formation, the space between them shimmery with energy, like heat waves from the pavement on a summer day. "Et voilà!" She bowed. "It will stay up until either you dismiss it or cross a threshold. If you keep it going for more than like a half hour, it will give you a wicked eye twitch, though. I haven't figured a way around that yet."

Nat was testing the spell, trying different motions. "Maybe both hands? That might distribute the effort equally."

"One's arms would fatigue fairly quickly, I would think," Lily said, mirroring what Nat was doing. They huddled next to each other, discussing other possibilities for dispersing the effort of holding the umbrella up.

Aislynn was spinning hers in the air above her. She smiled through the force field of brightly colored leaves she held around herself. "This is an excellent spell, Walker."

"Agreed," Junelle called from a few yards away. She had made her umbrella out of twigs and pine needles, arranged in an elaborate geometric formation.

"Oh, wow," Brenn breathed. "Mine is so pathetic next to yours." A droopy dome of brown and grey leaves slumped over Brenn's head. She tried a few different gestures to perk up her umbrella, but it got floppier and more shapeless instead. A wet leaf dropped down and plastered itself to her forehead. "For crying out loud," she ground out, flinging the leaf off her head. Her eye started twitching, and she faked a sneeze so she could disperse her umbrella without the rest of the coven noticing how she struggled.

Using even that tiny an amount of magic made her ears ring again. She massaged her jaw and neck to ease the tension, making her movements as small as possible. She had thought that drawing on the coven's collective strength would make up for the lack in her own abilities, but she could barely feel their connection tonight.

Following Brenn's lead, the coven dropped their umbrellas and stood around awkwardly. Lily gave them all handi-wipes. Aislynn spoke first. "So, are we just...going home now?"

Dani piped up. "Uh, I have a new potion if you all want to test it. I did some initial trials, so it's safe and all, but I'd love to see how it works with other people."

She pulled out a palm-sized plastic food storage container. She popped the top off and held it out to them.

Nat peered into the box, one eyebrow raised. "Dani. Those are gummy bears."

Brenn was glad that Nat had said what she was thinking so she didn't have to.

"Au contraire, my friend. These are potions in gelatinized form." She shook the box. "Think of it as a...more shelf-stable jello shot. And it will definitely make you float." She paused and cocked her head to the side. "Well, not float so much as, hmm, *loosen* your relationship with gravity."

Six stunned faces stared back at her as she beamed. "It's an experiment!" She offered the container around.

"No..." Nat whispered, a note of disbelief coloring her tone. "Seriously?"

"Holy shit." Junelle cackled, making a clutching motion with both hands. "Gimme gimme!"

Lily looked shocked for a minute, and then a grin spread across her face. "Yes, please. That's...seriously cool."

Brenn couldn't remember ever having seen Lily actually grin before. She picked a yellow bear out, looking at the moon glow through its translucent body.

Walker popped a gummy in her mouth and handed the container to Aislynn. "Ais, do you want an arm?"

"I'd appreciate it, especially for the landing part." Aislynn carefully stood, entwining her arm with Walker's as they chewed.

As soon as Brenn swallowed the last bit of her bear, her body shivered violently. Her tinnitus got briefly overwhelming, then went away entirely. The sensation running over her skin was like someone had poured a bucket of cold water on her. Then she got very warm all over, and she felt like she was standing on marshmallow. Taking an experimental step forward, Brenn nearly fell on her face. She recovered and took several floaty steps towards Aislynn and Walker. "Can I join your person chain? This is so weird."

Aislynn took her hand, and the three of them bounced around the park. Lily figured out a way to do a very high leap and then float gently back to the ground. Dani, Nat, and Junelle were trying, with varying amounts of success, to run vertically up tree trunks. Aislynn figured out she could essentially lie on the air by holding a tree branch and occasionally doing a pull-up. Walker spun around like a small child, then jumped as high as she could, whirling herself violently into trees and lamp posts, shrieking with laughter. A pair of evening grosbeaks glared disapprovingly down at her from a branch high in a tree she had crashed into.

The seven of them bounced around until the effects of the

gummies wore off a couple of hours later. "Dani, that was incredible."

Dani, breathing heavily, wobbled a curtsy. "Thank you much. And that was just my first formulation."

"What...what are you trying to achieve?" Nat asked with fascination.

"Actual floating, babe. The problem is keeping an upper limit on it so you don't fly off into a flight path."

They slowly made their way back to the downtown side of the park. Lily stopped them on the sidewalk. "I will be readying my spell this weekend. Would you be available early next week to try it with me?"

After agreeing on Tuesday, each witch went to her respective vehicle. Except Junelle, who waved cheerily. "I live on Talisman."

"I didn't know that. You're so close! I'll text you the next time I bring Charles Mayhew here if you want to hang out." Brenn said. She whistled for her familiars, sitting on her bumper until they showed up. Brenn still felt like she was floating.

Fifteen

THE NEXT MONDAY, Brenn had phone call after call, starting at seven in the morning. She was busy non-stop from the beginning of October until after the winter solstice. She paced back and forth in her office, snippets of her conversation floating out into the hallway. "John, you know that when women are economically secure they invest in their communities? Who better to know this than the women interested in...her family has owned and run the business for more than two hundred years...no, there is not a man that you could speak with. It's me or nothing...if the world went to shit for you tomorrow, what's the bare minimum order that would keep you afloat? John, her order covers 85% of that and she has a solid track record..."

She noticed Audrey loitering in the hallway. She covered the mic of her phone. "Do you need something? I'm going to be a while still. You okay to get to school?" she whispered.

"Yeah, I just was wondering if you need me to help? Before I go?" Audrey asked around the fingernail she was chewing on.

"No, don't worry about it. I'll see you after school, okay?" At Audrey's nod, Brenn went back into her office, uncovering her phone. "John, that is completely unreasonable. If you can't get the order together, we can find someone else. No, of course I don't want to, but I don't know why..." She waved to Audrey, still standing in the doorway, and pointed to her watch. Audrey looked at the clock on Brenn's wall, sighed, and disappeared, presumably to put her coat on and leave. Brenn frowned a little but then went back to her phone call. Charles loudly scolded her as he had to swerve around the dirty socks that she had taken off and thrown from her office.

After she hung up, Brenn sagged bonelessly in her chair. She hadn't realized how much she relied subtly on her magic to smooth negotiations with her suppliers until it wasn't there anymore. Her head was pounding.

BRENN WAS WAITING in the kitchen when Audrey got home from school. "Hey, kid. Want a snack?" She called at the sound of the door closing.

Audrey slumped into the room, desultorily taking a cookie from the plate Brenn held out. "Thanks. Do you have any powdered wormwood? I need three grams for school."

"We can check. I'm not sure if we do, but we can go get it if not." She watched Audrey break little crumbs off the edge of her cookie. "You okay?"

"Yeah," Audrey sighed. "I also need you to sign this permission slip." She produced a crumpled sheet of paper from her bag.

Brenn took it, signed, and gave it right back. "Do you want some time to decompress? You can use the lying room."

Audrey shrugged. She grabbed a sparkling water from the fridge, and the next thing Brenn heard was the slamming of the lying room door. She guessed this was the nightmare teen hormones everyone talked about. Oh, wait. Teen hormones.

She knocked on the door. "Audrey? Can I talk to you for a

minute?" At a muffled 'yeah', she opened the door. "I don't know how to ask this without it being terribly awkward, so. Uh, are you having boy troubles? Or girl troubles? Or person troubles?" She tripped over her words. "It's fine if you are dating or sexually involved with someone, though if you are, there are a few things we need to do."

"Brenn, no." Audrey's face was beet red. "I'm not dating or...the other thing."

"Having sex?" Audrey nodded, refusing to meet Brenn's eyes. "Well, okay. I guess it's good you aren't if you can't even say the word. You'll let me know when you are ready, though? So we can talk about safety?"

Audrey flung her arms over her head. Her voice was muffled. "How do you know when you are ready?"

"I don't really. I. Um. I didn't have sex until college. I'm asexual, and so I don't know what it feels like at your age, the whole crush and lust thing. And aromantic, so I don't date. I mean, I know academically what happens in your body, I just haven't experienced it. That kind of desire, I mean." Brenn tripped over her words.

She flopped back onto the floor. "I am making a mess of this. I only wanted to say, if you are having troubles with romance or sex, you can definitely tell me, and I'm not going to judge you. Or scold you or whatever."

"I'm okay. I just have a lot to do for school and stuff." Audrey's blush was lightening.

Brenn studied her, trying to decide how much to push. "You want to talk about it? I'd really like to hear."

Audrey talked to the ceiling. "We have this presentation thing to do at school. We can pick our own topics. I thought maybe I could research magic loss and cures, you know, to help you. But there are a couple of kids who are being super mean about it, because I guess it doesn't really happen that often? Or something. But, like, how would they know? They aren't doctors, they're in high school." She picked up steam as she went on. "And my teacher said I could research whatever I wanted to, but I should pick a topic that was easier because I'm new to magic, and then those kids heard about it, and now they won't leave me alone about it and are being real—"

Brenn sat up, cutting her off with a swipe of her hand. "Audrey. You can't let anyone, *anyone*, know about my magic. That is a can of worms you cannot open, unless you want to be sent away."

"I didn't say anything. I just did a little bit of research," Audrey said defensively. "I'm not stupid."

"I never said you were stupid. But this is really important, and I need to know you understand that." Brenn thought about the news of her problem spreading through town, about her clients hearing. Her breath caught. "Please, please, tell me you picked a different topic."

"Yes, I picked a different topic! I know I don't know anything about magic or how school works or what I should already know or anything!" Audrey got up and stormed out.

Before she could get up herself, Brenn heard keys jingle and the side door slam. She curled up on the floor, wondering what she'd said that had set Audrey off so intensely. Sure, she could have been less vehement, but Audrey knew they needed to keep her magic issues a secret. And she knew that Brenn was working on it.

She longed to be with her coven, wished she could confide in them about all her problems. Ever since the sealing, she could faintly feel each of them through the connection that she thought of as an invisible cord. It was a physical relief to be in the same space as her coven sisters, and she desperately wanted to let herself relax into it. But she had to hold herself back until she managed to fix her magic.

Audrey did know Brenn was working on it, but Brenn hadn't really showed her how. There had to be something they could do together. Brenn wasn't going to subject her to *Middle-Aged*, but maybe another book. She sat back up. The family grimoires.

Brenn vaguely recalled an enhancement spell that her parents would never let her or her sisters attempt. She, Cleo, and Noelle had been huddled around the library table one afternoon, jostling for the best position to read the spidery letters. They were so engrossed they hadn't heard their mother walk in.

"Your great-great-aunt Lorraine created that one. She was extremely reckless." Her mother snapped the book shut, narrowly missing Brenn's fingers.

"Sorry, Mama. We wanted to see what kinds of spells our family made. We weren't going to cast any." Noelle said, her face shiningly earnest.

Sasha had raised an eyebrow. "No? That isn't your wand I see under the table? Noelle, your sisters are far too young to attempt spell work like this. I thought I could count on you to be reasonable." She caressed Cleo's plump cheek. "And your baby sister's magic just started coming in."

She ushered them out of the library. "There will be a charm on that grimoire from now on. Not one of you will be able to open it until your magic has settled."

By the time they had each turned twenty-one and were in possession of their full abilities, not one of them was concerned with an antique enhancement spell nobody was sure even worked. The grimoire had scores of much more useful spells, and the memory faded.

Brenn had to flip through two dozen grimoires before she found the one she was thinking of. Clutching it with both hands, she strode back through the house to the kitchen. "She's still gone?" she asked Mayhew.

Mayhew bobbed his beak up and down.

"How long has it been?" He clacked his beak five times. Two and a half hours. The sun had set a few minutes ago, and Audrey knew the downtown well enough. She was probably fine. Brenn ate an apple, leaning against the sink. Maybe she should text her and find out where she was. Chewing slowly, she ran through their earlier conversations in her head. Brenn admittedly could have handled that better.

No, she should definitely text Audrey. She'd figure out where Audrey was, and convince her to talk with Brenn when she got home, so Brenn could clear the air and invite her to help. Having a plan lifted her spirits a bit.

The door creaked open as she was picking up her phone. She hurried out to the foyer. "Hey, do you want dinner? Did you get everything you need?"

Audrey lifted the bags she carried. "Yeah, and I'm not hungry. I'm going upstairs now if that's okay."

"Actually could you hang out down here for a while? I wanted to ask for your help with something."

"I guess." Audrey put her bags on the chair, and kicked her shoes off. "What do you need help with?"

A tendril of hope wound around Brenn's heart. "You weren't doing anything wrong by choosing that topic for your presentation. And I have a handle on trying to fix things. But there are a few things we could do together to try to get my magic back, and you would learn some new stuff, which is good, right?"

"Okay, yeah. That would be cool."

Audrey trailed behind Brenn to the kitchen. Brenn picked up the leather-bound journal. "This is one of my family's grimoires. It's a collection of the spells and rituals and other magic my great-great-aunt Lorraine did."

She let Audrey flip through the pages delicately. She stopped her on a page toward the end. "That's the one I was thinking we should do."

"Enhancing Ability to Countermeasure Weakness? This will work?" Audrey moved her finger back and forth as she slowly read the spidery cursive. "Do you have all the supplies for this one?"

"Let's go check," Brenn said as she herded Audrey towards her storeroom.

A mere ten minutes later, they were all set up to perform the spell in the dining room. Brenn filled in where Audrey stumbled over the language of the incantation.

"Ready?" Brenn asked. They both hovered their hands over the components laid out on the table and chanted in unison. The chrysanthemum petals they had scattered among several other ingredients rose into the air and swirled in lazy circles. The air grew crisp and cold. As they finished the spell, a thin fog spread above the table. There was a quiet popping sound, and the fog vanished.

"Did you feel that?" Audrey's voice was high with excitement.

Brenn focused her attention inward. "I don't feel anything. I don't think it worked for me."

"Oh." Audrey's face fell. "It feels fizzy."

"Huh. I'm glad it worked, even if it wasn't the way we hoped." Brenn handed Audrey a notebook and pen. "Write down what you feel."

Audrey set them on the table. "Why bother? It didn't work."

"Because data is always useful. We should keep track of the things we try." Brenn flipped the notebook open.

Audrey scoffed. "We haven't taken notes on anything else I've done. Just put down that we failed and the spell feels fizzy." She shoved back from the table. "I'm going to bed. If you figure out something that will work, you can come get me then." Her footsteps sounded heavy on the stairs.

"What just happened?" Brenn asked the empty room.

Sixteen

THE COVEN MET BACK at the clearing with mossy stone benches. It was only the second time they had been there, but already it felt as familiar as home.

Nat bumped her as they walked down the path that meandered through the soft grey-green grass. "Everything okay? You seem quieter than usual. And I can feel some stress coming off you."

"Oh, through the cord? I'm sorry. Audrey has been kind of hot and cold with me. And she's been hanging around Noelle a lot lately, which makes me wonder what Noelle has been saying to her." Brenn lifted her head to sniff the autumn air. Someone was burning leaves, and the smoky smell had ridden the breeze all the way over to them. "God, it smells good out here."

Walker loped up on her other side to join their conversation. "So, do you think that's going to be a problem?"

"No, but I have no idea how to talk to her. I don't know what is going to set her off. Is that a teen thing, you think?"

Aislynn raised her voice from behind them. "She had been on her own for a while, right? She's probably still getting used to relying on you and is pushing the boundaries to figure out where they are."

"Teens also are the picture of self-absorption. Audrey does have more experience with the harsh reality of the world than most children, but she is still a teenager." Lily magically nudged a rock off the path with a graceful twist of her wrist.

"We had a sort of misunderstanding yesterday. I was annoyed and said some jerk-y things, and she took off for a few hours." Brenn pushed her sleeves up off her hands. "We made up when she got back, but I don't know. I don't know if it's just that she wanted some space or if she was running away for a couple hours."

"Maybe you should focus on spending more one-on-one time with Audrey," Nat said. "She's likely so used to doing what she needs to just survive she doesn't know how to recognize when she's safe."

"You think so?" Brenn brightened. "I'm trying to make her feel that way, but maybe it hasn't been enough."

Nat wound her arm through Brenn's elbow. "It's only been a month. Give her a little time."

THEY GATHERED in the circle of benches. Lily led them in the ritual this time, to cast the searching spell she had designed. She placed thirteen chandelier light bulbs in the sand on the platform and put one type of each of the different leaves and feathers they had collected together in the middle. Two sprigs of eyebright and a clear quartz point held them down in the sand. She drew thin arrows in the sand, pointing from the leaves in the middle to each of the lightbulbs along the edge.

Lily dusted a few grains of sand from the fingertips of her gloves. "It's ready. You will need to make this gesture." She put her right hand in front of her left eye, then swiped her hand to the right as though she was wiping something away from her eyes. "Then blink twice, and recite this incantation. 'Eyes open, eyebright. Lights on, revelation'. Then close your eyes for the count of three. Keep repeating that until all the bulbs have lit."

They practiced the motions and muttered the incantation to themselves for a minute. One by one, they looked at Lily.

Brenn let her mind wander while she waited for everyone else to ready themselves. It made sense that Audrey was testing her to see if she was a safe adult. Maybe she should sign them up for volunteering or a cooking class or something to do together. And casting with the coven tonight should give her a boost, magically speaking.

The advice from her friends eased her mind considerably. Her shoulders relaxed. It didn't seem like they thought she was a total failure yet. And her magic was okay when they cast together, so she didn't have to reveal that either. She'd just power through, and everything was sure to get better with a little time, like Nat said. Reading more of *Middle-Aged* would probably help too, she thought grudgingly.

Brenn would have to work more at regulating her emotions though. If she was letting her stress leak out, who knows what else she might let slip at a vulnerable moment?

She heard Lily say, 'let's begin' from far away. She hastily put her hand up with everyone else, making the wiping motion, a long blink, the incantation, then the two short blinks. Each time she repeated the action, she thought she saw each bulb go dark but looking again, they were all lit.

As the thirteenth bulb lit up, the pile of items in the middle of the circle swirled around three times, then lay still. The bulbs dimmed slowly, then went dark. Lily exhaled. "It appears to have worked. Now whenever we recite the incantation, directing our intentions to one person, that person should be given a vision of something they seek to see. Shall we test it? I volunteer to be the first subject, as it is my spell."

They each turned towards Lily, reciting the incantation together again. As the last word faded, Dani gasped loudly. "Hey. Hey. Something didn't work right." Her voice trembled.

"Dani? What's wrong?" Junelle flicked her fingers up and five orbs of light floated in the air above her. She whisked them over to Dani as she crossed the circle.

Walker carefully turned Dani's face to peer into her face. "Look at her eyes."

Dani's eyes glittered in the soft light. From across the circle, Brenn couldn't see the difference between her iris and sclera.

"Oh, wow. Oh, *wow*. Dani, can you see?" Aislynn fumbled for her purse. "Let me grab my penlight, I want to take a closer look."

Dani was staring at them in wonder. "I think I can see our magic." Her normally gold-brown eyes sparkled silver.

Brenn immediately broke out in goosebumps. "What do you mean, see our magic?"

"Have any of you ever used mica powder? Or mixed a pigment into a liquid? Like food coloring?"

"I've used mica and pigments," Junelle said carefully, staring at Dani's eyes.

Dani was looking at the spaces around them. "So you know when you add mica to something and swirl it around? And it kind of keeps swirling itself? That's what this is like." She trailed her fingers dreamily through the air in a figure-eight shape.

Walker looked confused. "Is it like light trails when you, ahem Brenn, do psychotropic drugs?"

"Sort of," Dani said in nearly a whisper.

Lily ran through the ritual again. "This should have worked. I don't know what went amiss. The setup was precise and correct, the motion was the same, then blink twice, incantation, closed eyes, repeat."

"Oh no." Brenn hid her face in her hands. "Oh no." Her voice was muffled. She opened her fingers to peek through them.

"I did a long blink first, then the short blinks after the incantation. Oh, Dani, I'm so sorry. Can we reverse it?" Her stomach dropped, and she fought the urge to vomit.

Lily's mouth dropped open. "Oh. Oh." She rubbed her chin thoughtfully. "By introducing that element of reversal, I think you triggered an opposing response. So instead of the sight coming to me, it went to Dani since she was standing directly across from me. But the sight was to allow me to control when I get visions, not to see magic itself."

Dani sounded breathless. "I actually don't mind this. I can see the shape of the spell. And all the magic hanging around you all. It's...it's amazing."

Walker tipped her head to the side, her eyes moving back and forth from Dani to Lily. "Maybe it acts on a subconscious desire? I can feel that you," she pointed to Lily, "want more control, and you," her finger swung around towards Dani, "are pretty much always desperate for more knowledge. It just got kinda...literal?"

Lily was frantically taking notes. "That is plausible. I want to consult a few spell theory texts, but I think you may be on to something."

"How long do you think this will last?" Nat was examining Dani's eyes. She kept muttering and flicking tiny spells into the air, watching how Dani reacted to each.

"It was supposed to be permanent," Lily moaned.

Six heads whipped around to look at her. "Permanent? You really should have warned us first." Aislynn's voice was sharp.

"I know, but I thought it was only going to affect me, didn't I?" Lily sniped back.

"Well, it's done now." Walker turned back to Dani. "Do we need to take you to the hospital? Are you going to be able to function?"

"I think it's going to be fine." Dani took out her phone and scrolled through it. "I can read through it and see the real world through it. If I don't think about...using? the sight, I can kinda ignore it." She backed up from the circle. "I want to try something real quick."

She cast a glowing orb in front of her, like the ones Junelle made but larger. Dani moved her hands in the air, like she was shaping clay, and her orb changed shape. She made a rubbing motion, and the orb changed color. "Yeah, this is actually fucking cool. I can see the shape of the spell and adjust it on the fly."

"Holy shit." Nat pointed at Lily. "You make a record of this and do that research. That's an incredible spell." She looked thoughtful, then concerned. "And very powerful. This does not go beyond the coven."

She pulled a small carved snake from her pocket. "Everyone, a forefinger on the snake. We are binding this knowledge to coven only."

They crowded their fingers on the snake and swore. Dani gasped at the result of that too. Brenn's nausea subsided to a general unease and a horrifyingly shameful amount of jealousy. She'd changed her friend's body, possibly on a cellular level, and all she could think was how much she wanted to see the magic herself.

Seventeen

BRENN WAITED for Audrey the next morning, nursing a cup of coffee. The residual shame she carried from permanently altering her friend's eyesight pounded through her head like a hangover. How could she have been so careless? And why did she *always* have a headache lately? She handed Audrey a mug of tea and the sugar bowl to doctor it up the way she liked.

"Oh, thank you," Audrey said gratefully. She put two spoonfuls of sugar in her tea, slurped it noisily, then added another.

Brenn grimaced. "So I've been thinking. Since you've been at Noelle's so much, maybe tonight we could stay here and hang out, do a mini movie marathon? Whatever you like. We can go to Be Kind and get actual videos if you want to go retro." She shuddered a little at the idea of VHS being a vintage novelty.

"Oh, I can't. I'm babysitting for Noelle and Jasmine tonight, and then I was planning to sleep over there. Noelle said she'd drop me at school before she went in to work."

Brenn was taken aback. "Oh. Okay. When did you plan this?"

"Last night when you had coven stuff. It's not a big deal."

Audrey set her teacup in the sink with a clatter. "It's okay, right? I mean, it's family."

Sure, it's family, all right. "Yep. Totally fine. Are you going to come home after school?"

"I was going to go straight there. I have a Charms and Chums club meeting at the end of the day, and then I'll get dropped off at Noelle's. I have a change of clothes in my backpack."

"Gotcha. Well, call me if you need anything. Five kids can be a lot." She wondered if she should talk to Noelle about using Audrey as a babysitter. She decided to wait and see how it went first. Maybe Audrey would hate babysitting, and the situation would resolve itself. One could hope.

"Sure, thanks, Brenn." Audrey snatched an apple from the bowl on the counter, flicked an almond at Mayhew, and rushed out of the house.

"Okay, bye? See you tomorrow? Ugh." She groaned and put her head down on her arms.

THE DAY STRETCHED OUT LONG in front of her. She got work done early; it was a surprisingly light day on that front, especially considering how busy the beginning of the week had been. She tidied, then deep cleaned the house. The Moon House finally started slamming doors to annoy her into stopping. "Okay, okay, I get it. No more cleaning."

She prepped a week's worth of meals for Charles Mayhew and gave Charles a thorough brushing. She tried reading on the back porch, but it felt too lonely by herself. Her miniature room brought her no comfort, as the scene Audrey was working on still littered the work table.

She set herself up in the lying room but couldn't get her

mind or her body to relax. She gave up after an hour of tossing and turning and staring at the ceiling aimlessly.

Outside, it was a picture-perfect autumn day, sunny and brisk with a playful breeze that rustled the yellow and orange leaves on the trees in her backyard. Brenn shrugged into an oversized flannel shirt and went out to toss acorns in the air for Mayhew to catch. "What do you think I should do today?" she asked him.

The crow dropped the acorn he was carrying in the mound by her feet. She hugged her knees, chin resting on one. He clacked his beak. "Get girl?"

"No, I can't, she's helping Noelle and Jasmine." He made a dismissive gesture with his head. "It's fine. If my stupid magic problem keeps on like it has been, she's going to need someone besides me."

"Fool witch," he croaked at her. "Don't know."

"Rude," she responded, affronted. "It was a serious question. I cannot focus on anything today."

Mayhew nudged an acorn at her. "Hot bath. Self-care." He fluffed his feathers and shook them back into place.

She scoffed. "I'm not taking a bath at two in the afternoon."

He hopped away, then flew up to the back of a patio chair. "Cards? Try again. New card."

"Yeah okay." She sighed.

Inside, she took her deck to the library table, even though picking them up made her feel a little nauseated. She still had a hard time believing she'd missed the equinox card. Brenn cradled the deck to her chest, willing good intentions and optimism it.

She shouldn't have bothered.

The deck just showed her blank cards, no matter how many she pulled or how thoroughly she shuffled. "Fine!" She threw up her hands. "I'm going to drink that damn tea, and then we'll see what you do!"

She brewed Mina's luck tea according to the handwritten

instructions inside. After two cups, Brenn was feeling extremely mellow. There were sparkles at the edge of her vision every time she turned her head.

Putting her supplies in the lying room, she set herself up for optimal painting time. A glass of water and a cup of brushes within arms' reach. Paper already taped to a board and propped on her tabletop easel. Another cup of that marvelous tea. Her best playlist on her phone.

She laid back on the cushions with a contented sigh and closed her eyes.

She woke up three hours later with no dream.

This was becoming a very serious problem.

BRENN HAD MANAGED to doze off in front of the television when her phone rang. She startled awake and answered it without looking. "Audrey? Is everything all right?"

"Not Audrey and everything is fine." Noelle. Damnit, Brenn needed to stop answering her phone without checking caller ID first. She rubbed a goo from the corner of her eye.

"Oh. Why are you calling me? Does Audrey need something?" Brenn patted her pocket for her keys. She sat up, blinking the sleep away.

"No, everything's fine. Sorry to bother you this late." Brenn twisted around to look at the clock on the mantle. Ten-thirty. Noelle had a very different definition of late than she did. She switched her attention back to Noelle, who was still talking. "...and so we got back a little earlier than expected. Audrey is great, she's sleeping in a blanket fort with all the kids in the twins' room. Getting them to school tomorrow might be a little rough."

"Sorry? Did you need something else?"

Noelle's tone got officious. "Actually, I wanted to talk to

you, again, about what is best for Audrey. She's lonely, Brenn, and needs to be in a more appropriate situation."

"Noelle, come *on*. We've talked this to death."

"No, Brenn, hear me out. We can get her back to her family, and I'm sure they would let you check in, if she wants that."

Brenn gritted her teeth. "No, Noelle, you listen. Audrey's parents are dead. She's been through a dozen foster homes and got kicked out of each one because her magic went wild. She doesn't have extended family. I checked."

"Oh. Well, why didn't you tell me in the first place?"

"Because that was her private information, and she gets to choose who to share it with. Except in this case, I guess, since you won't leave well enough alone."

There was a beat of silence as Noelle recalibrated her strategy. "Maybe we should start looking for magical fosters, then, get her to someone with experience and the willingness to raise a child."

"Noelle, did Audrey say she wanted to leave?"

"Well, no, but—"

"Has she said she doesn't want to live with me?"

"Not precisely, but Brenn, she's lonely. She needs more attention than you're giving her. And I know you think this is your way of helping our community but—"

Her sister was relentless but, in an even more infuriating way, was not wrong. Brenn had been spending more time with the coven and preoccupied with her own issues. She had to admit to herself she wasn't as hands-on with Audrey as she should be. Time to soften her approach. "Nono, you might be right. Give me another chance. I can cut back on my coven stuff and spend more time with Audrey. Please, Noelle." She let a little emotion into her voice. "Please. Don't uproot her again so soon."

Noelle sighed deeply. "Okay. You can try another few weeks, and we'll see where we are then."

"Fine. I'll talk to you in a few weeks. Goodnight." She hung up before Noelle could say goodnight herself, not caring how blatantly rude it was. Brenn was mad at Noelle and even angrier with herself. She stomped into the kitchen to get a sleeping draught. There was no way she'd be able to calm down enough on her own. She was, however, a little impressed at how complicated her life had gotten in just six weeks.

Eighteen

LEAVES CRUNCHED under Brenn's boots as she walked the six blocks to Violet's house. There was a house on the way that she always thought of as the Pumpkin House. Every year during September and October, the residents carved at least one new jack-o-lantern every day and set them out in scraggly rows on the hill of their front lawn. There were over seventy out already. Brenn's favorite this year was the one carved to look like Doc Brown, complete with cornsilk hair and goggles.

She was still considering what theme she would do if she carved that many pumpkins every year as she strode up the brick path to Violet's door. The doorbell tinkled out a different melody for every person who rang. Brenn's ring was the title bit from Here Comes the Sun.

"Bunny! To what do I owe the honor?" Violet hugged her tightly. Brenn was transported back twenty years, showing up on Violet's doorstep with problems that seemed too big for one person to handle.

"Hi, Auntie Vi. I need some advice."

"I'm always here to help you. Come in, come in." She

escorted Brenn into the cozy living room and disappeared to the kitchen to make tea.

Brenn wandered around the comfortably cluttered living room, taking a piece of raspberry hard candy from the tin on Violet's secretary. Rolling the candy against the back of her front teeth, she perused the bookshelf to look for books that were new since the last time she was over. Violet kept piles of books all over the house, the shelf in here the only place where they were neatly arranged. Both Brenn's mother's and father's families were big on reading. She was in the fifth grade before she realized having a fully stocked library in one's house was not incredibly common.

Violet deposited a tray with a teapot, two cups, and a sugar bowl on an overstuffed ottoman. "What's troubling you, Bunny?"

Brenn took the cup she proffered. She sipped her tea as she tried to figure out where to begin. "Well, Audrey, I guess? I mean, she's a great kid and doing really well, considering she started from nothing six weeks ago. School is good, as far as I can tell, and she's made a few friends. But then Noelle is always around her."

Violet made a knowing noise. Brenn kept going. "Yeah, exactly. So, not only is Noelle spending a lot of time with her, she keeps hounding me to get rid of Audrey. She doesn't think I can do anything, ever. And now, I think Audrey is picking up on that and is pushing me away."

She stared into her teacup. "Which feels like I'm not being fair because who am I to this kid? But if I can't get Audrey to want to stay with me, I don't know what Noelle is going to do. She might end up in a much worse situation than she was in before. So what do I do?"

"That is a lot." Violet took a sip of her tea. "What outcome are you hoping for here? Do you want to adopt Audrey? Help her to be a functioning witch and then send her on her way? Are you trying to spite your sister? I don't think we can make any progress until you figure out what you want."

"I don't want to adopt her. I'm not a parent. And I don't know." Brenn sighed. "I want her to be safe and happy, and I like having her live with me. I like it a lot, actually."

"And you think Noelle will get in the way of that?"

"Uh, yep. I might partly be doing this to irritate Noelle. Ugh." She tugged her shirt collar away from her neck. "But does that matter if it does good too?"

"Well, dear heart, I think the reasons we do things are often more complex than we'd like to admit. Maybe you'd prefer a mentor relationship with Audrey rather than a familial one?"

"Honestly, I like our relationship," she said, motioning from herself to Violet. "I want her to come to me when she has problems and know I'm a safe adult for her."

Violet smiled, putting her cup on its saucer. "That's an achievable goal. So, you need to show Noelle that Audrey is going to thrive with you, and that you are committed to this, and to show Audrey that you are a safe person for her to trust. When you say she's pushing you away, how so?"

"Well, she disappeared on me Monday night for several hours. I was being kind of a jerk, but she just took off."

"Brenn, when you would show up at my door, why was that?"

"Usually because Mama was too busy with Noelle or Cleo. And Poppy wanted us to figure things out on our own. I was... frustrated? No one was listening to me, and when I got too obnoxious, they told me to go play by myself until I could calm down."

"And how open have you been with Audrey about this? Perhaps if you are open with her about your own upbringing, she will extend some understanding your way as well."

"Yeah, but how? Just say, 'oh Noelle was a super overachiever, Cleo was a wild child who was always in some kind of trouble, so my parents were busy with them, and I didn't need as much attention, so everyone left me alone and I guess that's what I've been doing to you'? That doesn't sound whiny?"

"I don't think it does. That is a reasonable place to start." Violet leaned forward and put her hand on Brenn's. "You are smart and capable and kind. You can find a solution that serves everyone."

"Thanks, Auntie Violet." Brenn rubbed her eyes to disguise that she was tearing up. She should have come here sooner. It was so easy for her to forget that Violet always saw the best parts of her. "What should I do to make her feel involved?"

"Remember, Audrey is new both to magic and to Briar Vale. That gives you two excellent points to connect with her. It's Friday the thirteenth, there are activities all around town. You used to love going to events like that with me when you were that age."

"Oh yeah, remember that year there was the cheese-making festival?"

Violet shuddered. "Maybe avoid things like that until Audrey is more settled."

They spent the afternoon reminiscing and brainstorming things for Brenn to do with Audrey. When she was ready to leave, Brenn hugged Violet for a few beats longer than she usually did. "Really, thank you. For today, but also for everything you did for me as a kid. You're the reason I didn't move out of town permanently."

Violet cupped Brenn's face in her hands. "You are a delight, and I love you. I'm so happy to have known you at all stages of your life, even the ones in which you might stumble."

Brenn had to blink back tears.

~

BRENN FOUND Audrey curled up on the sofa on the screened porch when she got home, intently scrolling on her phone. Charles was lying in the curve of her waist, and Mayhew snuggled under a curtain of her hair. Brenn pulled out her own phone and snapped a photo surreptitiously.

"Hey, guys. And gal. What have you been up to?" She sat on the other end of the sofa. Charles opened one eye to gaze at her. Audrey made a noncommittal sound without looking up.

"That's very interesting. I'm so glad we had this in-depth chat." Audrey still didn't look up. Brenn poked her foot.

She sniffed and tucked them under the cushion. Brenn poked her leg. "Hey, I am being serious now. I'd like to talk to you about this week."

Audrey sighed heavily and put her phone down. "What about this week?"

"Well, first, I'm sorry about Monday. I was stressed, and I took it out on you, and that wasn't fair. And then I know I'm cold when Noelle is involved. I'm glad you like her, I want you to have lots of people to support you. But you don't understand how complicated our past really is."

"Well, you could tell me. I'm fifteen, not stupid," Audrey said sarcastically.

Brenn tucked her own feet up under her. "Well, you know I'm the middle child. Noelle was always perfect, and Cleo was always more fun, and everyone in my family just kind of left me alone to do my own thing. And sometimes, that's what I wanted. But I also never felt like a part of my own family. So I think I've been too hands off with you, because I don't know how to make you feel involved, and I was afraid of being smothering or pushing too much too fast."

She pursed her lips, trying to find a way to say what she felt without being an overwhelming weirdo. "I really like having you here. I'd like us to get closer. I was talking to Auntie Violet earlier, and I realized I'd like our relationship to be like the one I have with her."

"Oh, like an aunt."

"Yeah? Family but not a parent? Do you think that would work for you?" Brenn held her breath for a beat.

Audrey looked at the floor. "I guess. I don't really want to live anywhere else."

Brenn quietly let her breath out. This was a good start. She could work with 'I guess'. "Okay. So could you not just take off on me anymore, please? Give me a heads-up. I don't care if you go do things on your own, but I do need to know where you've gone, since I'm responsible for you. And I like to know you're safe."

"Yeah, sorry." Audrey went to pick up her phone again.

Brenn waved a hand at her. "And maybe we could focus on getting to know each other better? Like while we do fun stuff because we live in a town full of magic that loves holidays and festivals and reasons to put on ridiculous events? Because I don't know if you noticed, but it is Friday the thirteenth."

Audrey started to smile in spite of herself. "Okay? What do you do on a spooky day like today?"

Brenn grinned at her and started singing the opening lines of *A Whole New World* loudly, drawing out the word 'splendid' for several bars too long.

"Noooo," Audrey moaned, covering her ears. "That is too scary!"

Brenn added some dance moves to her singing, and Audrey mock-screamed and ran out of the room.

BRENN TOOK AUDREY TO HEXES & Vexes first, where they ran a class at the top of every hour for making good-luck charms. They each made a charm for the other. Brenn made

Audrey a tiny Charles and Mayhew sitting in an acorn. Audrey made Brenn a mini cassette tape upon which she etched 'good luck mix tape'. Brenn immediately put hers onto her key chain while Audrey cradled hers in her hands, peering at the details.

"So, the movies don't start until 8:30. Dinner? Bookstore? Visit Dani at Phoenix?" Brenn flipped the page of the event pamphlet she picked up when they walked in. "Oh, Gothic Misfortunes is doing a workshop."

"Workshop for what?" Audrey asked, idly.

"Collage zines of spooky plans, ill wishes, or nightmares for mine enemies." She rattled off the options in an exaggerated spooky voice.

"Ooh, yes. Let's do that and get food at the theater."

Audrey made a zine of ill wishes featuring an alarming amount of teeth. Brenn made an autumn spooky plan zine full of things she and Audrey could do together.

They went to a double feature of *Scream* and *Friday the 13th* at the Grove Outdoor Theater, nestled in the woods east of the town proper. The Grove had a few folding chairs left in the corral behind the ticket counter, waiting for patrons to drag them out on the lawn and magic them into something a little more comfortable. Out in front of the screen, there was a smattering of armchairs, bean bag chairs, hammocks, love seats, settees, and one group of teens who had made themselves an army of playground spring riders. Watching them hurl themselves back and forth wildly made Brenn a little nauseous, so she made sure they picked a spot on the opposite side of the theater lawn. They hauled a couple of folding chairs behind them.

"Would you like to make us some more comfortable seats, my lady?" Brenn pointed theatrically at the chairs forlornly sitting on their open patch of grass.

"Uh, okay. Really?" Audrey glanced around at the crowd, biting her lip.

"Nobody is going to judge you. Make whatever you want."

Audrey did a weird dance, flailing her arms around and wiggling her hips. She put her hands up like claws, and the folding chairs ballooned into two ornate porter's chairs with tiny fairy lights lining the hoods.

"Well done," Brenn said as she walked a slow circle around them. "These are really impressive."

Her approval grew when she sat down. It was like sitting in a cloud, but not wet. The canopy of the chair blocked out everything but the projector screen, and Audrey had thoughtfully included a cup holder in one arm. Brenn bent forward to talk to Audrey about getting snacks before the film started. They flipped a coin to see who had to go stand in line. Brenn won, and she didn't even use magic to juice the results.

THEY WERE LAUGHING as they stumbled into the house, earning disapproving looks from both Mayhew and Charles as they disturbed their naps. "Here," Brenn said. "I made this for us."

Audrey flipped through the zine. "We can do this stuff? This looks fun."

"I was hoping so. Cider and donuts tomorrow?"

"Yum, definitely." She stopped on a page near the end and pointed to the images Brenn pasted in. "Can I decorate the house for Halloween? Or is that too much? I could maybe only do my room?"

Brenn raised her eyebrows. "You can decorate if you want. Don't be surprised if the Moon House...adjusts things to its liking, though. We can stop and pick up some things while we're out tomorrow."

Audrey clattered up the stairs, shouting over her shoulder. "I'm going to start a list! Text me if you think of things I should add!"

Brenn just shook her head, shrugging in commiseration at Charles Mayhew. "She's gonna decorate, guys. If you don't want your room done, you should go tell her now."

They both snuggled back down on the pillows they were using.

"Yeah," Brenn snorted. "I think we are going to get in a lot of holiday spirit all year round."

If she was being honest, it wasn't the worst thing in the world. She may even—grudgingly, mind you—enjoy it.

Nineteen

SATURDAY MORNING, Brenn was woken up by a ghost. It was a ghost made of a scrap of linen, animated by Audrey, who was giggling maniacally in the hallway. She pulled the covers over her head. "You are a teenager! Shouldn't you still be in bed? Like until a decent weekend hour? Like noon? Or one?"

"You promised donuts." Audrey singsonged, hanging off the door frame. "And cider!"

She made her ghost bounce up and down where Brenn's head was under the duvet. "And autumn spooky fun!"

Brenn stuck an arm out of her blanket cave and batted the ghost away. "Booooooo. Give me a half hour."

AUDREY WAS WAITING at the kitchen island, a tumbler of iced coffee next to her. "You're up! I made you an iced pumpkin spice latte!" She slid the tumbler towards Brenn. "Check the fit, please."

She stood up and spun. Audrey was a picture of autumn wholesomeness in tan corduroys and an oversized yellow and rust plaid shirt hanging open to show her tee, which was illustrated with a ghost holding a pumpkin full of flowers. Her hair was up in a crown braid, and she clutched Brenn's zine so tightly it was a little crumpled.

"The 'fit' looks great." Brenn had just thrown on a fisherman's sweater and jeans. "We'll need to load the truck, and then we can head out."

"Did you notice my decorations? I was up for a while last night, and borrowed a few things from the miniature room, and I put them up this morning."

There were more linen ghosts floating around the house and piles of velvet pumpkins scattered around in open corners. "Very nice. I like the levitation spells." She nodded at the ghosts hovering above her head. "Got your list?" She took a long sip of her drink.

"Yep!" Audrey struck a cheerleader pose, arms in the air triumphantly. "Donuts! Donuts! Let's go, donuts!"

~

SHADY APPLE ORCHARDS WAS PACKED, people milling around the picnic tables or waiting in line for a hay ride. Audrey ran over to the waist-high apple sculpture and hopped up on it. "Brenn, can you take a photo?" she asked. They did an impromptu photo shoot, with Audrey coercing Brenn to be in as many photos as she took.

Brenn finally called a time out. "We need to get in line now, if we want donuts this morning."

The line moved quickly for being so long. A new tray of donuts was being put into the display case as they were walking up, the sugar crystals sparkling in the light. The man behind the counter perked up as he saw them. "Brenn! First donut of the season?"

"Hey, Ravi. Yeah, I'm really behind this year." She put an

arm around Audrey's shoulders and pulled her up to the counter. "This is Audrey. Her first donuts of the season too."

"What kind are they?" Audrey asked.

"Cinnamon sugar cake donuts. We also do pumpkin spice, but these ones are for purists." Ravi bagged a half dozen for them, calling down the counter to the woman manning the cider kettle. "Two hot ciders, Mal, and a half dozen donuts, family discount."

"Ravi."

"Brenn." He matched her tone.

"All right, thank you." They took their donuts and cider outside, picking a table that was in full sun. Brenn tipped her face up, and breathed deeply. The air smelled crisp and just a smidge smoky. She cracked an eye open to find Audrey watching her. "Deep breaths. Autumn air. Nothing better."

Audrey did the same, clearly placating her. Brenn shoved a napkin at her. "Whatever. Eat your donut."

The donuts were still warm, soft and cakey inside, spicy with cinnamon. The sugar crunched in their teeth. The cider was bright and apple-y with the perfect tang to balance the sweetness of the donuts.

"Okay, I am never eating anything else ever again." Audrey started on a second donut. "This is incredible."

Brenn licked cinnamon sugar off her fingers. "Yep. Sacred Grove does donuts and cider too, but I am a Shady's girl through and through."

"Maybe I should try Sacred Grove also. For science."

"Tomorrow?" Brenn asked.

"Fine." Audrey fake pouted.

AFTER THEIR EXTREMELY HEALTHY breakfast of four donuts, Brenn handed Audrey her planner, open to the page listing the deliveries she had. "Normally, I wouldn't have Saturday deliveries, but with Halloween coming up, I'm swamped."

"Yeah, I can help!" Audrey hopped up into the truck. "Are you guys super into Halloween because of the whole witch thing?"

"Ha. Not really, actually. The big holidays for us are the solstices and, to a lesser degree, equinoxes. Winter solstice is when we go all out. And there is usually a festival or event every month or so. Halloween is mostly for the tourists. It's basically a huge party for the entire week leading up to it and then all day on the day itself. You'll see."

They ended their run at the Witch's Way Hotel. Brenn stood off to the side of the front desk, sorting through two boxes of hard candy that had gotten mixed, picking out the ones that were branded for Witch's Way. Audrey was perusing the stand of tourism brochures, every so often saying 'hmm' and sticking one in her tote.

From the open elevator, a grating voice loudly said, "Amanda, I'll ask at the front desk." The woman bustled over to where Brenn was standing. "You got a Meijers in this town?"

"No, ma'am, we don't, but we do have Teeny's Wondermart." Brenn quickly assessed her, then leaned in and lowered her voice conspiratorially. "Don't be put off by the name. They've got a huge selection, lots of the more common national brands." She glanced around and leaned even closer. "Lower prices, too, not like the markets you'll find in the middle of town."

Brenn straightened back up. "If you are heading there now, I can give you directions from here."

The woman beamed. "Aren't you just an angel! Amanda, isn't she an angel?" Amanda agreed enthusiastically.

"Well, isn't that a sweet thing to say." Brenn managed to

respond without letting any sarcasm leak into her voice. "Why don't we step outside, and we can get you on your way."

She led them outside, gesturing widely and pointing down the street. After a few pained smiles, she came back in.

Audrey raised an eyebrow. "How could you manage to be so nice to that lady? She was so annoying."

"Someday, we'll have a chat about the difference between nice and kind." She grabbed the pile of candy she had been sorting. "It doesn't cost me any more to be kind than it does to be a jerk."

She gazed over Audrey's head, thoughtful. "And in a slight majority of situations, you tend to get better results with kindness. Like sending annoying people on their way quickly."

Audrey nodded but had a skeptical look on her face. "Can I ask you a question? About magic? Or doing magic, I guess?"

"Course you can. What's up?"

"Are there rules?" At Brenn's questioning look, she kept going. "Like for when and where you can do magic? Like in front of regular people? Non-magic people?"

Brenn folded the flaps of a box of candy down and nestled it back on her cart. "I mean, there's nothing official. No one is going to come haul you off to magic jail if you use it in front of normies." She pursed her lips. "Well, unless you are using magic to hurt people on purpose. But there's not, like, a formal set of laws."

The front desk clerk signed the invoice Brenn handed him. She held the door open for Audrey. "Though you should be cautious who you practice in front of. You've seen how people react, and there might be times when there isn't a more experienced witch around to fuzz people's perceptions."

"Huh?" Audrey jumped out of the path of a middle schooler riding their bike down the sidewalk, wearing a mustard yellow velvet suit. "Did you see that?" she asked Brenn, staring down the street at the kid with her mouth open. She rubbed her elbow where she had bumped it against the building.

Brenn was already shouting after the kid. "Warren! Don't run people down on the sidewalks!" She shook her head. "Those kids. Anyways, the reason we don't get harassed by normie people here is because there are wards at each of the Lemonee's gas stations and around the border of town. Those wards... encourage people to make excuses for what they've seen, that square with their usual outlook, so they write off magic as clever tricks, or them being tired and imagining things."

Audrey looked deep in thought for the rest of the ride back to the Moon House.

AS IF SHE'D spoken it into being, on Wednesday evening Brenn got a frantic call from Janine Patel, Mayor Ackerman's executive assistant.

"Brenn! The wards that hold the glamours are failing. Is there any way you can get new dandelenses? Please tell me you can get some."

Brenn wasn't sure she had heard Janine correctly. "What happened to the wards?"

"The lenses are clouding. At least a third of each one. Every ward needs to be replaced." Janine's voice was strained.

"There's not even two weeks until Halloween. Those take at least six days to make, you need a day to install them all, and then the wards still need to charge for ten days. And that's if you can get enough made in time. Can't you just cancel some events and keep the tourists in a smaller space?" Brenn twirled a pen in her fingers.

"The mayor is desperate." Janine lowered her voice to a panicked whisper. "We are so screwed if we can't get this fixed. Every single hotel room and campsite is booked solid. I shouldn't say anything, but a couple of state council members are coming. I guess there are some rumors flying around about how we handle tourists."

"Oh. Shit. Huh. I don't have enough bittercress dewdrops right now; I think I maybe have enough for four or five wards. And those would only last about forty-eight hours anyhow," Brenn mused. "It's not the right time of year to harvest more. I wonder if...hang on a minute."

She pinned her phone between her shoulder and her ear as she fumbled in a file box. Holding a sheaf of papers, she flipped through them as she said, "So I once got these things from this witch that might...yes! Would hazelgaze mirrors work instead? I have a contact up near Traverse, in the Pere Marquette forest. They might be able to whip something up for us."

Janine hummed a little before answering. "This is embarrassing, but I don't know what those are. Can we get enough for sixteen wards?"

"They're mirrors, obviously, made from metal and ceramic fired in hazel wood. Since hazel is such a soft wood that burns super fast, you need serious skill to maintain the fire for as long as it takes while also shaping the mirrors." Brenn copied down the address from the invoice she held. "Like train-for-twenty-years-before-you-are-trusted-to-do-it-on-your-own skill."

"That sounds very difficult. You sure they will work?"

"You should be able to substitute the mirrors for the dandelenses as long as you have the right lanterns to put them in. I can't really help you with that part. Maybe call Tunie Estrella." Brenn clicked her tongue as she thought. "They operate like candles, sort of? But with cold fire instead of regular fire. I think Atlas can make some with wicks that will last a week, maybe two? If you get someone else to start making the replacement lenses, I can probably get us the mirrors as a stopgap to carry us through the holiday."

"That would be amazing. It'll really work? The mayor would

owe you a huge favor," Janine said in a rush, sounding both hopeful and dubious.

"I'll go tomorrow. Takes a little more than a day for them to make the mirrors, so I can drop 'em by on Saturday if I get them." Brenn dismissed Janine's effusive thanks. "Wait until I get back before you thank me."

THE LAST TIME Brenn had gotten hazelgaze mirrors from Atlas, the payment they'd asked in return required some tricky magic on her part. She considered for a long minute, and then went upstairs to Audrey's bedroom. "Hey, so. Since you helping me last week went so well, you up for something a little more complicated?"

Audrey slid off the bed and bounced over to the door. "Yes! Right now?" she asked eagerly.

"Tomorrow. We need to go find a witch out in the forest north of here, and get them to make us a bunch of hazelgaze mirrors."

"What're those?" Audrey sat back down.

"It's a way to make a glamour ward in a hurry. Something happened to the dandelenses in the ones the city council maintain—"

Audrey interrupted her. "What's a dandelens?"

"Uh, it's a framework of minuscule lenses strung together. They look like a dandelion seed head." At Audrey's questioning look, she clarified. "The puffy white part of the dandelion you blow on and make a wish?"

She made the shape of a sphere with her hands to illustrate. Audrey nodded, and Brenn continued. "A ward made from them can last for decades with minor maintenance, so it's kind of a big deal. And with the sheer number of regular people coming to town we have to have something to mask the magical stuff. So the two of us are going hiking!"

Audrey got up and started grabbing clothes from her closet. "Can't you do the Halloween stuff without magic? Like regular places do?"

Brenn laughed. "No. If we had several months, sure, but in not quite two weeks? Nope. Besides, the glamours mask the day-to-day magical stuff here too. We have nine thousand magic people in town. What are you doing?"

"I'm gonna need hiking clothes, duh." She leaned deeper into the closet.

"Carry on," Brenn said. "I'll go prep the rest of our stuff."

They were up before sunrise the next morning. Brenn was in the middle of rinsing her coffee mug when she remembered that Audrey was still a minor. "Damn. Your school. Do I call them? What's the absence policy? Where did I put that handbook?"

"Email," Audrey mumbled through a mouthful of cereal.

Brenn stared at her expectantly. Audrey swallowed and said, "You have to email them. It's the address on the school website."

Brenn made finger guns at her. "Go put our bags in the truck. I'll be out in a minute."

The drive up to Northern Michigan was stunning in October. The leaves were a vibrant rainbow of reds and oranges and yellows, with the deep viridian of pines poking through. The day was perfectly clear without a cloud in the sky. Mayhew rode on a little perch Brenn had fashioned for him between the seats, and Charles was snuggled down in a cup holder.

Audrey cleared her throat, which Brenn had learned meant she was going to ask about something she wasn't sure she should. Brenn hid a smile.

"Why didn't we take the car that's in the garage? Wouldn't it get better gas mileage?"

Brenn glanced at her. "And how do you know about the car in the garage? I thought it was covered."

Audrey blushed. "I was putting my bike away and saw it."

"Uh-huh," Brenn teased. "It's fine, you can be curious. The car belongs to my parents. The Moon House is the house I grew up in, and a few years after I was done with college, my parents moved to a condo and the Moon House became mine. But they didn't have enough parking at their condo, so I store their car in my garage. Sorry, it's nothing exciting."

When they arrived at the edge of the forest, Brenn put the truck in park. She turned to Audrey, her face serious. "So the witch we are going to see is named Atlas. They live up here all alone, so they can be...prickly. The mirrors we are asking for are very energy intensive to make, so they are going to ask us for payment that might be difficult to get. That's why I brought you. I will likely need your magic to help."

"But I barely know anything," Audrey protested. "I don't want to screw it up."

"Just let me do the talking when we're with Atlas, and I can guide you through all the magic stuff," Brenn reassured her. "And there's no use worrying about anything else before we know what Atlas is going to ask for. Be polite, but talk as little as possible."

Audrey's eyes got wide and she snapped her mouth shut. Brenn patted her on the hand as she started the truck again. "It will be fine. Weird, but fine."

They pulled up to the strangest cabin either of them had ever seen. Several trees were integrated into the building and the upper floors wound around the trunks. Every window was a half-circle, making the cabin look as though it had dozens of droopy, sleepy eyes. Moss dripped off the roof and slid down walls, pooling on the forest floor. Smoke poured from one sloping chimney, and multi-colored steam hissed out of three different metal pipes.

Brenn turned off the engine as soon as they turned off the dirt road, gliding to a stop next to an outbuilding that looked as if it had been built by a beaver. "Atlas prefers that the only live mechanical devices on their property are ones they made themselves," she said in answer to Audrey's quizzical look. "It's a whole thing."

They stood awkwardly by the truck until a bell chimed and Brenn led them to the cabin's door. She knocked, waited, and then knocked again. There was a rustling in the woods to their right.

Atlas rounded the corner, arms full of unidentifiable metal tools. They stomped into the beaver dam building and Brenn and Audrey heard a metallic-sounding crash. Audrey pointed to the building, mouthing, 'should we'. Brenn shook her head quickly, stilling as Atlas reappeared.

They scratched their head, causing their grey curls to stand out even more wildly. Glaring, they motioned Brenn and Audrey to enter the cabin. Atlas shut the door sharply behind them. "What?" they snapped. "This is not a guest day."

"Atlas," Brenn said respectfully. "Nice to see you again, sorry to intrude. Briar Vale is in a crisis. We need sixteen hazelgaze mirrors to patch our wards."

Atlas huffed. "Sixteen, huh." They crossed the room and opened a drawer built into the wall. "Got five."

"Could you possibly make us some more?" Brenn winced in anticipation. "Tonight? With wicks that can last a couple of weeks?"

The room was silent for a moment. Atlas swung their head around. "Tonight? Tonight." They stared out a window, fingers flicking quickly as though they were counting. "Gonna cost."

Brenn sucked in a relieved breath. "Of course. What payment would you like?" She had packed the truck with a wide variety of items and ingredients, and crossed her fingers it would be something relatively easy.

Atlas hummed and smacked their lips. "Need three darksome branches given freely from a mirage tree. Two moved in this year, either is fine."

Damn. Not easy. Mirage trees moved around, and the forest up here was healthy, which meant lots of undergrowth to wade through. It could take them days to track one down, and then they had to convince it to drop three branches. She pushed down a flash of annoyance. "Of course. Do you have advice on what direction to take?"

Atlas opened the door and pointed vaguely east. They stood there until Brenn and Audrey sidled past, then slammed it shut after them. Audrey scowled at the cabin. "You weren't kidding," she said to Brenn.

"Told you. But really, they're good people. Little weird, but if you only saw other humans once every three or four years, you'd get strange too." She started for the truck, but stopped short at the sound of the door opening again.

Atlas stood on the threshold, hand outstretched. "Chocolate." They made a grabbing motion.

Out of sight of Atlas, Brenn smirked as she strode to the truck. She tossed a box across the yard and Atlas caught it neatly. They peered inside, nodded once, and disappeared back inside.

Audrey gave a disbelieving laugh. "Okay." She got her backpack out the truck and slid it on. "How do we find a mirage tree?" she asked Brenn. She held her jacket pocket open for Charles to scamper into.

"We go that way," Brenn said, pointing east. "I don't suppose you have an affinity for plants?"

Brenn sent Mayhew ahead to scout while they still had light. After they had been hiking for a couple of hours, the forest started feeling different. The sounds of insects and birds and animals became more melodic. The light filtering through the forest canopy seemed to float in the air instead of slanting like normal. And the trees, well...

"Brenn!" Audrey whisper-yelled. "Why are there purple leaves? And pink ones!"

Brenn grinned at her. "Because magic. If you didn't have any ability, they'd just look like regular leaves to you. But since you do, you can see how the trees store the extra magic." Brenn caressed a leaf that was a particularly virulent shade of pink. "That's what makes a mirage tree. The leaves can't hold any more magic and it starts to leak. But since it's been sort of... processed through the tree, the magic bends reality around the tree."

"Whoa, that's cool," Audrey breathed, her face close enough to a branch that her words stirred the leaves. She jumped back as the branch reached out and ruffled against her head. "Sorry, tree," she said as she patted its trunk. "You startled me."

The tree wiggled under her hand like an excited puppy. Brenn watched, feeling very pleased with herself. Audrey's naturally sweet disposition would be an asset in convincing the mirage tree to help them. Mayhew swooped down to Brenn's shoulder, a berry in his beak. She scritched his chest feathers. "Feeling snacky?"

"We should keep going, as cute as it is to see you commune with that tree." Brenn took a few steps, but then turned back to Audrey. "Hey, what direction do you feel like we should go?"

"Me? I don't have any ideas," Audrey said doubtfully. She gave her tree one last pat. "What are we even looking for? Palm trees and water?"

"Funny. The more magic in the tree, the blacker the leaves. And as the magic leaks out, it kinda sparkles. So, tree with glittery black leaves," Brenn said. "Trees have community, and community has a shared language. Your tree might have an idea where the mirages are. Concentrate on your tree. See if you get a feeling for which way we should look."

Audrey's tree shimmied a little behind her. She turned to it, startled. "Uh. Um, it says this way," Audrey told Brenn, pointing further into the forest. "Thanks, tree. You are the prettiest plant I have ever seen in my whole life."

They hiked in silence until the sun started setting. Brenn was about to suggest they stop and make camp when Audrey cried out.

"What is it? You didn't hurt yourself, did you?" Brenn demanded.

"No. Look!" Audrey pointed between the thick trunks of two ancient pines. A faint sparkling glimmer glowed in the haze ahead of them.

"You found one!" Brenn was so proud she could burst. She quickly picked her way through the brush, Audrey clumsily following. The sounds of the forest faded away as Brenn gazed at the tree. "This is the first mirage tree I've seen in person. It's *beautiful*." She blinked back tears.

The mirage tree was a towering paper birch, with bark that gleamed silvery-white in the dusk. Its leaves were a velvety black dusted with sparkling specks of magic that swirled and glittered. Standing next to it made the hairs on the back of Brenn's neck rise, and she shivered in delight.

"What do we do now?" Audrey asked Brenn out of the side of her mouth.

Brenn slid her pack to the ground. "Ask it to give us three branches."

Audrey stepped forward cautiously. "Excuse me, tree? Could you give us three of your branches?" She stiffened and asked Brenn, "Do they have to be a certain size?"

"Oh. Atlas didn't say, so they must not care." Brenn made a clicking sound with her tongue. If she were collecting them for herself, she would probably get a variety of sizes. Since she didn't have a clue what Atlas would use the branches for, she would have to make an educated guess. "Maybe different sizes? So they have some options?"

Audrey nodded. "Um, could we have three different size

branches? Just whichever ones you can spare? We need to pay for these mirrors that are going to protect our home…"

As Audrey explained the situation to the tree, Brenn moved around her in the darkness as unobtrusively as she could manage, nestling small ceramic bowls in the pine needles covering the ground. In some of the bowls, she put oils. In others, stones and glass beads, or little clay figures, or a pinch of spices. She sprinkled a few grains of salt on the ground between the bowls, enough to sketch a circle but not enough to harm the soil. She had Charles gather some pieces of fallen bark, upon which she chalked sigils. Using a glow-in-the-dark compass, she marked the cardinal directions on her casting circle with the bark.

Brenn brushed bits of bark off her palms and turned on a few LED tealight candles.

Audrey finally noticed what Brenn was doing, and her voice trailed off. "Fake candles?" she whispered.

"I'm not going to light a fire when we are asking a tree for a favor," Brenn hissed back. "It would be disrespectful." To the tree, she said at full volume, "Hello, friend. Audrey told you what we are looking for and why. I'm here to do this for you."

Brenn held her right hand palm up and her left hand palm down above it, in front of her heart. She moved her left hand forward like she was sweeping something off her right palm. As she did this, she said, "Light as air, release." She felt a small tingle but not the vibration of a spell fully cast. She was glad she wasn't alone.

"Audrey," she prompted. Audrey caught on quickly, mimicking Brenn's actions. They cast the spell four times, once in each direction, north and south, east and west.

Brenn steered Audrey out of the circle when they finished, bending close to tell her, "The trees have no way of releasing any magic on their own. This will let it skim off the top. Like when you get a haircut and your head feels lighter. It can siphon the magic into the stuff in the bowls, or use it to do...that." They watched in wonder as the glass beads rose from the bowl and floated. The tree used the beads to draw pictures in the air of places it had been. Brenn, Audrey, Charles, and Mayhew settled on a fallen log nearby to wait for the tree to use its magic.

Audrey wondered aloud what Atlas wanted the branches for. "Can they make wands out of it?"

"You can with some kinds of magic trees, like the wand wood in Briar Vale. I'll take you down there after Halloween if you want. It would be a waste to use this wood for wands though. Like using actual gold to put a star on a first-grader's spelling test. It's overkill and a waste of resources." Brenn shushed her. "I think its done."

The tree shook itself and three branches fell into the circle. Brenn quickly packed up her casting supplies, smudging her sigils off the bark chunks with her thumb. She gave the tree a little bow, saying thank you and taking their leave.

Their prize secured in a duffle bag, Brenn and Audrey debated between setting up the tent or just hiking back to Atlas's cabin. The lure of an actual bathroom was too strong, and they made the trek back. They found a note on the door, tersely granting them permission to use the facilities and sleep indoors. When they woke the next morning, Atlas was nowhere to be found, but sixteen shiny mirrors sat on the work table in the middle of the room.

"Oh, perfect," Brenn said as she wrapped them in soft flannel and put them in a box. She left the branches on the table.

On the drive home, Brenn tapped Audrey on the knee. "Thank you for coming with me and for your help. I honestly don't think I could have done it without you. And you really helped our town."

"No problem," Audrey said, blushing furiously.

Twenty

A WEEK BEFORE HALLOWEEN, Audrey managed to talk Brenn into painting her nails for the holiday. "I love painting nails! I can do them super cute, like sparkly spooky nails. I won't change the length or anything. Look at mine!" She held her hands out for Brenn to inspect. She had delicately painted dancing skeletons on a solid color background, each nail a different shade of pink or orange or purple.

Brenn let Audrey cajole her into it, though she would have said yes eventually. But now, sitting on the floor, massaging oil into her cuticles, she was a little trepidatious. Audrey had nearly twenty bottles of polish lined up on the coffee table and was currently examining ten brushes that looked exactly the same to Brenn.

"I'm thinking a matte base that is twilight sky with trees, so like, purple and navy? And shiny gold stars and crescent moons, for the Moon House," she patted the hardwood floor, "and maybe some bats and ghosts? I have some pigments too, so I can do glow in the dark and maybe color shift."

"I am fully at your mercy." Brenn presented her hands.

Audrey stuck the tip of her tongue out while she concentrated, like a little orange cat with a blep. She kept up a steady stream of chatter as she worked, talking about school, Halloween, magic, and the cute things Charles Mayhew did that morning. Brenn replied when appropriate, but otherwise just relaxed and let her natter on. It was so nice having Audrey living there.

She considered what it would be like if it were permanent. Summer afternoons lazing at the lakes, bringing Audrey to all the festivals, especially to the Quickening Days celebrations with the whole town at the solstice, dinners, and reading, and, yes, nail painting for every holiday—it was all too easy to imagine. Charles Mayhew would love being doted on constantly. Brenn stared at her as she finished nail number nine, wondering what the process was to make Audrey her ward officially. She stared intently enough that Audrey looked up at her, embarrassed to be studied so closely.

Audrey tucked a stray piece of hair behind her ear. "What?" she asked, bashful.

"Sorry, nothing. Just thinking and staring into space." She was about to ask if Audrey would be interested in staying with her permanently, but her ringtone preempted her.

"Oh, hell. It's Noelle. I promised I'd answer the next time she called. Hang on a minute, and then we can finish the last nail." Brenn contorted herself to get up without smudging her freshly painted nails. She gingerly grabbed her phone, walked down to her office, and bumped the door closed with her hip. She had a premonition she didn't want Audrey to overhear any of this conversation.

Noelle sounded entirely too cheerful. "I have some interesting and great news. About an hour outside of Chicago, there is a boarding school precisely for kids in Audrey's situation. All kids whose parents or guardians are unable to guide their magical educations. She'd be with her peers and have intensive training to make up for the years she missed by being in the normal world."

"Noelle, no. I'm not sending her away."

"If this is about money, don't worry. Everything is covered, tuition, room, board. And I contacted some former students about their experiences. They all gave it glowing reviews, Brenn. It's a nurturing environment. And it's close enough you could go visit her on the parents' weekend. I pulled some strings to make sure you could, even though you aren't her legal guardian or parent."

"I don't know how else to say this to you. She's. Not. Going. To. Boarding. School." She drew in a deep breath to explain exactly why that was, inhaled a bit of dust, and started coughing uncontrollably. Brenn opened her door, peering down the hall to make sure Audrey wasn't in sight. Muffling her coughs, she went to the kitchen to grab a sparkling water.

"Brenn, I don't understand why you are being so stubborn. Look, if you want a child, we are witches, there are ways for you to have a baby. We have a world-class fertility witch in town. You aren't limited to having a baby with someone who has a penis. My kids are proof of that."

"The penis isn't the problem in that scenario. Or, well, I guess it is actually. But the bigger issue is the whole pregnancy then baby thing."

"Well, we can look into other ways for you to have a child. There are plenty of interventions—"

Brenn set her water down on the foyer table with more force than she meant to, and some sloshed out of the can. She wiped it up with her sleeve. "Get off my case. I don't want kids, Noelle. Period. No matter how many times you bring it up! No kids! I never have and never will!" She hung up over Noelle's protests.

Brenn took a minute in the foyer to calm down. Maybe it would be worth the week-long coma to persuade Noelle to knock this the hell off. She growled at herself in the mirror.

Audrey was very quiet when she got back to the living room. Brenn gave her a questioning look, but Audrey got back to work painting Brenn's pinkie nail with a brush that was barely three bristles. The air in the room felt heavy. Her nail was getting a little warm. Maybe the heater kicked on?

She turned her head towards the vent to listen but didn't hear the furnace running. Suddenly, her nail was extremely hot. Brenn looked back at Audrey and saw a spray of sparks fly from her brush. "Audrey! What's going on?"

Audrey looked up, stricken. "I'm sorry! Did I burn you?" She fanned Brenn with her hand, but a gust of wind flew out from her. The bottles of polish cascaded onto the floor, spilling a rainbow puddle on the hardwood. The dancing snake lady miniature shot sideways into the wall and, with a loud crack, broke into several pieces. "No! No!" She jumped to her feet, holding her hands together so tightly her knuckles were white. She shouted over the rushing wind, "I'm sorry!"

In the middle of the whirlwind, Brenn yelled back, "Can you make it stop?"

She saw Audrey make a couple of different complicated gestures, frantically reciting spells. The room got much hotter. Brenn stood up. She tried a few spells of her own, but nothing she did had any effect.

"Audrey! My magic isn't working. I can't get yours to stop. You have to concentrate!" Brenn shouted.

Audrey shook her head wildly. "You have to! I can't!"

Brenn did a dampening spell that Violet had taught her when she was trying to contain her own teenage magic. Instead of tamping Audrey's magic down, it made all the lightbulbs in the room explode.

Audrey shrieked as a shower of sparks rained down, throwing her arms over her head as she cringed away. There was an eerie quiet as the room went still. Audrey cautiously peered out from between her arms, and gasped. She rushed out of the room.

Brenn sat on the floor amid the mess, bewildered. What on earth just happened, she thought. "Audrey, it's okay. We have other lightbulbs. I can clean this up, most of the miniatures just tipped over. I can fix the amethyst lady." She leaned around the sofa to call down the hallway. "Audrey?"

There was a soft sob, and Charles chittered. Audrey sniffled deeply, then answered him quietly. "No, I made a mess. Again. No, her magic isn't strong enough right now."

Brenn never realized how clearly a person could hear someone in the foyer. Growing up, there was always enough noise in the Moon House that she hadn't noticed. She sat straight up. With dawning horror, she thought back to how loud her voice was when she told Noelle that she never wanted kids. She scrambled to her feet to go explain to Audrey what had happened. She heard a door close upstairs.

Mayhew clacked his beak at her when Brenn tried to follow Audrey. "Not yet, not yet."

SHE STUMBLED out onto the front porch instead and called Dani. She was close to tears when Dani picked up.

"Dani? Dani, I seriously fucked up," she gasped. "Damnit. Damnit."

"What's going on?" Dani was succinct in her concern.

"Noelle called." Dani groaned, and Brenn bobbed her head in silent agreement. "Yeah, well, she wants me to send Audrey to boarding school—"

"Oh no, did Audrey overhear that? That's really bad—"

Brenn cut her off. "Nope. She heard the part where I shouted at Noelle that I never wanted kids."

Dani whispered, "Oh shit." She let out a noisy breath. "Brenn, that's kind of worse."

"I know." Brenn moaned. She pounded her fist on the porch railing. "We were having a really good time too. I'm such an idiot."

"I mean, not brilliant. Not your best moment."

"What do I do? Like, what do you do when Lydia is mad? Or hurt?"

Dani made a long hmmm noise. "Usually, she likes space right after so she can process what she's feeling. And then we talk about it the next day if she wants."

"Okay, okay. Space to process. That makes sense." Brenn pulled the wool throw off the porch swing and wrapped it around her shoulders. She stared at the sunset, resting her head against the porch post. "How long do you think I should leave her alone?"

"You guys already ate dinner?"

"Yeah, we ate early tonight."

"Maybe try knocking on her door in a couple hours? But I wouldn't push it. Lyd would get irritated we were invading her space on top of whatever else we did to upset her."

Brenn nodded to herself. "Yeah okay. That sounds good. Space, then be open to talking if she wants."

"That's what we do. Good luck, and let me know how it goes, okay? And if you want me to check with Lyd to see if anything else is going on with Audrey, I definitely can."

"No, I don't think it's anything but me being a jackass because I let my sister push my buttons yet again. I'll text you tomorrow."

"I'll be waiting. Well, not in a creepy way. Or a demanding way. A supportive way." Dani's voice was warm in her ear. "Whatever. Talk to you later."

Brenn said goodbye and sat on the porch swing until the moon was high overhead, dreading the coming morning.

Twenty-One

THE NEXT MORNING, Brenn procrastinated taking her shower. Once she showered, she would have to go downstairs, and downstairs, she'd have to face Audrey and figure out how to apologize thoroughly enough. She'd had the worst time trying to fall asleep last night. Her conversation with Noelle kept replaying in her head in excruciating detail. She ended up failing at procrastinating, too, getting downstairs before Audrey had even woken up.

She sat at her desk, sorting and filing an old box filled with half-illegible notes scrawled on scraps of paper. After the two hours she spent trying to distract herself this morning, her office had never been cleaner. Brenn kept picking tasks that would fill up some time, but she was painfully efficient. Maybe she would dust the storeroom next. The stairs creaked, and her jaw tensed. She got up to stand in her doorway, waiting for Audrey.

"Audrey? About last night? I'm so sorry. That conversation wasn't even about you at all." She stuttered to a stop as Audrey gave her a smile and shoulder shrug.

"It's okay. I'm sorry for making a mess. Do I need to help you clean it up?"

Brenn gave her head a little shake. "Um, you seem weirdly okay."

"Yeah, I overreacted. I obviously didn't know what you were talking about. I shouldn't have assumed it was about me." Her voice was bright but thin. She gave Brenn a tight-lipped smile. "There's an after-school program thing that helps kids practice controlling magic, so I'm going to do that today."

"Oh, okay. You sure everything is okay?"

"Yep." Audrey jabbed a thumb towards the living room.

Brenn waved it off. "I cleaned it up. It's fine."

"Good," Audrey said and walked past her into the kitchen. "I'm running late. Could you write me a note?"

"Yeah, of course." Brenn felt put off her stride by the entire conversation.

SHE TEXTED Dani after Audrey left in a flurry.

Brenn:

> So, Audrey seems…fine?

Dani replied almost instantly:

> fine how?

Brenn:

> She apologized for making assumptions, and
> making a mess, and accepted my apology.
> So…fine?

Dani:

> huh.

how was the vibe?

Brenn:

Weird. But then it IS weird. She seemed
normal when she left for school. Maybe more
tired than usual?

Dani:

i guess play it by ear? follow her lead?

Brenn:

That was my plan.

Dani:

good luck.

Brenn went back to work, discomfited. Dani obviously had
more experience with teenagers than she did, and she supposed a
person should trust experience. It still felt like something essen-
tial had snapped and would always be weakened, even if she
managed to knot it back together.

THE WEEK COULDN'T GO by fast enough for Brenn.
She and Audrey danced around each other, unfailingly polite,
but the air between them felt brittle. She was hoping that having
Cleo as a buffer on Saturday would help smooth the situation
out again.

Unfortunately for her, as soon as they arrived at Witchery
Aesthetica, Cleo sent them out with a foot-long shopping list.

She physically pushed them out the back door. "Thank you, thank you, you are lifesavers! Brenn, I'll text you if I think of anything else, okay?"

The door slammed shut before Brenn could respond. Taken aback, she looked from the list to Audrey to the list. "I guess...we should go shopping?"

Audrey gave her the same look. "That was...I mean...what?" They started laughing. The chill between them thawed a bit.

THEY MADE it through a third of Cleo's list and were debating whether they should drop the stuff they had back at Witchery or do one more stop first. Brenn's phone rang, her mother's photo popping up on the screen. She flashed it at Audrey and hurriedly said, "Can you go get the stuff here alone? So I can answer this?"

Audrey gave her a thumbs-up and went into the store.

"Hi, Mama," she said, holding the phone with her shoulder while she struggled to rearrange the bags she held. "What do you need?"

"Do I need a reason to call my daughter?" Her mother's voice was cool and a little hurt.

"No, but you usually have one."

"I was calling to check on you and Audrey. Cleo said you were assisting her today with some errands."

"We are. We're in the middle of them, actually. And there's still at least twenty more stops to make, so I should let you—"

Her mother interrupted her. "Noelle told me she gave you the information about the boarding school she found. Darling, I fail to understand why you refuse to make decisions for that child's best interest."

"She doesn't want to go live anywhere else, Mama. She's doing well here. I think she should have a say in her future."

Brenn sidled over to a bench, dropping her bags on the seat. She massaged her fingers.

"Of course she doesn't, Brenn. You are acting like you have no responsibilities, and she can run around however she likes. Children need discipline. You are treating this situation like the 'fun' auntie and not a serious guardian."

Brenn sighed as quietly as she could. "That is not actually what's happening. I don't know what you're hearing from Noelle, but we're fine."

"Brenn, do you remember the puppy you begged us for? Do you recall what happened to that puppy? You never walked it, you constantly forgot to buy its food, and we had to spend a week calling everyone we could think of to rehouse it. You have shown that you weren't responsible enough to provide for its basic needs, much less guide its development in an appropriate way. And now we are discussing a human being. You have to make the responsible decision for Audrey. You are the adult. You cannot leave her to her own devices."

"For crying out loud, Ma, I was *eleven*. It was one instance of irresponsibility when I was a literal child. That's what childhood is for, making mistakes and learning from them. You do realize that was more than twenty-five years ago, right?" Brenn burned with the desire to say what she actually wanted to: *You were the adult. Where were you when I was struggling with a brand new responsibility? Why didn't you help me figure it out? How did you not realize I didn't know what I was doing?*

But she swallowed it down. That would just lead to a fight. Well, probably not a fight since her mother would never validate Brenn's feelings and thus never accept there was anything to fight about. But it would certainly make her life harder in the end and not affect her mother at all.

"You cannot make mistakes like that when living beings are involved. All I am asking is that you seriously consider what is truly best for Audrey, what will give her the best foundation for her future." Sasha delicately cleared her throat. "I know you have made a respectable, fulfilling life for yourself. Your father and I are proud of you. Remember, you have a good head on your shoulders. Tell Cleo we will be down tomorrow to see her holiday displays. I love you. Bye now."

Brenn shoved her phone in her pocket. She clenched her fists until her knuckles cracked. The worst part of the entire situation was that her mother and Noelle had a point. Audrey probably would learn more at a boarding school, and it likely was a good school, if Noelle had vetted it. But Brenn desperately wanted Audrey to stay. If she could fix her magic, not only would she be a better teacher for Audrey, but she would also relieve the pressure of keeping such a huge secret from everyone else. Tears pricked her eyes and made her nose itch. She angrily swiped at her face.

Audrey came out, bags swinging from her wrists. She didn't seem to notice how quiet Brenn was, keeping up a steady stream of chatter as they walked back to drop off their spoils to Cleo.

When they got home, Brenn made an excuse to shut herself in her office. She pulled *Middle-Aged* out of a desk drawer, staring at the cover contemptuously. The damn book hadn't done a single thing for her yet. What was even the point, she thought, annoyed. She dropped it back in the drawer, slamming it shut.

Instead, she tried to think of every magical exercise she had done as a child, in school, and under the instruction of her parents and Violet. She grabbed a notepad, and her pen flew as she wrote down every one she could remember. Why didn't she think of this earlier? Start at the beginning, that was the ticket.

BRENN WOKE on Sunday morning to Audrey shrieking her name. She practically flew down the hall, skidding a little as she rounded the corner into Audrey's room. "What? What's the matter?" she gasped, her eyes sweeping the room for what could be wrong.

Audrey wiggled an arm out from under the duvet she was clutching around herself and pointed to the windows with a shaking hand. "Look. You didn't do that?"

The central window in her room had turned from a clear pane to stained glass, a silvery crescent moon set in a purple ground.

Brenn slumped into the chair at the desk. She rested her head on her hand, yawning widely. "It's the Moon House."

"Huh? I know this is the Moon House, but why did the window change?" Noting Brenn's nonchalance, Audrey padded over to the window.

"No, the Moon House did it. All the buildings here are sentient to a degree, but when the same family stays in a house for many generations, the house tends to develop a close relationship with them." She pulled her bonnet off and massaged her head, fluffing her curls. "It will make...adjustments to itself it thinks the family will like. I think the Moon House might consider you family now."

Tears shined in Audrey's eyes as she stared at the window. She gently touched the edge of the window.

Brenn yawned again. "It's a special thing, for sure. I'm going to go get freshened up for the day. You want to help me pack some orders?"

Audrey nodded as Brenn left, never looking away from the window.

FOUR HOURS of packing orders later, Audrey stretched and groaned. "Oh, my old bones."

"Don't start. Your bones are barely out of the rubbery kid

phase." Brenn twisted her back to one side and then the other, a series of cracking noises emanating from her body. "*Those* are old bones."

"We need to load these into the truck, and then we'll be done for the day." Brenn slapped the pile of boxes. She wheeled a folding wagon out of the closet and started stacking boxes.

As they loaded boxes into the back of her truck, Brenn shivered as the unseasonably cold October wind cut through her threadbare flannel shirt. "Brr. I should have put a sweater on."

Audrey sniffled. "No kidding. This wind is freezing." She looked around, pursing her lips. "I'm going to try something."

She stepped into the driveway, out of the shelter of the garage, and lifted her hands. She sang a snippet of what sounded to Brenn like a playground rhyme and a warm current of air swirled around them. "Yes! I thought that would work." She pumped her fist in the air.

"Nice job," Brenn said. "Where'd you learn that one?"

"Oh. Nowhere? I just thought it would work? The wind has always felt kinda...friendly? To me." Audrey smiled in satisfaction. She took one step towards the garage, and then a loud popping noise made the smile slide off her face. "Uh, Brenn?" She turned, facing the backyard. Her voice grew panicked. "Brenn!"

Alarmed at the tension in Audrey's voice, Brenn dropped the box she was holding and strode quickly out of the garage, immediately seeing the problem. There was a diminutive meadowsweet bush next to the path, its branches completely bare. A towering lilac that stood next to it was shaking violently, then abruptly stopped, all its leaves dropping to the ground in one swoop. It stood still. Then the tree closest to the lilac started shaking and lost all its leaves. Audrey's eyes were wide. "Help!"

Brenn clapped her hands twice and made a wiping motion in the air. "Stop!" she said, her voice ringing out in the yard. The breeze picked up, and all the trees started shaking. "Audrey. I need you to do the same thing I just did, with me this time." She mimed the motion, and Audrey nodded.

In unison, they clapped twice, wiped the air, and told the trees to stop. There was sudden quiet. Brenn bobbed her head once. "Okay. Cool." She went back into the garage.

"Brenn. What...was that me?" Audrey wrung her hands together.

"Probably. Looks like your warming spell goosed the bushes a little." Her voice was muffled a bit as she shoved boxes further into the truck. "Why?"

"Why? I just stripped all the leaves off the bushes! And a tree!" She swung her arms wildly, gesturing to the bushes and trees and the fresh piles of leaves underneath them. "I know these ones aren't as magic as the ones in the forest, but their leaves!"

Brenn heaved the last couple of orders in and knocked the door shut with her hip. "So? They were done with those leaves for the year, you just hurried up the process." She patted Audrey on the back. "Don't worry about it. They expect it. Maybe a little more slowly, but no harm done."

The wind picked up again. "So cold! Let's get inside." She jogged to the back door, Audrey following slowly.

"YOU AREN'T MAD?" Audrey moped over her mug of hot chocolate.

"No," Brenn scoffed. "It's fine. I told you, your magic is going to flare for the next few years. We know that. We expect it to."

"Brenn?" Audrey asked in a small voice. "Out there, the first time? Was that your magic not being strong enough to stop me?"

Brenn set the oven mitt she was holding on the counter. "It might have been. Or it just might have been that your spell didn't want to listen to me. The important thing is that we stopped it, okay?"

"I guess," Audrey said doubtfully.

"I'm not worried about it, Audrey," she said. She felt like she should be concerned, but that leaf-dropping magic was just a normal teenage flare. Everyone she knew had it happen to them at least a few times, and it almost never resulted in any real, lasting damage.

Brenn started to reassure Audrey again, but the oven timer dinged. She pulled a pan of French bread pizzas out. "Ready to eat? You want to do half and half, or split them as is?"

Audrey stretched up on her stool, trying to see the pan. "What flavors again?"

Brenn pointed to one and then the other. "Pumpkin, garlic, and sage. Margherita."

"Half and half, please." The promise of food seemed to calm her down better than Brenn had.

They ate in companionable silence at the dining room table. Brenn leafed through a catalogue of scientific equipment, while Audrey propped a dragon novel up against the vase of flowers in the middle of the table. Charles was running his paws over his whiskers as he laid next to his empty plate. Mayhew was perched on the window sill, watching leaves swirl around in the wind. Every few minutes, he snapped up one of the nuts Audrey had laid in a rough line for him on the sill.

Brenn basked in a wave of contentment. This was nice, all of them casually going about their lives together. As she watched Audrey flip the pages of her book, a frisson of anxiety wound through her. Audrey was going to need a stronger witch looking out for her, and soon. Brenn grimaced as she thought about her failed attempts yesterday to bolster her abilities. Mayhew hopped around to glare at her as if he knew what she was thinking. She shook her head at him, tipping her head slightly towards Audrey. He puffed his feathers and flew out of the room.

Audrey looked up as he swooped past. She glanced at the clock on the wall and put her bookmark in her novel. "I'm at a good stopping point. Is there anything else we need to do today?"

"I could use a hand filing today's paperwork, but that's about it."

Audrey got up and took their plates into the kitchen. "Coming?" she asked from the hall.

In her office, right in the middle of her desk, Brenn found the card Nat had given her the day they'd met. She swung her head around to look at Mayhew. Subtle.

"What's that?" Audrey asked.

"Nat's phone number. Mayhew must have been tidying up after me." She tossed it in a drawer.

The filing took not even half as long as usual, with Audrey helping. Her body fully in the closet, putting the last folders in a drawer, Brenn almost missed Audrey's question.

"How do you, you know, actually find this stuff?" She was twirling an ornate copper key in her fingers.

"Like, the stuff my customers order specifically? Or just in general? Or how I specifically find them?"

"The last one. That's part of your special powers, right?"

Brenn considered her for a long minute. "I'll show you." She took the key from Audrey. "I *will* show you," she started again, "but I don't want to hear that you spread this information around."

Audrey pinched her forefinger and thumb together, drawing them across her lips and miming a key turning in a lock.

Brenn rolled her eyes. "Okay, yeah. Come here." There was a flat file cabinet in the corner. Each drawer held dozens of maps, all hand-drawn by Brenn. The first drawer was full of branching maps of people-names, and some of random words. The second held maps that were illustrations of elements: crystals and rocks, plants, flowers, bodies of water, weather. In the third were terrain maps for places around the world: urban, rural, and wild. The bottom three drawers were stuffed full of area maps: cities to street level, each state in the US as well as Puerto Rico and DC, and each province of Canada and every Mexican state. Some of farther-flung countries, some foreign cities. All in all, Brenn had amassed nearly three hundred of these, all made by her own hand.

She took out a map of Briar Vale, painted in fine detail. Smoothing it over the top of the cabinet, she said to Audrey, "This is technically called dowsing. By holding a pendulum over a map, it can indicate where I will find something." She took her pendulum out of a small velvet-covered box. It was a gold chain about four inches long, with a gold ring attached to one end and a vaguely triangular rock on the other. The rock itself was drab grey, with white lines scoring the surface and a hole near the wider end.

Brenn held the rock out for Audrey to look at. "This is a rock I was called to on the day I turned twenty-one. We were up at Lake Superior, and the weather was really rainy and gloomy. I could not get out of my head the feeling I needed to go wading in the lake, so I finally did. This rock was waiting for me." She slipped the ring over the middle finger of her left hand. "It's both a hag stone and a wishing rock."

"What are those?" Audrey asked.

"A hag stone is a rock with a hole through it, and wishing stones are grey rocks with white or pink stripes through them." Brenn held her pendulum over the map. "What should we look for? A person is probably going to give us the best results."

Audrey made a clicking noise with her tongue as she thought. "Um, Cleo?"

"Cleo. Gotcha." She whispered inaudibly to the stone. Brenn slowly moved her hand around the map in concentric circles starting from the center. As her finger hovered near Witchery Aesthetica, the pendulum tugged her finger down gently. Brenn frowned at the hesitation she could feel in the chain. "So this says Witchery. Text Cleo and ask her if she's there."

Audrey tapped on her phone, and when it dinged, she looked amazed. "That's exactly where she is."

Brenn slipped the pendulum off, making a mental note to try cleansing it in moonlight soon. Maybe it had a build-up of energy, and that's why it was so wishy-washy. "There you go. I tell the...magic? I guess? what I'm looking for, and ask it to help me pinpoint where I can get it."

She slipped the map onto her desk and pulled out stacks from the other drawers. "And I don't really have to even know the specific name of what I want. One time Dani asked me for a wood that burned pink, and that's how I found raspberry wood, which only grows in one tiny copse of trees in Canada."

"That's so fucking cool," Audrey breathed. Then blanched as she realized what she'd said and clamped a hand over her mouth.

Brenn chuckled. "I don't care if you use swear words, relax."

Audrey gave a fake grimacing smile showing all her teeth. "Okay. I don't think I've sworn in front of anyone here yet."

"I mean, different people have different preferences, but I'm not bothered."

"Yeah okay." Audrey traced a finger over one of Brenn's weather maps. "So what do you use this one to find?" She drew a circle around an illustration of a thunderstorm with purple-white lightning, and the paper burned under her fingertip. She yelped in panic.

Brenn tossed old paint rinse water on it to put out the burgeoning flame. "Maybe we will avoid you touching my maps for a while."

Audrey babbled apologies as Brenn blotted up the water and hung the paper up to dry. "Not your fault. At least I hope you weren't trying to set fire to my livelihood." She turned and saw the horrified look in Audrey's eyes. "Kidding! That was a joke. Really, I can fix it, it's okay."

She ushered Audrey out of the room and shut the door behind them. Brenn wanted to get them out of her office before anything was damaged beyond her ability to fix it.

Twenty-Two

BRENN POKED her into Audrey's room. "You about ready?"

Audrey was sitting at her desk, the lights of her mirror highlighting the indecision on her face. "Do you think I should cover up my birthmark?"

"Why would you?"

"I dunno. Fairy princesses have perfect skin?"

"Audrey. Your birthmark isn't a pimple. It's not a blemish." She crossed the room to look at Audrey in the mirror. "Your skin is lovely. Look at that teenage glow. Millions of people spend lots of money every day to achieve that. We can have Cleo do a glamour to make you literally glow if you want."

"I know, but whoever saw a fairy with a giant mark on her face?" She touched it lightly as she spoke.

Brenn pinned a copper-colored curl that escaped the artful pile on Audrey's head. "Audrey." She waited until she made eye contact. "Whoever saw a fairy?" she asked deliberately.

Audrey reluctantly snorted. "Yeah, okay. I just don't want anyone to make fun of me."

A shock of anger rippled through Brenn. In a very measured

voice, she asked, "Has anyone here said anything to you? Because if so, I would love if you'd give me their first and last names. So I can find them. And have a chat. A nice, *friendly* chat."

"No, no, no no no, not here, ever. I swear." She cast her eyes down. "Some of my foster parents gave me makeup to cover it up so I wouldn't scare their kids."

"For fucking crying out loud." She gently tipped Audrey's face back up to look at her from the mirror. "I know this is hard to do, but ignore people who say anything about the way you look. Your birthmark, the size of your body, your hair, your style, whatever. Those mean things are never on you. It's always about them. People very often choose to be idiot assholes, and you definitely don't have to give them any credence."

Brenn tilted her head to the side. "Would you think I was scary if I had a birthmark like yours? Or ugly?"

"No! No way."

Brenn spread her hands. "Well?"

She squirmed in her chair, eyes downcast. "Yeah, okay, whatever, I'll be kind to myself."

"Thank you. Now I'm going to go finish my own costume." Brenn went to her own room, where she put on a red and white striped sweater, a pair of fake round black-framed eyeglasses, and a red and white striped hat topped with a pompom.

Brenn entered the hallway at the same time as Audrey, who stopped in her tracks to shriek, "Waldo?"

"Oh, you found me." She made a face. "And yes, Waldo, because it is the easiest costume I could think of that also would be warm."

THEY WERE AT THE DOOR, gathering the last of the things they'd need with them for the day when Audrey decided she wanted a photo of her costume. Brenn lined up the shot, and

Audrey flicked her sparkly play fairy wand around. There was a flash of light, and once their eyes recovered from the brightness, Mayhew and Charles were hopping around with agitation. They both were bright purple.

"Charles Mayhew!" Audrey choked out.

Brenn tilted her head and snapped a photo of them. She cackled, then ran a hand over both of them, turning them to a lavender. "Audrey? Can you?" She gestured to her familiars.

Audrey bent over them, apologizing profusely. She did the same motion Brenn had, and they turned their regular colors. Mayhew scolded her as he flew away to preen atop the banister, and Charles chittered angrily, then accepted a few pets on his head.

"Audrey," Brenn said. She tossed her a couple of almonds when she looked up. She jerked her chin towards Mayhew at Audrey's questioning look.

"Oh! Sorry I turned you purple, Mayhew." He took an almond from her palm with a clack of his beak, then grabbed the second one much more gently.

"Looks like you're forgiven. Ready?"

"Yes," Audrey whispered. She gave Charles Mayhew one last guilty look before Brenn ushered her out the door.

DOWNTOWN BRIAR VALE was a riot of pumpkins, bats, and ghosts. And, though unknown to the out-of-towners packing the sidewalks, actual real-life magic-doing witches. Every business that catered to tourists had a Halloween special, with secret specials for town citizens. Audrey and Brenn started their afternoon at Witchery Aesthetica, helping Cleo restock the witch kits. They cleaned out the back room of her stock only thirty minutes after they arrived.

"Thanks for coming, lady friends. Brenn, your costume is

lame. Audrey, you look fantastic." Audrey preened at Cleo's compliment as Cleo escorted them to the front door. "Go have some spooky fun."

Brenn scowled at Cleo. "My costume is not your concern, thank you. If you need anything else today, call Noelle." Turning her back to her sister, she asked Audrey what she wanted to do first.

Audrey did an exaggerated shrug. "I have no idea. You're the one who lived their whole life here."

"Right. We'll start north and work our way down." Brenn strode off briskly, securing them seats on a wagon stuffed with hay. "Hey, Fred, looking good," she said, greeting the palomino horse hitched to the wagon.

UP AT THE FAIRGROUNDS, they watched a pumpkin catapult contest and fed the animals in the pop-up petting zoo. A goat stole the hat from a child dressed as a pirate, and the petting zoo attendant chased it in circles, trying to recover the pilfered hat. There was a small craft fair, where Brenn bought Audrey an apple-spice scented candle in a jar shaped like a cauldron and two enamel pins, one a glittering crescent moon and the other a flowery pointed witch hat.

They wandered across the Miller Bridge to the library, which transformed into a massive haunted house every Halloween. It took the librarians three full days to spook-ify the building, and it was the highlight of the day. They ran into a group of Audrey's classmates at the entrance, and Brenn sent her ahead with them. She wandered through the haunted house, stopping to chat with the zombies and mad scientists and assorted monsters she knew when their assigned areas were clear of people.

Brenn blinked in the late afternoon sun as she exited the

library. Audrey was talking animatedly with her school friends at a picnic table down by the river behind the building. Brenn wandered a short way down the riverside path, sitting on a bench near the gazebo to wait for Audrey. A classic doo-wop girl group dressed as brides of Frankenstein sang spooky songs, using the gazebo as a stage. She adjusted her hat and closed her eyes as she listened to a melodic version of Season of the Witch.

Brenn jumped as someone kicked her foot. Audrey loomed over her. "Sorry! I didn't know you were waiting."

"I've been enjoying the atmosphere. Or the vibes? Is that what the kids say?" Audrey rolled her eyes. Brenn slid over on the bench so Audrey could sit. She gestured at the singers with her chin. "Do they go to your high school?"

"The Velvets? Yep. They sing at assemblies a lot. Like a weird amount." Audrey pulled a few pieces of candy from a pocket in her dress, offering one to Brenn. "They're really good, though. I guess they've been together since, like, fourth grade."

Brenn stood up. "No thanks. Dinner though?"

The stretch of Tower Road next to the library hosted out-of-town food trucks that drove in every year. Brenn and Audrey gorged themselves, paying a visit to nearly every truck there. They discussed, and Brenn decided her favorite truck was Snack Quest, which served a wide global selection of dumplings that could only be ordered by rolling a d20 and accepting whatever fate decided to give. Audrey went back to Stick 'Em Up three times, double-fisting kebab skewers each trip.

They wrapped up their night in Garden Park, at the annual horror short film festival sponsored by the art film theater.

It was nearly midnight when Brenn turned at a familiar chorus of voices shouting, "Waldo!" Dani smiled under the paper mâché UFO balancing from her shoulders, iridescent streamers floating around her like a tractor beam. Walker was wearing a cat ear headband, and Nat was dressed as a mermaid. Junelle was a dapper Willy Wonka, and Lily had dressed up as a stereotypical witch, black hat and all. Aislynn wore a white rabbit onesie.

She waved and tapped Audrey on the arm to let her know she was going to see the coven. "Hey, you guys look great."

"Nice costume. Did you pick Waldo so you could wear a sweater and a hat?" Dani flicked a few strands of tractor beam out of her face.

"You know it. Roswell?" She motioned to Dani's UFO.

"Every year. Nearly hometown pride. So where have you been hiding? It's been forever since we've seen you."

Brenn wrinkled her nose. "I know. I've been trying to focus on Audrey, and you know, Halloween keeps me busy every year. I didn't miss any meetings, did I? I didn't see anything in the group chat."

"Nah, we've been a little quiet the last couple weeks. We were thinking about getting up to some mischief tonight, though, if you're up for it." Nat smoothed her scales over her hips. "This costume is a lot," she complained to Junelle.

Junelle scoffed. "You look amazing, so I don't want to hear it. You come to me and just say, 'can you make me a costume' but don't tell me anything more, you are getting what you get."

Brenn laughed. She had missed being around the coven, but she hadn't realized how big that empty space was until they were here in front of her, filling it with their camaraderie and warmth. Walker tweaked the pompom on her hat. "I wish I'd thought of this. Brilliant."

Aislynn unzipped her suit a bit. "This thing is so much warmer than I expected. So Brenn, you coming with us?" She fanned herself with her hands. Lily noticed and used her hat as a fan to help.

"I'm here with Audrey, so I don't know if I can—" she was interrupted by Audrey wrapping a hand around her arm.

"I don't mind. I'm ready to go to bed." Audrey waved and said hi to the coven.

"You look wonderful," Junelle said. She ran her fingers along Audrey's wings. "These are a really nice construction. Did you do them yourself?"

Audrey half shrugged. "I did them with the Charms and Chums club at school. So mostly?"

"If you're interested in sewing or costuming, I'd be happy to teach you. I do a lot of both in my spare time."

"Thanks, Junelle. I'd like that. Probably not for a while, though?"

"Sure thing, kiddo. You can get my number from Brenn whenever you're ready." Junelle waved to a group of women dressed as honeybees. "I'll be back in a few minutes," she said over her shoulder, already walking away.

Brenn turned to Audrey. "If you're ready to go, I'll walk you home." She addressed the group. "And then I can meet you all wherever."

"Let's just meet here. The kebab cart is right over there, and I'm starving." Dani started for the food cart across the street.

"You okay walking back yourself?" Walker asked Brenn.

Audrey spoke at the same time. "I can walk home by myself, it's not that far."

"Yes," she said, pointing to Walker. Swiveling to Audrey, she said, "And no, I'll walk you home. You're going to need help getting out of those wings."

"Oh yeah." Audrey smiled sheepishly as she said goodnight to the coven.

"I'll be back in thirty minutes or so."

∿

AUDREY YAWNED SO WIDELY her jaw creaked. Rubbing her face, she said, "Thanks for taking me around today. It was super fun."

"Of course. It was fun to do with someone new to the whole

thing." Brenn unlocked the door, greeting the house, its wood warm under her hand. Audrey rubbed it perfunctorily and said hello through another huge yawn.

"Okay, let's get you to bed. Arms." Brenn twirled her finger in a circle so Audrey would turn.

She put her arms out, and Brenn detached the iridescent fairy wings she had worn all day. Audrey sagged her shoulders, heaving a contented sigh that turned into yet another yawn.

Brenn pointed up the stairs. "Bed. You sure you'll be okay?"

Audrey nodded.

"I don't know when I'll be back, but if you need anything at all, you text me, got it?" Brenn watched her until she disappeared into the upstairs hallway, the corner of her mouth curled up.

BRENN WALKED SWIFTLY BACK to the coven. Her joints felt tight with a buzzy excitement. She felt like a teen herself again, the night stretching out in front of her, offering endless possibilities.

Nat and Dani shouted happily when Brenn was in sight. Walker was watching Lily bounce balls of light off her fingers, the light changing colors every time it touched her skin. Aislynn was haggling with a woman wearing an usherette tray crowded with tiny bottles.

Brenn strolled up to Nat and Dani. "Where's Junelle?" she asked.

Nat pointed over to the group of women Junelle had joined when Brenn had left earlier. "I'm pretty sure she has a massive crush on one of the honeybees over there."

"Ooh, which one?" Dani craned her neck. "They're all pretty cute."

Nat shrugged. "No idea, but I concur."

Walker noticed Brenn had joined them and touched Lily's arm, pointing to her. Walker shouted Junelle's name, wildly waving her arms. She and Aislynn came back at the same time.

"What'd ya buy?" Dani pestered.

"It's a selection of perfume samples. I tried to catch her last year, but I never could find her." Aislynn handed her a black cardboard box that made a clinking noise as it moved. "What's the plan for the rest of our night?"

Lily raised a hand. "There is a labyrinth in the park south of Thorn Lake that looks intriguing. You are magically sealed in and cannot leave until you solve it. There is supposed to be a prize once you do."

"I'm good with that." Nat offered around a cellophane bag of bat-shaped hard candy.

The labyrinth was a huge hit. Brenn and Dani laughed so hard they got hiccups. The prize turned out to be an alchemy goblet. The person holding it can fill it with any liquid, which will immediately transform into champagne. The coven squabbled over who got to try it out first and then over its future custody. They ended up back at Nat's house, where Dani drunkenly wrote out a goblet schedule for the next year.

~

WALKER SLUNG an arm around Brenn's neck. "You sure you don't want an escort home?"

"Nah, it's like four blocks from here, and you guys are going in the opposite direction." She extricated herself and left in a flurry of goodnight kisses.

"Don't call me if something spooky gets you!" Walker called after her.

"I'll delete your number!" Brenn threatened back, laughing.

Waving to the members of the Motorheads as they zoomed past on their golf carts, she was surprised to see it was after three in the morning. She hadn't meant to stay out that late. She'd have to leave a note for Audrey in case she slept through breakfast.

When she turned from East Pleasant onto Star Street, she felt a little uneasy. She stopped, listening hard. The night was cool and clear, and she was alone on the street save for a few rabbits and fireflies. Sounds of the Motorheads faded as she stood there a minute more, but there was nothing else disturbing the quiet.

The feeling got worse as she approached Waxwing. It didn't look like anything was amiss on the street—the neighbors had all left their porch lights on, and between those and the gentle glow of the street lights, she had a decent view. She walked faster, thinking she'd feel safer once at home, cozied up in bed after checking on Audrey.

She stopped in her tracks as she came around the last curve. There was an ominous darkness where Moon House stood. Goosebumps popped up all over her body, and, skin crawling with fear, she broke into a run.

BRENN DASHED UP THE PORCH, putting a hand on the jamb near the door listing on its hinges. "House," she gasped. Its wood felt cold. Acid crawled up her throat as she banged into the house. "Audrey?" She shouted. "Charles? Mayhew?"

Wind howled through the house, slamming open doors against the walls. The foyer was a complete disaster—furniture tipped over, the mirror broken, pictures hanging drunkenly on their nails. Debris poured from every doorway. Brenn's stomach twisted painfully. She whipped her head back and forth, trying to decide in her panic whether to check the rooms down here first or to run up to Audrey. Whirling around, she bolted up the stairs.

Audrey stood in the middle of her bedroom, staring blankly forward, mouth open in a soundless scream. Brenn's heart skipped a beat. She fought against the tempest surrounding Audrey, wading through a river of books and clothes and blankets. Audrey's desk chair smashed into Brenn's side, knocking her over. She crawled along the floor, keeping low to avoid the worst of the wind.

After what felt like an eternity, Brenn reached Audrey. She grabbed the girl's shoulders and shook her. "Audrey! You have to wake up! Audrey!" Brenn shouted. Audrey didn't respond, just kept sightlessly staring at some point behind Brenn. Brenn pinched the delicate skin on the inside of Audrey's wrist with her fingernails.

Audrey blinked. "Brenn," she gasped. "What's happening?"

"Your magic! You have to control it!" Brenn yelled.

Audrey shook her head wildly. "I don't know what's going on," she yelled back. "I'm not doing this!"

Her door slammed shut. Brenn kept one hand on Audrey's shoulder and extended her other arm. She clawed at the air, desperately searching for a source of magic to draw on outside herself, to nullify Audrey's. The magic that usually flowed through the Moon House was gone, and Brenn couldn't feel Charles Mayhew. A perverse bolt of relief flew through her at that absence. She hoped it meant they had managed to get somewhere safe.

A heavy glass water bottle smashed into her wrist, bringing her back to the pressing trouble. Brenn howled in pain. She yanked for the invisible cord that connected her to her coven, but as soon as she touched it, she felt it slip away. "Fuck!" she screamed. She grabbed Audrey's face. "Audrey, you have to work with me!"

Audrey just sobbed.

Brenn took a deep breath to steady herself and *reached*. Reached further into herself than she ever had before, seeking her deepest reserve of magic. She painstakingly forced it towards Audrey, shaped it into a blanket to tamp down Audrey's power. Brenn was concentrating so intently, she didn't hear the storm subside. Only when it was completely quiet save for Audrey's shuddery hiccups did she notice that it had worked.

"Oh, thank fuck. Are you alright?" Brenn's entire body was trembling. Her vision started going black on the edges. Audrey's voice sounded faraway and tinny, and the last thing Brenn heard was Audrey shrieking her name as Brenn slumped to the floor.

Everything was dark when Brenn woke up. She rubbed her eyes and hissed in pain. Her whole face felt bruised. There was a pillow under her head, which wasn't surprising, and a hardwood floor under her body, which was. It was a struggle for her to focus her thoughts enough to realize she was lying on the floor of Audrey's bedroom. She rolled to her side and something crunched under her hip. The memory of the evening came flooding back:

Audrey, her eyes wide and unseeing, terrified in the middle of an uncontrollable storm.

Brenn bolted up from the floor, ignoring the pain that threatened to put her back down. She was afraid to look around, and more afraid not to. She groped for her phone, flicking on the flashlight function.

The mess in Audrey's room flowed outward from her bed, and the dread Brenn was holding blossomed into full-blown panic. "Audrey?" she shouted. There was a rustling noise from her bedroom. She burst in to find Charles and Mayhew huddled in the open cupboard of her nightstand. Dropping to her knees, she ran her hands over them both, feeling for injuries. Once she was sure they were safe, she put Charles in the pocket of her jacket. Mayhew hopped to her bed.

"Where is Audrey?" She flipped the light on and gasped.

The destruction in her room was nearly as bad as it had been in Audrey's. She started to ask Mayhew again but then saw the thing that made her heart drop. The moon window was shattered. Milky glass glinted from the floor. "Mayhew, where is Audrey?"

"Go. Go." he said. "Note."

"Note? So she's alive?" She followed him as he flew downstairs into the kitchen. There was space on the island where bits of rubbish had been hastily pushed aside, and lying there was a folded piece of paper with 'Brenn' scrawled in a shaky script. Underneath was Audrey's account card.

She nearly tore the tear-stained paper in her hurry to read it. 'Brenn, I'm sorry. I'm so sorry I hurt you. I broke the Moon House— everything's broken. I don't know what happened. I'm too dangerous for your magic to fix so I'm going away so I can't hurt anyone else. I'm sorry. Charles Mayhew are OK, I made sure. I told them to get help if you didn't wake up. I'm sorry. Audrey."

Her stomach heaved, and she retched into the sink. What the fuck was she going to do. She splashed some water on her face. Hotels. Motels. She knew Audrey had some cash, she could get a room without much trouble if she managed to find a vacancy.

She staggered through the drifts of torn paper maps in her office, opening the safe secured behind the false back of the closet to grab an angular grey stone. "Charles Mayhew? Could you fix the windows and the door while I go look for Audrey?" She tossed her last magic storestone down and released the energy for Charles and Mayhew to use. "If there is magic left in that when you're done, could you clean up? Start down here?"

"Fixing house." Mayhew said, flying back up the stairs.

Brenn grabbed her keys.

Twenty-Three

THE FORTUNE HOTEL had two dim lamps lighting the lobby and a very sleepy-looking clerk behind the desk. Brenn tried not to appear as panicked as she felt. "Excuse me, did you have anyone rent a room tonight? My friend got into town late and said she was getting a room, but she didn't tell me which hotel."

"Sorry, hon, we've been booked solid for weeks." The clerk yawned. "Let me look real quick to make sure we didn't have a cancellation, though."

Brenn picked at a hangnail as the clerk checked their reservation log. "No, sorry again, hon, we didn't book any rooms today, they were all prior reserved."

"Thanks for looking," Brenn said. She went to leave. To her back, the clerk said, "I think you're gonna run into the same thing at all the hotels and motels in town; we're real busy around Halloween. Well, not the Sprite, but nobody stays there. You might want to check the campgrounds too."

The story was the same at every hotel in the downtown area. She drove up the row of motels, no-vacancy signs taunting her every fifty feet. It took her an hour to get through every motel, even the Sprite, and she braced herself to drive out to the two campgrounds in Briar Vale.

No luck at any of the places she stopped. She racked her brain for other places to check. The only friend Audrey was comfortable enough to stay with was Lydia, and Brenn knew she was at the haunted house lock-in. Noelle! She fervently, selfishly hoped Audrey hadn't gone to Noelle, but at least she'd be safe if she had. Her truck tires squealed as she took the corner too sharply.

Standing in the street outside of Noelle's house, she was suddenly stuck. How to see if Audrey was inside without alerting her sister? She didn't want to go peek in all the windows like some predatory creep. She needed night-vision goggles that could see through walls. Or infrared vision, like the movie Predator. *Infrared vision.*

Rhyming was a shortcut to strengthen a spell. She used the same motion Walker had showed them for her umbrella spell and, feeling foolish, recited "from the street, body heat." Her view of the street went blurry, and as she blinked to try to clear it, faint, pulsing, human-shaped lights began to shine in the blur. Two from Noelle and Jasmine's bedroom and five more from the kids' rooms. That was it. It was unlikely Audrey was there in place of one of her niblings. She glanced around at the lights in the other houses on the street, a small part of her impressed it worked.

When she released the spell, the world swooped around her. She stumbled against the truck, fighting a sudden nausea. If she was going to use that spell again, she would have to rework it. The energy sink was too high. She reeled as she climbed into the driver's seat. It was almost six in the morning, and even though most places in town took November first off, people were going to start noticing her lurking. Noelle finding out Audrey ran away would give her enough leverage to take Audrey away once Brenn did find her.

Defeated and fighting to keep her eyes open, she decided to go home and get an hour of sleep. There were dozens of towns and cities in southwest Michigan where Audrey could be staying. She needed a plan and a nap instead of just driving back and forth aimlessly.

~

BRENN WOKE WITH A START, her neck aching from sleeping on the living room couch. For a split second, she didn't know where she was, but then the whole horrible night came flooding back. Her head was splitting. "Charles Mayhew?" she called out into the eerie silence of the house, staying as still as possible.

Charles scampered in, his gait lopsided as he carried a travel-size bottle of painkillers in one tiny arm. He dropped it near her hands, then ran up her body. Putting a paw on each of her cheeks, he peered into her left eye and then her right. He chirped at her softly and, seemingly satisfied with what he saw, hopped onto the back of the sofa.

Mayhew waited on the coffee table until Charles had finished, then tapped the bottle of water sitting there closer to Brenn.

"Thank you, guys." Brenn rolled to her side as slowly as humanly possible, trying not to jostle her head. She washed the pills down, and fell back onto the cushion with a moan. "Oh my word, I feel awful. I don't know how I'm even alive."

Mayhew nuzzled her. She stroked his back. Her hand stilled. "How much of your magic did you use on me?" she asked, stricken. "Why did you do so much? Are either of you hurt?"

Charles spun in a circle, chittering furiously. His words made her sit straight up.

"The Moon House is in a coma?" She stood up then immediately sat down again. Her head in her heads, she asked Mayhew to grab her a granola bar. "Yeah, of course. You two do whatever you need to wake it back up. Don't exhaust yourselves, though."

Mayhew set the granola bar next to her on the sofa, and shifted from foot to foot as she ate it. When he'd decided she had enough, he hopped to her knee. "Girl school. Late."

"Huh?" Brenn asked him and then realized in the same breath what he was saying. "I have to excuse her absence. Right. Right? We'd know if she were there, right?"

"Go check," Mayhew said and flew off.

He was gone for only the time it took Brenn to down the rest of her water and stumble down the hall to plug in her phone. He looked troubled when he came in. "No girl."

Brenn sighed and pressed her fingers to her temples. "I'm going to email the school and then we can make of list of places to look for her. Shit."

The rest of the week, as she drove to every town within fifty miles, her stomach hurt. She survived on coffee and handfuls of almonds. Every time she crossed another place off her list, she thought of somewhere else Audrey might have gone, erasing her progress. The impromptu Peeping Tom body heat spell she'd done in front of Noelle's house was proving much more difficult for her to recover from than she'd expected.

She called the town hall of every magical town in Michigan, Wisconsin, Illinois, Indiana, and Ohio, to see if there had been any new witches passing through. Those calls went the same way, mild concern that deepened into great suspicion. A little part of Brenn was relieved when she was finished, humiliation was difficult enough to deal with, even without a healthy scoop of exhaustion and panic on top.

Brenn was appalled when she saw herself in a mirror. There were deep, dark bags under her eyes, her skin was dry and dull, and she had deeply etched frown lines on her forehead she couldn't massage away. Audrey had been gone for four horrible days already. Brenn knew she was pushing her limits, but four days should be enough time to bounce back from that spell. She had to now try magical means to find Audrey.

She spent a full day cleaning the mess she had ignored in her frantic travel, though she couldn't bring herself to touch Audrey's room. She was horribly guilty about neglecting the Moon House. Charles Mayhew's magical fixes had at least brought the house out of its weird coma, but it was not fully awake yet. After she cleared out the debris on the first floor, she polished all the wood in the house until it shone, repaired and washed windows until they sparkled. She brewed pot after pot of healing tea, leaving steaming bowls in every room, wafting the steam into every corner. She walked the entire house, running her hand over every wall, attempting to transfer as much of her love into it as possible.

When the house gave her a splinter on her second time through, her knees went weak with relief. Brenn admitted out loud to the Moon House she had been procrastinating. She was terrified to her toes that her magic wasn't going to work at all.

Sitting at the kitchen island, her stomach twisted as she looked at the deck of cards in front of her. Brenn shuffled them slowly. She put the edges up to her lips, whispering a request to find Audrey. She flipped the top card. Blank. She swore viciously under her breath, and flipped another card. This time it showed a dead end, a dark hallway from which nothing would emerge. Another card. A locked door, the key lost. Again. Blank. What in the ever loving hell.

She furiously turned the deck over in her hand, flipping through each card. Every single one had an image she'd painted on it, not a single blank card in the bunch. She shuffled again. Shoving aside the cards on the counter, she flipped a new one from the deck. Blank. Blank. Blank. She dropped the deck, ground the heels of her hands into her eyes, and screamed in frustration.

CHARLES HELPED her stitch her maps back together, and Mayhew lent her his magic while she held the pendulum over the patchwork papers. She didn't get even a faint tug. She drew a new map, nothing. She used her grandparents' maps, nothing. She spent three hours painting a new map, pouring her fear and need and, yes, love into every brush stroke. Still nothing.

She lay miserably in her lying room, not bothering to turn on the aurora or any music. Tears rolled slowly from the corners of her eyes into her ears. Charles crept up next to her, putting a wet paw on her face. "Sorry about the puddle, guys." Oh! Puddle. She could try scrying for Audrey's location.

THE LIBRARY DOWNTOWN had an excellent selection of books and pamphlets on scrying. She loitered around the doors, waiting for the librarian to come unlock them. She snuck in under a low-visibility cloak like some kind of thief, desperate to find a book before For Whom decided to announce her failure to the entire town. She checked out the first handful of books she found on the subject and speed-walked home.

After six hours of attempts, she admitted defeat. Idly flipping through a pamphlet that had been shoved inside one of the library books, she found instructions for a farsight prism that would let her see through the eyes of her subject. She tipped the book so Charles Mayhew could see it. "Huh. Maybe this?" Couldn't hurt at this point.

BRENN COULDN'T BELIEVE she didn't have a single suitable crystal in her entire house to make a farsight prism. Damn. She ran through the undelivered inventory she had still in the truck but came up empty. She needed to stay away from her family; there was no way she could convince them nothing was wrong. She didn't want to go to the coven. Once they found out how colossally she'd fucked up, they would want nothing to do with her. Blowing out a noisy breath, she racked her brain for who might have the crystals she needed and the ability to accept a brush-off explanation.

Ken might. Well, he almost certainly would. If she was going to go to Glass Moon, she needed to shower. She could smell herself, which was always a bad sign.

~

"BRENN!" Ken stopped punching numbers on his calculator. "I don't have a supply delivery today."

"Nope, just something for me today. I have no appropriate crystals to show Audrey how to set up a farsight prism if you can believe it." That was not entirely a lie. She didn't have to feel bad about it.

Ken called towards his back room, and his husband Liam bustled out. "Brenn!" he said warmly before turning to the counter. "What do you need, my dear?" he asked Ken.

"Our friend needs farsight rocks," Ken said, leaning over to fix Liam's collar.

Liam snapped his fingers jauntily at Ken, who handed him a little wire basket. He swiftly strode around the shop, gathering five different crystals, gently wrapping each one in a square of tissue paper. Ken passed him a box, and he tucked them inside, nestling a piece of black chalk in as well. "Black chalk usually gives you more clarity, absorbs any glare coming off the image."

She signed the receipt, thanking them profusely.

Not that it was any good. Once she had it activated, the prism only showed her a hazy grey darkness. She wasn't strong enough to bend the magic like she needed, to direct it forcefully enough to focus. Brenn massaged the space between her eyebrows. She felt like she was missing something obvious.

~

THE ENHANCEMENT SPELL! The one she and Audrey had tried a few weeks ago had given her a bit of a boost; it couldn't hurt to try it again. Brenn dashed into the library, skidding a little on the rug. Picking a plain brass key from the bowl of trinkets on a side table, she unlocked the cabinet that held her most valuable books. "Come on, come on," she whispered urgently, running a finger down each shelf, bumping across a rainbow of leather book spines. "Where did you put yourself?"

Somehow the grimoire ended up hiding on the bottom shelf, all the way in the back corner. Its leather binding had been burnished into a deep black-brown that seemed to absorb all light shone on it. She flipped through the pages as quickly as she felt was safe, the paper brittle with age. She recalled the spell was near the end, but she went one page at a time, looking for anything that might be helpful.

A small cloud of dust burst up from the binding, and she sneezed twice. The next page had the spell she was looking for, Enhancing Ability to Countermeasure Periods of Distress and Weakness. Huh. She didn't remember the part about distress being there when she and Audrey had used the grimoire. Well, it wasn't wrong.

Brenn gathered her supplies and prepared the ritual. She repeated the incantation under her breath a few times to familiarize herself again, the language tangling her tongue. Once she started the spell, however, it rolled out of her mouth like she had made it up herself. There was a popping sound and a chill through the room when she finished.

Instead of the burst of energy she was supposed to feel coiling around her, she felt a slow leak of magic. It was strangely cold. She slumped back in her chair. "Damnit. Damnit!"

Mayhew squawked. "Empty witch. Empty witch. No focus."

Brenn looked at him crossly. "Shut UP, Mayhew."

He muttered out a muffled half croak, puffing his feathers out and settling with a haughty wiggle.

Damnit, he was right, though. A nexus probably would help.

She dug around for the wand she had collected and carved when she was twelve, and puberty would make her magic spark and fizzle—sometimes literally, as though she lived in a never-ending cloud of static electricity. Brenn wished she had taken Audrey to the wand wood to collect her own. Her regrets were accumulating rapidly.

She left a trail of random stuff behind her as she tossed things from her closets behind her in her search. Charles ran around returning small items to their places, but he was fighting a losing battle. "Charles, leave it. I'll get it later, I promise."

He chattered at her, paws waving wildly. He pointed at all the detritus and then back at her, accusingly. She threw her own hands up in the air. "Fine! If it makes you feel better, go ahead."

Finally, she felt an electric shock from the recesses of a box in the closet of her old bedroom. She pulled the wand out. It was thirteen inches long, a pale birch branch with a slight spiral and a dyed plum-colored grip. She had felt so grown up the day she finished it. It had been at least two decades since she'd last used it, but the wood still gleamed.

Brenn swished it through the air experimentally. A trail of purple light curved from it like a neon sign. That will do.

Once she got back to the library, Mayhew nodded at her

approvingly. "Wand." he said, hopping across the table to stand next to the grimoire. She stroked the glossy feathers atop his head.

"You were right. I apologize for being cross at you." She squared her shoulders and did the spell again, using her wand to absorb the magical energy it was supposed to produce. This time, the wood grew warm, her hand tingling as she held it. "Fellas, it worked! Let's find our girl."

She took the map she had painted earlier that week and tried to find Audrey again. There was a slight dip when she passed her wand over Michigan, but she couldn't get any more precise than that. She held the wand in different positions, and tried both hands, and dowsed with both eyes open and then both closed. Not a single thing she did resulted in more than a gentle tug. Usually, when she was looking for something, her pendulum would pull straight down on the map like a magnet.

Brenn turned to try a different map and nearly fell over. The room swooped around her, and she had to hold the edge of her desk to stay upright. Charles skittered up her chair, leapt onto the desk, and put his tiny paws on her knuckles. He chirped insistently at her.

"Yeah, yeah. I hear you. I will take a nap. A *nap*." She noticed just how dry her eyes felt. "And yes, I'll eat real food."

She wearily stumbled down the hall and collapsed on the living room sofa.

Twenty-Four

BRENN WOKE with a start to the doorbell. The morning sun slanted into her eyes, and she blinked. Her head felt wrapped in wool.

Junelle was on her porch, pacing back and forth, ringing the bell every few minutes. Brenn silently rested her forehead on the wood, willing Junelle to leave.

She started knocking instead. "Brenn, I know you're home. I can feel you in there," she called.

Brenn sighed in defeat. She cracked the door just enough to see her friend. "Hey, Junelle. What's going on?"

"What's going on? That's what I'd like to know. Can I come in?" She craned her neck to try to see around Brenn's body into the house.

"It's really not a great time. I overslept, and I really am not company-ready. I'll call you later..." she trailed off as Junelle shook her head no and pushed her way into the house.

Junelle whirled around once she was inside. "Brenn. I subbed at the high school this entire week, and Audrey wasn't there a single day. No one seemed to know what was going on." Her eyes got wide as she noticed the mess surrounding her for the first time. "What happened? Brenn, are you in trouble? Is Audrey okay?"

Brenn's face crumpled. "No, everything is bad," she managed to get out through her tears. She sobbed into Junelle's thick cable-knit shawl. "I think I might need some help."

~

SHE TOOK the tissue Junelle held out, thanking her tearily. "I'm sorry for losing it at you."

Junelle waved her off. "Babe, something is clearly wrong."

"Audrey ran away." Brenn swallowed back the bile rising in her throat. Saying it out loud made her want to curl up in shame.

"Ran away?!" Junelle's voice climbed several octaves.

Brenn could barely force the words out. "On Halloween—"

"Halloween! Oh, Brenn." She started to ask her another question but instead motioned Brenn to continue.

"So, on Halloween, when I finally got home, the house was dark and Audrey was in the middle of...a wind storm, I guess. Windows breaking, stuff flying around, everything trashed. I tried to calm her magic, but it was too strong and I passed out. When I woke up, she was gone. She did leave a note. Hang on, it's in the living room." Junelle followed her as she strode into the living room and rummaged around in the pile of junk on the table. Tearing up again as she unearthed the note, she held it out to Junelle.

It took Junelle no time at all the read the note. She looked up at Brenn quizzically. "Why would she think she had to leave?"

Brenn groaned. "That is a terrible combination of my idiocy and her background. You know what happened at her foster homes, right?" Junelle nodded. "Yeah, so let me tell you how I grew up."

She told Junelle about Noelle being perfect and Cleo being

the baby. How they sucked up all their parents' attention, leaving her to be left on her own. "So I was used to solving my problems by myself. And I am overly sensitive to Noelle constantly picking at me." She raised her hands and shrugged. "Soooo, when Noelle called, insisting that I send Audrey to boarding school and have a 'real' baby of my own, I lost my shit and yelled at her that I didn't want kids. And Audrey heard."

"Oh, no," Junelle breathed. "You hit her where it hurts."

Brenn hid her face in her hands. "I know. So Audrey went upstairs and wouldn't talk to me, so I called Dani for advice because Lydia is just a year older. She said they always have to let Lydia work it out in her head first before talking about things, so that's what I tried. I left her alone that night, and then she seemed fine. Everything was normal the next day."

Junelle tipped her head to the side, studying her. "Brenn, what happened when you were upset with your parents? Say you got angry with them because they said something insensitive?"

Brenn snorted. "We weren't allowed to get mad at our parents."

Junelle's eyebrows shot up, and she pressed her lips together tightly. She made a little 'tsk' noise. "We are going to circle back to that one, but for now—hypothetically," she spread her hands out in front of her conciliatory, "when you were upset with your parents, what did you do? How did you react?"

"I'd go to my room for a while until I could calm down enough to say I was fine and not sound like I was lying."

Junelle gave her a prompting look.

"Oh. Oh, no."

"And if you didn't have someone like your Aunt Violet that you knew you could rely on in a pinch, and you had been taught your whole life that when you make destructive mistakes, you'd be kicked out, don't you think you might decide it would be less painful to leave than to be sent away from the one place you let yourself love?"

Brenn smooshed her cheeks in towards her mouth. "Oh, fuck. I screwed that up, I'm so stupid."

"No, you're not. And going to Dani for advice was a sound first step. But Brenn, if you asked Aislynn about her teenage daughter or even me about my students, you would have gotten completely different answers." She stepped around the coffee table to sit next to Brenn on the sofa and gripped her in a tight hug. "Babe, I know you've been on your own a lot, but now you've got a half dozen of us ready to help you with whatever you need. Granted, you decide to become evil, we're going to have a different kind of chat."

Brenn choked out a laugh.

"And look, you've been caring for a traumatized teenager for *two months*. Of course you'll need help. It would be a lot easier for everyone if you'd just asked instead of me having to barge in here and force you to accept my assistance." Junelle handed her another tissue, scooching over on the seat to give Brenn room to compose herself.

She sniffled a few times, then looked at Junelle with watery eyes. "How do I fix this? How do I find her? Nothing I've tried is working."

"Tell me what you've tried and the results you got, and we'll go over it together." She took a pink spiral notebook and a purple enamel pen covered in teeny gold stars and moons from her purse. Looking expectantly at Brenn, she wrote the number one on the top line of a blank sheet.

"Well, I went around to all the hotels and motels in town. Even the Sprite. And to the campgrounds. Lydia was gone, so I knew she wasn't at Dani's, and I checked Noelle's. I confirmed surreptitiously that Cleo hadn't let her stay at her apartment. Then I called every town hall in the directory here and in Wisconsin, Illinois, Indiana, and Ohio. I drove around every town and city and village in southwest Michigan."

"That's thorough. But that's all stuff anyone could do. I

mean, it's good to know, but I was thinking more along the lines of what magical means have you tried?" Junelle drew a line down the center of the page and wrote the number one again.

Brenn twisted her fingers. "There's something I need to tell you. Something you all don't know about me and is probably going to make you never want to speak to me again."

Junelle's eyes went wide. "Uh. Did you murder someone? Are we having that evil chat right now?"

"No, I didn't murder anyone. So, all through August, my cards kept telling me something big was coming. I had done a few protection spells in case it was bad, you know, basic stuff. Then on the first of September, all I've pulled have been blank cards."

"I'm not seeing why we'd be upset about that."

Brenn winced. "That is also the day my magic started fizzing out."

"I'm going to need some clarification on that one, Brenn." Junelle tipped her head to the side, watching Brenn calmly.

"Like I'm not as powerful. And spells don't work properly, or at all. It's like I'm a ten-year-old again. I'm pathetic." She wiped a hand down her face. "I know I should have told you all before we sealed, but I've been working to fix it, and I thought with the power surge from the coven, maybe I'd get back some. I don't know what I was thinking. I guess I wasn't."

"Is this what that drug thing was about? Fixing your magic?"

"Yeah. For Whom gave me this book. You've got to see this thing, it's ridiculous. Except it came from For Whom." She gave Junelle a significant look.

Junelle nodded along. "And that cart is never wrong."

"But I've done all this stupid shit and nothing is working."

"Let's ignore that for right now. What magical means have you tried to find Audrey? We'll start there, make sure we don't repeat anything that doesn't need to be."

"Wait. What?" Brenn pinched her lips between her teeth. "You're going to help me? I lied to you for weeks."

"Your magic was on the fritz when Nat asked you to join the coven, yeah?" Brenn nodded. "So I trust Nat, and none of us got a whiff of you being not powerful enough to join us. After we find Audrey, we'll focus on getting you back up to full power, okay?"

Brenn sniffled again. She was getting really damn tired of crying. Never in her life had she cried this much. "I tried my cards, my maps and pendulum, scrying in water and crystal and mirrors, a far sight prism, an enhancement spell from my great great aunt, and then a new map I made."

Junelle looked half shocked and half impressed. "You really covered the basics, didn't you? Well, we are definitely going to want to repeat some of that. Maybe Lily has another seeking spell we could modify. Or I wonder if Walker could pull anything from Audrey's stuff to indicate where she wanted to go."

As Junelle rattled off the list of things they could try, Brenn's heart started pounding again. "She's been gone for more than a week, what if she's hurt? What if she can't call me? Junelle, what if she's—"

"Nope, we're not going to spiral. I'll call everyone and get them over here. You go take a steaming hot shower, and we will figure this out together, as a coven. You have any chamomile and lavender?"

"In the kitchen, the tea cabinet. Armoire on the wall."

Junelle prepped her a muslin bag of calming herbs and flowers. "Hang this in the stream of water, and breathe the steam for a good five minutes before you get in, okay?" She pressed it into Brenn's hand and steered her to the staircase. "While you're doing that, I'm going to call everyone."

Brenn nodded, not trusting her voice not to crack.

FEELING MUCH MORE human after her shower, Brenn padded downstairs. She was wearing a gigantic sweatshirt and jeans that had holes in both knees.

The foyer was spotlessly clean. A flash of embarrassment went through her, and she consciously pushed it away. She found Junelle in the living room, organizing the books strewn around the floor into stacks.

"Brenn! Sorry I didn't get more done, but these miniatures are amazing. Did you make them? Did you charm them?"

"Yeah, I'll show you my workroom sometime." She shuffled over and kicked a pile of dirty socks towards the door. "You don't need to clean my mess."

"I haven't done much, just listened to your house to see how you like your housekeeping, and then it was a couple of quick spells." She sat back, her hands on her knees. "So I called everyone. Walker and Dani are on their way in a bit. Nat is gathering supplies, and she's going to stop at Vitamin M before here. Aislynn's husband is away at a conference, so she can't come until tomorrow because she doesn't have anyone to watch her kids last minute, and Lily won't be here until tomorrow either, as she's out of town."

"Thanks for making the calls. Did you tell them what's going on?" Brenn picked at a hangnail.

Junelle put the last of the scattered books in a stack. "I only told Nat about your magic. I figured you should tell everyone else yourself. They all know about Audrey and how long she's been gone, though."

Brenn clasped her hands behind her back to stop herself from picking at her skin. She made a face. "Junelle, I don't know if I can tell everyone."

The doorbell rang.

~

DANI AND WALKER were on the porch, straining under armfuls of pillows and blankets. There were three folding cots on the path behind them, like a line of ducklings. "Brenn! Why didn't you call me? I would have come over right away." Dani bustled in. "Where should we stash all this? I didn't know how many beds you had, so I thought we should bring some supplies with us."

Walker shifted her armload around so she had a hand free and squeezed Brenn's elbow as she walked into the house. Dani whistled, and the cots rolled themselves in as well.

Brenn watched, speechless. Dani misunderstood her silence. "Oh, don't worry! We won't leave you with a mess."

"Uh, no, that's not...uh. Why?" She gestured at the cots.

"Well, we're going to need places to sleep, and I am too old to do a sleeping bag on the floor."

That did not clear anything up for Brenn. "But...why would you need to sleep?"

Dani looked surprised. "We aren't leaving until we find Audrey. If you couldn't do it in a full week, I'm guessing it will take us at least a day."

"Dani!" Walker chided.

Dani drew back. "What? She needs someone to be a realist. Obviously, we'll find Audrey, but I'm not going to pretend it's gonna be fast. Brenn's whole business is finding things. She is a *professional*. Her skills are superior."

Brenn looked between them, overwhelmed.

Walker dropped her blankets on the foyer chair. "I concede the point. I just don't think it's especially helpful to be so blunt about it."

Dani just sniffed. She put her blankets and pillows down atop Walker's pile, then peered around the Moon House. "I can't believe we've been friends for three years, and I've never been inside your house before."

"Oh, yeah. Sorry. I don't know why." Brenn started to tell them about her house, but she caught a glimpse of Nat struggling up the walkway, loaded down with bags. Instead, she went out to meet her. Nat gratefully let a handful of totes slide down her arms into Brenn's hands.

"What is all this?" Brenn asked.

"This and that. Spell components, food, bourbon, a couple bottles of wine, a change of clothes for me, Jelly's travel bag, books. Anything I could think of that we might need." She laid her hand on the outer wall of the house for a moment. "Oh, hello." She cocked her head to the side like she was listening, then laughed quietly. She turned back to Brenn. "This is a good house."

Brenn blinked. "Yeah, it is. How did you know to greet it like that? I haven't ever seen anyone besides our family do it that way."

Nat lifted her shoulders. "Just seemed like the thing to do."

Junelle was in the foyer when they came in. Brenn put the bags she carried on the floor. "So. Welcome to the Moon House. Library and living room." She pointed to the front, then waved a hand at the doors around them. "My office. Storeroom. Lying room. Bathroom. Kitchen, dining, and porch in the back. I've got an extra bedroom upstairs besides mine and Audrey's." Her voice broke when she said Audrey's name. Nat rubbed her back.

They decided to set up one cot downstairs in the lying room and stuck the rest in a guest room upstairs. Walker got to work organizing the mess in Audrey's room. Brenn wanted to stop her, an irrational fear that cleaning up meant cleaning Audrey out of the house, but the thought of Audrey coming home to a mess was worse.

Walker saw the emotions warring on her face. "Brenn? That whole reading desires thing I do? I know where Audrey prefers things." She gestured around the room. "It will be exactly like she left it. Before, I mean. Which is probably better than the reminder of what happened?"

Brenn scrubbed her hands down her face. "No, you're right. I just feel weird about it."

~

DOWNSTAIRS, Dani had commandeered the dining room table. She had two laptops set up, and Nat was stacking books on the other end. There was a pile of notepads and pens and sticky notes. Dani flipped a surge protector on. "Be careful of the cords," she warned Brenn, pointing at the floor. "We're going to get Aislynn and Lily on video chat so we can make a plan for tomorrow."

Brenn sank into a chair. Her limbs felt like they were attached to her with rubber bands.

Once Lily and Aislynn were up on the screens, Dani absently waved two moths off her shirt to go get Walker and Junelle. She dragged a couple more chairs over so they could all see each other. A few minutes of fiddling once everyone was seated and ready, and Dani looked to Brenn. "Okay, we're ready."

Brenn swallowed hard. "So, I know Junelle told you Audrey is missing. Her magic flared pretty badly on Halloween after I dropped her off here, when all of us were together at the labyrinth. When I got home, she was in the middle of a windstorm kind of thing. I tried to subdue her magic, but I passed out. When I woke up, she was gone."

Aislynn interrupted her. "How bad a flare are we talking?"

"The house was in a...coma? for a few days, and it didn't really fully wake up until Sunday? Yesterday?" Brenn searched her memories. "Yesterday morning. There were a couple broken windows, and the door had been splintered. Most of my maps were torn. It honestly looked like a tornado ran through here."

"Your maps?" Nat asked.

"Yeah. I showed them to Audrey the weekend before Halloween, so they were still sitting out. And I handmade all of them, so my guess is Audrey thought I'd be mad when I saw them destroyed, since they took so much work." She rubbed her forehead. "I tried everything I could possibly think of, but there's no trace of her." Brenn detailed everything she had tried. Junelle then stepped in.

"So I made a list of all the regular and all the magical things Brenn has done to track Audrey down. We will want to try a few of these again, with all of us together."

The coven spent several hours narrowing down their options and setting a plan of attack, mentioning spells and resources Brenn hadn't thought of herself. She slumped back in her seat, feeling a throb of relief so acute it was painful.

Nat's voice broke into her thoughts. "...so tonight, the four of us are going to stay here with Brenn, and we will prep as much as possible so we can get started right away tomorrow. What time do you..." Brenn's mind drifted again, Nat's voice fading to background noise. She should tell them now about her magic. They hadn't judged her yet for failing Audrey.

But sealing herself in a coven with them while lying about her magical ability was an entirely different thing.

She decided to wait until they had cast enough to find Audrey, shoving the guilt down deeper. At least then, her worst mistake would be fixed before they kicked her out.

BRENN SLEPT SURPRISINGLY WELL. Dani had given her a drop of a sleeping draught in a cup of tea, and it had been potent. She got out of bed feeling cheerier than she expected. Knowing they had a plan and that she wasn't on her own in this anymore lightened her mood.

When she got downstairs, she almost collided with Walker, who was rushing in the door. Walker held up the bags she was carrying. "I brought food. Lots and lots of food, so we don't have to leave in the middle of anything."

Brenn gave her a crooked smile. "That sounds really great."

She followed her into the dining room. Aislynn and Lily had already arrived, Lily deep in conversation with Nat and Junelle about the most accurate scrying methods. Aislynn was on the phone, giving Brenn a little wave when she saw her.

Flipping through three different books simultaneously, Dani, without looking up, asked, "Brenn, we are going to need quite a few unusual things. How well stocked is your storeroom right now?"

"It's okay. I try to keep some of the rarer items in reserve." She took the list Dani flapped at her. "Oh, damn. This is… comprehensive."

Walker read the list over her shoulder. "I'll come with you, be your pack mule."

Her eyes widened as she took in the organized chaos of Brenn's storeroom. "Oh, wow. I guess I didn't realize the scope of your operation." She started reading labels on the shelf closest to her. "So, when you acquire things for people, how specific do they need to be?"

"Not super specific. I actually met Dani because she hired me to find her wood that would burn pink."

Walker snorted.

"Oh, I know. Trust me. It was a bit of a wild goose chase; I ended up following leads through four different countries. And then I found it in Canada, of all places." She consulted the list and unlocked one of her cabinets. "I was so prepared to hate her on sight when I dropped it off, but we ended up friends instead." She pointed at the filing cabinets in the middle of the room. "Can you grab me one of those trays?"

Walker handed it to her, stretching over the table. "So you

can find things off just a particular quality? What about an extremely vague purpose?"

"Maybe? You looking for something?"

Walker blushed. "Not yet. But I've been dabbling in perfumery, and I have a couple of ideas. But, like, barely formed."

Brenn tossed her a rope basket. "Grab those spiky candles and put them in this." She tucked a few crystals in her own box. "When you do, definitely let me know. I'll show you how I dowse for them. And if you're with me, it'll be easier to focus in on exactly what you want."

"Cool." Walker grabbed the boxes Brenn handed her, balanced the basket of candles on top, and walked out with large strides.

BRENN'S STOMACH was churning with butterflies as the witches stood in a circle, ready to clasp hands and cast their first spell. She rubbed her palms on her pants, trying to dry them before subjecting Walker and Nat to the clamminess. She started to reach out but then balled her hands into fists and pulled them to her chest. "Nope. No. I can't." She backed out of the circle and hunched in a chair.

Dani looked at her in amazement. "Brenn. This is the whole reason we're here. We are going to need you to finish the circle so we can cast this spell. What's going on with you?"

"Oh, boy." Brenn said in a small voice. "I have to tell you all something."

She grimaced, showing her clenched teeth. "Or, well, Junelle and Nat already know, but the rest of you don't." She clutched at her throat, not knowing how to begin. "I don't have magic anymore."

"*What*?" The four of them said at almost the same time.

"No, no, wait. I do have magic, just, it's wrong. Wrong? Glitchy?" Brenn looked wildly at Junelle for help. She gave Brenn an encouraging smile and nod. Brenn powered through. "At the beginning of September, I started having trouble with anything that wasn't a child-level working. That's partly why I joined the coven. To restore my power."

She faltered as she heard one of them draw in a sharp breath. "I'm sorry. I'm so sorry I didn't tell you. And after sealing, I did get a boost. But that was only temporary. And then I told Audrey. Which is why she freaked out so thoroughly, she thought I wouldn't be able to curb the power that came out of her flare-ups."

"Well, it sucks that you lied to us." Dani looked wounded. "But why wouldn't you just tell me? I could have helped you."

Lily cleared her throat. "Brenn, I understand why you might be panicked at that, but you should have told us so we could make our own decision on how to proceed. However, what's done is done. After we find Audrey, I propose we focus on assisting Brenn recover her abilities."

"Obviously," scoffed Aislynn. She wheeled herself over to Brenn. "I'm going to scan you real quick, make sure it's not a physiological issue." Taking Brenn's hand in hers, she let her eyes go unfocused. The rest of the group stayed silent. After several minutes, Aislynn made a satisfied noise, and her gaze snapped back into focus. "All clear on physical reasons. Which means we're looking at either psychological or magical. You piss anyone off lately? Maybe have a curse on you?"

Brenn shook her head.

"Well, we should get you to someone who can check for that." The group devolved into chatter about who would be best to approach.

Dani raised her hand. "Uh, I'm right here? I can see magic now?"

"Right! What are you waiting for?" Aislynn gave her a shove.

Swatting back at her, Dani stood in front of Brenn. "Stand up. I guess you should try to use your magic?"

"Does it matter what I do? No?" Feeling supremely awkward, Brenn extinguished a candle and then tried to light it again. It took her a full minute to get it to light.

Dani watched her with her head cocked, the silver bits in her eyes shining brightly. "Huh. You look...faded. Like when you cast with us before, I didn't notice. But on your own it's like I'm looking at it through a veil."

Aislynn and Lily started talking to Dani at the same moment. Brenn stood there, not sure what to do.

She startled as Walker touched her arm. "That was a huge secret to be carrying for so long," Walker said. "You good? Need to sit a minute?"

"No. I. Uh. Hey," she raised her voice above the din. "You aren't going to kick me out?"

"Kick you out of what?" Nat asked, confused.

"The coven?" Brenn gripped the fingers of one hand in the other.

"What? No? Brenn, we saw in person what your abilities were when we performed the sealing. If anyone here had concerns about your power, or anyone's really, they could have raised them before we sealed."

Brenn stared at Nat in disbelief. She pressed her fingers together and held them to her lips.

Junelle half-smirked at her. "I told you Nat knew your abilities when she invited you."

"I know, but haven't I put you all in danger? I mean, Dani's altered forever because I fucked up that spell."

Dani raised a hand. "Hey, Dani is a-okay with being altered forever. Turns out to be an extremely useful skill, as you just saw."

"Okay, fine, but I hurt Audrey too."

"You were focused on helping Audrey control her magic

while she was using it. But Brenn, you also need to teach her how to deal with the effects of magic, like how to fix the mistakes she makes, not just stop them. We all make mistakes, and we clean them up. That is an integral part of using magic." Lily replied.

"Oh, fuck. You're right. I ignored...half of her education. Noelle was right. I should have put Audrey in a situation that would actually prepare her for being a witch." Brenn's face sank.

"Brenn, that's not what we're saying. You're too far in your own head. What we're saying is you shouldn't try to be everything for her by yourself. Let us in. Let us help." Junelle said. "And, need I remind you, you told us yourself that you *did* show her some reversal magic."

"That was nothing, just a few kiddie spells I couldn't even manage on my own."

"For fuck's sake. Wallowing isn't helping anyone right now. Brenn, you fucked some things up. You are trying to fix them. We are going to help. I've forgiven you, and I doubt I'm the only one. Work on making your first instinct to rely on us, not shut us out. Can we move on for the moment?" Aislynn glowered at her, which undercut the kindness of her words a bit.

Brenn half-laughed, half-sobbed. "Okay. Point taken." She dabbed at her eyes with a tissue. If she didn't cry again for five years, it would be too soon, considering how many tears she'd shed today alone. "Let me wash my face, and then we can start?"

In the bathroom, Brenn splashed handfuls of cold water on her face. It felt so good she almost wanted to cry again. She had a towel pressed to her skin when she felt a nuzzle at her ankle. She looked down to see Charles Mayhew waiting at her feet. "Hey, fellas," she said. "We are going to find our girl." The Moon House creaked gently, walls trembling ever so slightly.

Out in the foyer, she straightened a photograph on the wall, knocked askew. It was a portrait she, Noelle, and Cleo had done for their parents' 45th wedding anniversary. Voices floated out from the dining room, and she turned towards them, hand still on the photo. She thought about Noelle, pushing her toward a partner and children and responsibility, and Cleo, feckless and running headlong into life, unafraid. She thought about the things she had discovered *she* wanted for herself. Her life was never going to look like her sisters'. She had no desire for a partner or babies, and she was too much of a planner to throw herself recklessly into things like Cleo, trusting everything would work out.

But she didn't need the things her sisters had. She didn't need the things her family wanted for her. And now she had six friends in her house, helping her without the promise of anything in return. Six people who didn't judge her for being soft or vulnerable, who weren't going to make her justify every decision. Six people who wanted to lift her up because she was *her*, and that was enough.

From the doorway, she watched her friends arrange the components for a spell, waiting for her to return to complete their circle. She swallowed hard, a lump in her throat. "Hey," she started, her voice a croak. She cleared her throat. "Hey. I just wanted to say that..." She had to take a shuddery breath. "That I am so grateful and happy that I get to have you all in my life." She shrugged sheepishly, tears filling her eyes again. She dashed them away roughly with the back of her hand.

"Oh, babe. We love you too." Dani crushed her in a hug, among a chorus of agreement.

Twenty-Five

NAT MADE an irritated sound of disgust, throwing her hands in the air. "What is going on with this? It's like something is purposefully screwing with our magic."

"I ran into this too, on my own." Brenn rolled her head from side to side, trying to stretch the kinks from her neck. "I tried an enhancement spell, but I couldn't get any narrower than this general area. Which is like five states and a chunk of Canada."

Walker cracked her knuckles. "I'm going to go heat up some food. Anybody?"

The coven had spent the past seven hours casting every searching spell they could dig up, tried every method they could think of. The magic felt like it wanted to reveal something to them but then would skitter away, like two magnets repelling each other. Brenn looked at her friends' drawn faces and tired eyes, and something in her stomach pulled uncomfortably.

Aislynn tapped her hand. "Hey. We expected this, at least in part. Take some deep breaths. Maybe you should take a walk around the block, clear your head in the fresh air."

"I wouldn't mind a walk myself," Lily said. "Junelle? Dani?"

Junelle set the wand she was holding on the table. "Actually, whatever Walker reheated smells delicious. I think I'm going to eat." She left for the kitchen.

Dani scraped her hair back into a ponytail. "Why not? If I don't do that, I'll fall asleep." She raised her eyebrows at Aislynn, who shook her head.

"I need to FaceTime Ben. I promised Declan I'd read him a chapter of *The Hobbit* every night until we were done, no breaks. Thirty or forty minutes, tops. Oh. Brenn, do you have a copy?"

She nodded. "I'll grab it, and then, yeah, a walk sounds good."

Nat tossed the pencil she was using down on the table. "Mind one more joining?"

Walker came in, shoveling food in her mouth. "Break time? I could use a half hour of mindless TV, myself."

Brenn pointed her towards the television. "Help yourself."

THE FOUR OF them split into pairs when they reached the sidewalk, Lily and Dani ahead and Nat falling back to walk next to Brenn.

"So," she said, "what's your favorite movie?"

That startled a laugh from Brenn. "What? Why?"

"I figured you were probably sick of thinking about magic and searching and the whole situation, and this is break time. So, what's your favorite movie?"

"*Alien.*" Brenn said without hesitation. "Very closely followed by *Aliens*. Mayhew was almost named Jones."

Nat snorted. "I didn't peg you as a sci-fi gal. But it makes sense."

"Yeah? I love pretty much any kind of speculative fiction. What's yours?" Brenn rubbed her hands together to warm them up.

"*But I'm A Cheerleader*. That movie wormed its way into my heart and will not let go."

"I haven't seen that one."

"Oh, it's great. Super queer. Oh, but I don't think there are any aro or ace characters. So maybe not super queer for you. Still, worth watching, great cast, really effective set design and costuming." Nat brushed aside a strand of hair that blew into her mouth. "I have a copy you can borrow if you want."

"Would it be appropriate for a fifteen-year-old?"

"Yep. I think Audrey would like it. Text me a reminder, and I'll pull it out for you."

Brenn promptly texted her. Making future plans that included Audrey made her feel a little weird. She tried to ignore it. "Hey, what do you think they're talking about?" She motioned at Lily and Dani, her hand in her jacket pocket.

"They do look thick as thieves." Nat raised her voice so it carried forward. "What are you two whispering about?"

Lily stopped and turned. "I have been collaborating with Dani on a potion that should let me acquire some control over my visions. I think if I take it tonight before sleep, I might be more useful tomorrow. Dreams sometimes take us places we cannot access consciously."

Nat looked at Dani for confirmation. She nodded. "We've been testing different variations for about a month now? I think this one is the closest yet. Plus, we have nothing to lose." She winced. "I mean, we might as well try it. Because if it doesn't work, we aren't worse off."

When they got back to the Moon House, Walker and Junelle were sprawled on the sofa watching an old episode of *The Great British Bake-Off*. Nat flopped into an armchair, asking questions about the episode currently on. They had to wait ten minutes or so for Aislynn to finish reading to her son, and then Dani and Lily told the rest of them their plan.

Nat stood up. "I'd like to get in a couple more hours of casting if the rest of you are up for it, before we turn in."

Aislynn spoke up. "I actually need to sleep at home tonight; I have to be at the hospital at five a.m. with a patient tomorrow morning, and I can't really reschedule this late. So I can stay until, let's see." She counted on her fingers. "Nine thirty? That would give us about two hours."

"Anyone else need to sleep at home?" Nat asked. The other women shook their heads. "Alright, let's give it a few more tries, and then we can fight over beds."

THE CASTING DID NOT GO WELL. Something was blocking their access.

Nat massaged her temples. "She must be warded, but where would she learn that? Brenn?"

"I haven't done any of that with her. I mean, I told her how they work in really basic terms." She screwed her face up, thinking back. "She saw me put a shield on us the first day we met, but that doesn't feel like whatever we are running into here." Chewing her lip, she stared blankly at the wall. "It feels familiar to me, though," she mused.

"I doubt we will get any further now. Dani, shall we go finish preparing that potion?" Lily and Dani left the room.

Aislynn left for home, and Walker and Junelle coerced Nat into watching more *Bake-Off* with them. Brenn went up to her room, pretending to read while she worried. Charles Mayhew tucked themselves in for the night in their usual places. Usually, their presence acted as a soporific for her, but tonight she was too keyed up. It was a little after four before she fell asleep with her book lying on her chest.

SHE FOUND the entire coven crowded around her dining room table early the next morning when she stumbled down the stairs. Lily was painting with sure strokes in a sketchbook covered in green linen. They parted so Brenn could watch easily as well.

"What is that?" Dani asked when Lily sat back in her chair, shaking her hand out. "It just looks like softballs in front of some trees."

Lily studied her painting for a long minute. "I think it's hail." She traced a few spots with her fingers. "No, it is definitely hail. Perhaps Audrey is in a location where hail occurs regularly? These are big for hailstones, though."

They all stared at the painting. Dani snapped her fingers and went around to her laptop on the opposite side of the table. She typed furiously for a few minutes, then silently read her screen.

"Ah ha! The forecast for the entire state is sunny and clear and has been over the past couple of days as well."

"So she's not in Michigan?" Brenn's heart sank.

Dani waggled a finger at her. "I'm not done. I just need to..." she typed a bit more. "...and, yes! There have been two unusual storms in the UP, one was about a week ago, huge thunderstorms. The other was two days ago, at Tahquamenon Falls, which saw a hailstorm with softball-sized hail."

Brenn's breath left her all at once, and her knees wobbled. Nat pushed her towards a chair. Brenn's question came out on a breath. "Do you think that's her?"

Nat shrugged. "Do you know what's up near the Falls? Why would she go there?"

"It's isolated?" Walker offered. Aislynn nodded and added, "The forest up there is wild. There's a lot of magic in the air. Maybe she was drawn there without knowing why?"

Brenn gasped. "Holy shit, the Hyacinth Center."

"The what Center?" Junelle asked.

"My family traded for a tiny piece of land up there like two hundred years ago, put a sort of camp on it for gatherings. My parents use it every summer for their conferences." She frowned. "How would Audrey have gotten up there? It's warded to the..." Her mouth dropped open as she stared at her friends. "It's *warded*," she said. "You can't find it unless you have the key or an invitation." She stopped, a realization hitting her. "Or the fucking car."

She ran out the back door, flinging the garage door open with magic before her. She scrambled to the back stall, yanking off a tarp that was supposed to be draped over a small coupe. Throwing it behind her, she looked dumbly at crates and boxes stacked in a vaguely car-shaped configuration.

The coven found her there, vibrating with anger. She held her hand out towards the parking space, fingers spread like she was pointing with all of them. "That is where my parents' conference car is supposed to be. The car that is spelled to drive only between this house and that conference center on autopilot so they can work on the drive up. The car you don't need a license or experience driving to operate because it just does its own thing."

Walker whistled. "This is pretty conclusive evidence. How do we get up there?"

"I don't know who would have told her about..." She stopped as she heard Walker's question. "Noelle has the key. My parents wanted it in a separate location from the car for safety."

"Okay, so we get the key and then drive up? How long is the drive?" Dani pulled her phone out, opening the maps app.

"Five hours or so? If I can even get Noelle to give me the key." Brenn gritted her teeth.

Dani looked around. "Lily and I will go with you to get the key. Everyone else will stay here and get everything we need ready so we can leave right away."

Brenn nodded tightly. "I'm going to go inside and try to figure out a way to convince Noelle to give me that damn key."

JUST BEFORE BREAKFAST, Dani, Lily, and Brenn left for Noelle's house. Brenn was out of Dani's car before it had stopped fully. Every step she took to Noelle's front door left a footprint singed on the pavement. She rapped her knuckles sharply on the door, part of her pleased she didn't give in and pound on it with both fists like she wanted.

Ready to lay into her sister as the door swung open, she stopped abruptly at the sight of her niece. "Hey, Sav. I need to talk to your Mama. Can I come in?"

Savannah peered around her. "Hi, Auntie Brenn," she said distractedly. "Did you bring Audrey? I want to show her something in my room!"

"Sorry, cutie, just me today." Savannah pouted and led Brenn to the kitchen, where the rest of her family sat around their dining table. Jasmine took one look at Brenn's face and subtly stroked the edge of her phone, which immediately pinged. She flashed the notification at the kids. "Hey, kidlets, the Sweet Squares truck is out. Who wants to go have a waffle feast for breakfast?"

She shepherded their excited kids out of the house. Brenn waited until the sound of their voices faded before she spoke.

"Noelle, I need the key to the Hyacinth Center right now." She held her hand out, palm up.

Noelle looked at her skeptically. "Mama and Poppy trusted me to keep that key and the center safe. There is no way I'm just handing it to you. If you and your cute little coven need a place for a outing, there are plenty of spots around here."

Brenn nodded tightly. "Nono, you will give me that key, and you will do it now. Audrey has been missing for a full week, and I have been out of my mind trying to find her. And those women in my 'cute little coven'," she did the air quotes, "are the only people who have bothered to help me. It was a giant fucking surprise to find out not only that Audrey has apparently made it all the way to the Falls but also to discover the car is missing." She barreled on. "Who told her about the center, Noelle? Who told her how to get there? How the car works? Who was irresponsible enough to give an emotional teenager with the tendency to run fucking *blueprints on how to run away*? You've been so busy tearing me down to her that she didn't believe I was strong enough to handle her magic flaring, so when it did, she just took off."

Brenn drew in an angry breath. "How dare you? Every time I turned around, you were planting these criticisms in her head. Do you really hate me that much?"

"Brenn, calm down and talk to me rationally. Audrey is missing? And you didn't tell me for a week? You can't see how irresponsible that is? You don't get to yell at me for spending time with her while you've left her alone over and over." Noelle started clearing the table, ferrying cereal boxes and a jug of milk to the kitchen as she spoke.

Brenn slammed her palm on the table. "I can't do anything right, can I? I finally find a place where I matter and people who let me be soft around them, who value me as myself. Their support gave me strength to be a better person to help Audrey, no thanks to you or anyone in our damn family. But it's never enough! Now you are going to give me that fucking key so I can go get my kid!"

Noelle snapped her mouth shut, eyes wide. "Your kid? I didn't realize she was that important to you."

At that, the fury that had powered Brenn stepped back and let her despair take over. She huffed out a disbelieving laugh. "What did you think this was?" she asked tiredly. "I knew that girl barely two hours before inviting her into my home. I don't do things on a whim. I'm not spontaneous. You all never let me." She held up a hand to stop Noelle from speaking. "Every time I wanted to do something, I had to have a fifteen-point plan justifying every move I made. And only then did you all consider, just *consider*, giving me support or encouragement or even validation. You have an entire lifetime of experience being my sister. Have you ever bothered to see me?"

She clenched her fists. "Mama keeps berating me for a mistake I made when I was eleven. *Eleven*! Kids should be allowed to make mistakes without it being a lifelong statement about their worth. Hell, adults should be allowed to make mistakes without it hanging over them for the rest of time. But no, I make one mistake, and I'm irresponsible forever. Cleo treats me like I am so goddamned boring, because she thinks I only exist to clean up other people's messes. And you. You act like I am too incompetent to live. Like I couldn't possibly fully be a person without your supervision or advice."

Noelle looked stricken. "We didn't—"

"Yeah, you did." Brenn collapsed into a chair opposite her. "Please tell me. Just tell me. Are you the one who told her how to use the car?"

Noelle worried at the end of one of her braids. "She asked me at one of our lunches. I assumed you had told her what it does, because she already knew about the car. I didn't think she would ever use it."

"Well, she did, so it's a little late for recrimination now."

Noelle rolled her braid in her fingers faster. "What is your plan?"

"I'm going to go get Audrey and bring her back. That's the extent of the information you're going to get." Brenn stood up. "Give me that key."

Noelle let go of her braid, the end unraveled and frizzy, a note of discord in her usually impeccable appearance. She nodded and led Brenn towards Jasmine's recording studio at the back of their house. Noelle made a subtle gesture, and a small drawer popped open in the secretary outside the door.

Brenn scoffed. "You don't even lock it up?"

"Jasmine and I are the only ones who can open that drawer, so yes, it is essentially locked up." Noelle dropped the key in her palm. "You're just going up and then coming back, right? I can cover for you with Mama and Poppy for a couple days, but any more than that and it's going to be a problem."

"As long as Audrey is there, and wants to come back with me, yeah, one day." Brenn hadn't thought about Audrey not wanting to come back. She swallowed hard against the lump in her throat.

Noelle looked at Brenn, her brow drawn. "I'm sorry. Just be careful, okay? Have one of your friends drive."

Brenn stared at her for a long second, set off her stride by Noelle's sincere concern, and said, "Thanks. I'll drop this by when we get back." Clutching the key, she swept out of the house.

Twenty-Six

BRENN LOOKED DOUBTFULLY at the notes in her hand. "You really think she wants to hear this?"

"Why would she not? It's an apology and a plan for the future." Lily plucked it out of Brenn's hand. "It is cogent and respectful and establishes expectations."

"It's too formal." Brenn bit at a hangnail. "I can't say that and not sound like a robot."

"You can put it in your own words."

Junelle motioned at Lily to give her the paper. "It *is* too formal, Lil. But I do think apologizing for not doing enough to make her feel safe is an important point to hit. I'd reiterate that you overlooked her inexperience, and you're sorry that came across as indifference."

"Ooh, that's good." Walker stretched up over the seat to peer at the note Junelle added. "I think you have to figure out what exactly you want from the future. Which I can help with if you need it."

"You don't just automatically sense what people want?" Aislynn asked.

"Nope. I learned to shut that out real early on in my life. It's nice to know what people want from you, but it sucks to constantly feel like an object or a transaction."

"Ugh." Aislynn made a face. "I can see how that would get old really damn fast."

"I think I want Audrey to stay with me permanently." Brenn's statement cut through all the other conversation.

Dani looked at her in the rearview mirror. "That's a big step."

"I know. It feels right when I say it, though. That's how I felt when I started my business, and when I got Charles Mayhew, and when I moved back into the Moon House. I think this is the next part of my life falling into place."

"I thought you never wanted kids," Dani said, glancing at her.

"I don't want kids. I don't want to be Audrey's parent. But I do want to live with her and help her grow and be her family." Brenn watched the wind tugging the bare branches of trees back and forth. "It feels selfish to want, and considering all my bull-shit, that probably means it's a good idea."

Nat turned halfway around in the passenger seat. "Here's something I'd like to know. Dani, how does Brenn seem to you compared to how she was this summer? Like, before Audrey."

Dani licked her lips, then pursed them, thinking. "Steadier. You seem like you are more *in* the world. I don't want to say more substantial, because you weren't frivolous, but your energy seems bigger. Brighter." She flicked on her blinker, changing lanes to pass a slow-moving bus. "And I don't want this to sound like, 'oh, a child will complete your life, and that's the only way to know true happiness' because we all know that's not fucking true. But. Your life is a little bigger now, and I think that's been good for you."

Nat twisted further to look directly at Brenn. "There you go. You feel positively about that decision, the person who is closest to you right now thinks it's a good decision, we all think it's a good decision. All that's left is to ask Audrey what she wants."

Brenn clenched the key she had gotten from Noelle so tightly her hand cramped. "Give me the notes again. I need to write all this down."

~

THEY PULLED off the highway onto a dirt track winding through the forest. Nat rolled down her window. "Oh, wow. Do you feel that?"

Dani rolled hers down as well and stuck her arm out. "Oh, that's *magic* magic."

Brenn looked up. "Yeah, it's intense the first time," she said, distracted. "There's a turn-off on the right, just past that big boulder." She exhaled a shaky breath. "Hey. What if she's not there?" She bent over to put her head on her knees.

"Then we will tap into the magic of this place and try again until we find her." Dani steered the van skillfully around the sharp curves of the road. "How long are we on this deer track?"

"Until we get there," Brenn said, mostly to her lap. Aislynn rubbed her back.

"I have a good feeling about this. You want some water? A Xanax? Weed gummy? This potion I nicked from Dani's kit?"

"Hey!" Dani thrust her hand back, snapping her fingers. "Give it back, please."

"I was joking. I didn't take anything from your bag, I'm not an asshole."

"Oh. Good. Sorry." Dani slowed the van. "Uh, Brenn? I think this is where you come in." An imposing gate loomed over them.

Brenn held the key out in her upturned palm. "Brenn Maren. Open, please."

The gates swung open. "Well, okay." Dani said and pulled in.

~

THE HYACINTH CENTER campus didn't look that impressive at first glance. There were a few gravel parking spots in front of a long, low building made of stone and logs. No vehicles were parked out front. Several of the women exchanged anxious glances. Brenn instructed Dani to park in the one closest to the door, unconcerned.

"We have to go through the welcome center instead of the main hall proper since the Center isn't actually open." She put her jacket on and strode across the gravel. Drifts of leaves swirled around her ankles as she walked, piling themselves neatly at the edge of the grass lawn.

The rest of the coven followed, bunching up behind her as she unlocked the door. Directly in front of them, a desk stretched in a half circle, with a large picture window behind it. Through the window, they could see the main hall towering over the rest of the campus. Two hallways swept around an interior courtyard between the welcome center and the main hall. Right inside the door, there was a map of the area.

Nat and Walker studied the map together. "This is a really nice facility. I don't know how I've never heard of it." Nat said over her shoulder.

"Why would you? The only people who know about it are the ones who go to my parents' conferences." Brenn took off down the hallway to the left. "This way."

She led them into the main hall, which had a large central room scattered with round tables and chairs and smaller meeting rooms off the back side. There was a nondescript door in the middle of the wall opposite them. Brenn stopped and took several deep breaths. She pointed at the door. "That's the way to the resident cabins. If she's here, she'll be staying in one of those. Oh, boy."

A wave of anxiety paralyzed her. She couldn't get her feet to move another step. Her hand scrabbled in her pocket for her notes. Nat came up beside her. "You good?"

"I don't know." Brenn whispered.

Nat nodded and then, with both her hands, pushed her gently forward. "You're okay."

Lily crossed to the door, holding it open. The rest of the coven fanned out around her as Brenn walked through the door.

There was no one in the clearing. The cold November wind whistled through the bare tree branches, cutting through any warmth the sun gave. Brenn's eyes scanned the cabins frantically, her breathing erratic.

"Brenn?" Walker said, pointing to the cabin farthest from the center. There was a thin stream of smoke coming from the chimney. A sliver of a blue car could be seen around the edge of the building. Brenn got out a shaky 'oh', and then somehow she was at the door of the cabin, covering the distance in no time at all.

She lifted her hand to knock, but the door swung open. Audrey looked out at her, shocked. Brenn grabbed her in a crushing hug, silently sobbing into her hair. Audrey's hands slowly raised to Brenn's back, tentative at first, then clutching her in return.

With a giant shuddering sniffle, Brenn held Audrey out at arm's length. "Oh, my stars and moon, you're actually here. I was sure you weren't going to be here."

"Brenn? Why are you here?" Audrey looked like she was about to pinch herself to see if this was a dream.

"We came to bring you home. I'm sorry I made you feel unsafe. I want you to come home." The rest of Brenn's carefully prepared speech flew out of her head. "I wanted to say, uh. A bunch of things I don't remember right now."

Nat stepped onto the porch. "Hey, Audrey. Good to see you're okay. It looks like you have heat in this cabin?" At

Audrey's nod, she waved behind her to indicate the rest of the coven. "Do you mind if we come in?"

Brenn examined the cabin as the rest of her friends followed them in. It appeared Audrey had been taking care of herself fairly well. There were apples in a bowl on the counter and a pot of macaroni and cheese on the stovetop. Her books and some of Audrey's own were scattered on the dining table. A fire popped and crackled in the fireplace, radiating a cozy cheer.

"I think we have a lot to talk about." She said to Audrey. She grabbed a couple of wool blankets from the basket by the door. "Can we sit outside?" She was about to open the door when she wheeled around. "Unless you haven't eaten yet?" She pointed at the pot of macaroni, now in Walker's hand. Walker shamefacedly looked back at them, fork in her other hand, and said through a mouthful of pasta, "Do you mind if I have some of this? I'm starving."

To Brenn, Audrey said, "Oh, no, I finished a while ago. I just haven't put the leftovers away yet." She looked over at Walker. "You can eat it." Audrey grabbed a blanket from Brenn. The rest of the coven settled in around the fire, quietly talking.

Audrey and Brenn sat on the porch swing, wrapped in blankets. Brenn set them rocking gently with her toe. "This is the cabin we stayed in the most when my parents brought us up here."

Audrey stared straight ahead. Brenn felt like an idiot. Then she noticed how tightly Audrey's jaw was clenched. "Look, I really am sorry. I never wanted to make you feel like you couldn't make mistakes or that I would send you away if you did. And everything is fine back home, the Moon House is repaired, and it woke up and is okay, and Charles Mayhew are fine. I'm fine. I cleaned, well, we cleaned up," she gestured vaguely back at the cabin, "and my maps. Audrey, I made those maps once, I can do it again. And it will be easier the second time. I just—what did I do that made you feel like you had to run away?"

A single tear rolled down Audrey's cheek. She mumbled something that Brenn didn't catch.

"Hey, will you look at me?" Brenn snaked a hand out from under her blanket and put it on Audrey's arm. She looked at her. And Audrey promptly burst into tears.

"Don't apologize to me, it's all my fault. I always mess things up." Audrey's voice was garbled through her tears. Brenn put an arm around her shoulders, pulling her close. She rocked the swing faster without noticing she was doing it.

"Audrey, you didn't mess anything up." She considered a long second and then continued. "Well, actually, you did mess one thing up, and that was running away. I have been frantic the past week. Out of my mind trying to find you. From this minute on, I need you to promise me you aren't going to run again. I need you to promise to come to me and we will deal with things together, as a team."

"You. I mean, I don't. What?" She wiped her face. "You want me to come back?"

"We didn't drive three hundred miles for our health." Brenn bit her lips, deciding what she should say next. "I'm going to lay it out for you. I want you to come back with us. I want you to live with me, and I want to make our relationship more permanent. I don't want to adopt you. I was thinking of making you my ward? And then we could maybe have something like what I have with my Auntie Violet? Because I am not cut out to be a parent, but a friend and mentor and family? I definitely can do that. And I want to do that."

She met Audrey's eye. "Audrey, I care about you. And I *like* you. You're great, and you are going to have a great life. The Moon House likes you, Charles and Mayhew like you, all of my coven likes you. You have a home with us." She hurriedly added, "If you want, I mean. Oh, no, do you even want that?"

Audrey's chin wobbled. "Yes. A lot. I want that a lot." She

stuck her pinkie out, crooked. "I promise I won't run away again."

Brenn hooked her pinkie in hers. "So, what happened? What have you been doing the past week? How did you think to come up here?"

"Um, Noelle told me about it? How the car works, I mean. Don't be mad."

"I mean, I am mad. But I'll get over it, so don't worry about it."

Audrey made a face. "I got up here with the car. It's really cool. How does it work? It wasn't even scary on the highway."

"It has a spell that makes it only recognize the Moon House and here, and a spell to make it drive on autopilot safely, and it's got a bunch of sigils that prevent normal people from seeing it. I don't know the full extent." Brenn prompted her. "So you got here in the car...?"

"Oh, yeah. And Noelle told me about this cabin, and how things worked with the fireplace and stuff, and where the food is, and all that? So I've just been reading and stuff." Audrey tugged her shirt sleeves down over her hands. "I made it storm a couple of times."

"That's how we found you. The hail."

She nodded. "And then I've been using the reference room in the main building to try to find somewhere to move where people would be safe from me. And, like, taking walks and stuff?"

Brenn felt nauseated as Audrey talked about the places she had considered moving to. But she didn't want Audrey to feel like Brenn was brushing her off again, or invalidating her thoughts, so she let her ramble on for a while.

"...and Charles Mayhew are really okay? I mean I checked them before I left, but I was still worried. And the Moon House went cold after I hurt it. And hurt you." Her voice broke.

"It took a few days, but the Moon House woke up. We fixed

all the windows and stuff. And Charles Mayhew are fine; I know they'll be happy when you get back. And as you can see, I am a-okay." Brenn turned on the swing, tucking one leg up against the backrest. "So, what happened that night?"

"I don't really know. I was asleep, and I think maybe I had a nightmare? And then I was downstairs? I don't know. I was really tired that night."

Brenn was a little disquieted at that but pushed the feeling aside. "Okay. If you do remember anything, you'll tell me?"

"For sure. Sooo." She drew the word out. "What do I have to do to be your ward or whatever?"

Finally, an issue Brenn knew exactly how to take care of. "Well, I'll go down to City Hall," she looked at her watch, "tomorrow and set up an appointment for you, maybe next week. You'll need to become an official citizen first. For that, you'll need to take an exam and then swear an oath." She saw Audrey's alarm. "It's not a difficult exam, just a few questions about the town and working with magic, really basic stuff, and then they test to make sure you have an affinity for magic. I'll get you the booklet thing, it'll be fine. Then immediately after that, we walk down the hall to a different room and sign papers saying that we both want you to live with me and for me to be responsible for you until adulthood. And then done!"

"Oh. Okay. That doesn't sound too bad." Audrey chewed on the string of her hoodie. "What about the state and CPS?"

"There is someone at City Hall to take care of that too. There will be a record of you in the foster system and a record for your 'adoption', but anyone looking at them will just...not be concerned about it."

"That sounds...shady."

"I mean, sometimes we need to do things that seem unethical to protect ourselves. It doesn't hurt anyone, and it's not defrauding anyone or anything like that."

Audrey accepted that, and they spent another half hour

talking about logistics. Brenn's stomach started growling loudly. "Ugh, I'm starving. Let's go back in, you get your stuff together, and I'll get a snack, and then we can get on the road back home."

As they went back inside, Brenn flashed a thumbs-up at her friends. "Audrey's gonna get her stuff together, and then we can get back on the road if that sounds okay with all of you."

"Great! We may have eaten some stuff from the pantry." Dani said guiltily. "But we can leave some cash to replace it. Or whatever. Stop at a store up here."

"Nah, it's fine. They can deal with it next summer."

Junelle and Lily got up from their spots around the fireplace. "Does Audrey need any help with her things?" Lily asked.

Junelle wrapped an arm in Lily's and said, "Let's go ask her." They disappeared upstairs.

Brenn cut a hunk off a block of cheese in the fridge and washed and sliced an apple. She was stuffing it in her mouth as Nat came and stole a slice from her plate. "How do you want to divvy up for the ride home? Does the car need someone from your family to make it back?"

"It doesn't, but I wouldn't mind driving back just Audrey and me if the rest of you are okay with that."

"Of course we are. I'm going to go bring the van around. Do I need to go back the way we came, or...?"

"You can walk around the outside of the cabins. Or you can go through the main hall if you want. But from the back door here, there's a sidewalk that runs in a big circle around all the buildings."

Nat saluted her and left.

Junelle, Lily, and Audrey came down the stairs. Junelle and Lily each carried a duffel bag, and Audrey had an armful of used sheets. "Brenn? What should I do with the stuff I used?"

"Oh, here." Brenn flicked her fingers at the laundry. It flew into a washing machine in a closet by the back door. The machine ran furiously for a couple of minutes. The door to the machine banged open, and the sheets and towels flew themselves outdoors to shake the water off violently. They then delivered themselves, dry and folded, back into Audrey's arms. "K, can you take them back upstairs? Just put them in the linen closet."

Audrey's eyes bugged out. "What the hell?"

The rest of them, minus Nat, also looked at her in astonishment. "What?" she asked.

"So I guess your magic is full up," Dani said. "It's pretty. You're turquoise."

"Oh. *Oh*. I guess so." Brenn looked at her hand. "I guess I didn't notice?"

"For fuck's sake." Aislynn cackled at the bewildered look on Brenn's face. "Come here."

She scanned Brenn again. "There it is. You've got a good amount of extra adrenaline."

Brenn raised her eyebrows. "That's what fixed me?"

"I think it's because you stopped trying to fix it. You finally had a problem that you couldn't handle on your own, and I suspect the adrenal surge from the stress kinda gave your system a reboot. And then you stopped overthinking and just reached for magic, and it was there for you. But who knows." Aislynn shrugged, and wheeled herself to the door.

Walker said, "You also accepted actual support. Taking all that pressure off probably didn't hurt." She rolled her eyes up as she swept past, following Aislynn out onto the porch.

Brenn looked at Audrey with a bemused expression.

Audrey grinned at her. "Cool. I can't wait to see what your real magic is like."

Twenty-Seven

ONE WEEK to the day after bringing Audrey back to Briar Vale, Brenn Maren woke up from a dream she couldn't remember, with a vision that wouldn't let her go. She beamed into the pre-dawn darkness for a few moments before throwing off her quilt. She leapt out of bed in such excitement she bashed her shin on the stool she kept there for Charles.

"Ow ow ow," she complained under her breath as she hopped to the door. Throwing on the hoodie draped over her chair, she rushed downstairs. She silently thanked her past self for keeping her desk completely clear and her painting supplies neatly organized in the crate atop her flat file. She taped down two blank cards and started painting with sure strokes. The first card revealed itself to be seven wands carved from different woods, laid in a wreath-like circle around a lopsided heart. The second was a small crescent moon cradled in a larger crescent moon, with a swirl of sparkling stars scattered around them like sparks.

Well. Her subconscious certainly wasn't being subtle.

She set those aside to dry. Grabbing a stack of boards from the file holder she used as a drying rack, she started peeling tape from the cards she had painted the week prior. It was a modest deck, just a dozen cards, each showing a hand covered in symbols. She'd painted them in a gentle rainbow, with inked line art on top of the color, like her own cards. The gouache she had used gave them a lovely matte finish.

Brenn tapped the cards into a neat pile, and tied them with a bit of silk ribbon she had in her desk. She slipped them into the top drawer and locked it. Leaning back in her chair, she rubbed her eyes. She had a nagging feeling there was something she should be doing.

Audrey knocked on the door. "Brenn, we have to leave in like thirty minutes," she called through the door.

In her excitement that both her autumn and winter cards had shown up on the same day, and relief that she hadn't actually missed one, Brenn had completely forgotten that this was the day that Audrey would officially become her family and a citizen of Briar Vale. She scrambled up from her chair, her face flushed, trying not to shame herself into self-loathing for nearly letting Audrey down on possibly the most important day they'd have together. Normally Brenn would spend the next several days beating herself up for being a disappointment, but this morning she was simply grateful she was able to course correct in time. She banged her injured shin on a box sitting between her desk and the door in her rush, and swearing a blue streak, she limped back upstairs.

"What did you do?" Audrey asked her as they passed in the hallway, looking appalled at Brenn's grimace of pain.

"Bumped my shin twice in the same spot. It'll be fine, I'll go see Aislynn later." She detoured around Audrey into her bedroom. "I'm going to shower really quick, and then we can leave."

She poked her head back out to look at Audrey. "Really quick, I swear." Audrey just sighed as Brenn closed her bedroom door.

"HOW LONG IS this going to take?" Brenn paced outside the office where Audrey was taking her exam.

Noelle patted the chair next to her. "Sit down, Brenn. It will take as long as it takes. You're making me anxious with all your pacing."

Brenn sat down and twisted the strap of her bag in her hands. "I know, I know. I'm just worried. It took a lot of work to get here."

She took the piece of honey candy Noelle held out to her. "Thanks for being here, by the way. I know you don't like taking work off."

"It's the least I could do. And I didn't want you to have to wait alone." Noelle had come over to the Moon House last week when Brenn and Audrey had gotten home and actually gave them both a sincere apology, resulting in a tenuous peace between the sisters. Brenn suspected it was in large part because she had finally been completely honest with Noelle. And the yelling probably didn't hurt. There are some people who just wouldn't hear a person unless they were yelling.

Regardless, Brenn was pleased her big sister had shown up for her and Audrey. "Do you think—" she began to say, but the office door swung open. She stood up, dumping her bag onto the floor.

Audrey looked at her blankly for a second, then she grinned with her whole body. Brenn tripped over her bag in her haste to get over to her. "So? You're good?"

"Passed with flying colors, they said. Now we have to go to this office and sign some papers, and then the financial office again, and then we're done. I guess they have to give me a new card?" She handed Brenn a sticky note with a room number scribbled on it. She leaned around Brenn's body. "Hi, Noelle."

"Hello, and congratulations, Audrey. I'm so happy for you."

Noelle scooped Brenn's things back into her bag and held it out to her. "Do you want me to tag along for this part too?"

"Up to you. You can come with us or meet us back at the house at four for the party."

Noelle looked at them, assessing. "I'll let you have a private moment. See you in a few hours." They watched as Noelle marched down the hallway.

"She doesn't really ever relax, does she?" Audrey asked.

"Not really," Brenn sighed.

The rest of their morning went smoothly, and by noon Audrey was an official member of Brenn's family and the Briar Vale community. They went to the Clover Yard for lunch at Audrey's insistence and then to the wand shop at Brenn's.

They stood on the sidewalk, Audrey peering dubiously through the window. Brenn reached for the door handle. "I think if you give it a try with a wand *you* chose, it's going to feel less silly. I used a wand not two weeks ago to try to find you, so it's not exactly a kid-only thing."

Audrey grumbled but grudgingly tried at least three dozen wands. She rummaged in a section of shelving in a less trafficked corner of the shop, finding a box shoved all the way to the back, behind a stack of pink wands with gold inlay. She blew the dust off the top, coughing as it hung in the air. One end of the box disintegrated as Audrey opened it. Lying inside on a pristine bed of white linen was a fourteen-inch rowan wood wand, the faceted grip stained a deep charcoal grey the color of storm clouds, fading into a creamy near-white at the tip. The wand had a gentle wave along the length, giving it a graceful appearance. An inlay of silvery-white metal spread and forked across the wood just above the grip, looking like lightning bolts streaking across the sky.

Audrey lifted it out of the box with reverence. She mutely held it out for Brenn to look at. When she waved it experimentally in the air, a thin line of silver-purple light traced through the air, fracturing outward like electricity. "Oh," was all she could say.

"Yep." Brenn said with deep satisfaction. She motioned the clerk over. "We'll take this one. Maybe with a new box?" She pulled the linen out and gave what was left of the original box back to the clerk.

Audrey clutched it to her chest the entire ride back to the Moon House, cradling it like precious treasure.

$\sim$

A COUPLE OF HOURS LATER, she showed it off to all of Brenn's family. "I just felt it, back on that shelf, like I was supposed to have it."

"Yes, dear heart, that is often how we find our tools. It's a fine piece of workmanship." Violet smiled at Audrey as she handed the wand back. "I can feel how attuned it is to you."

"Really? That's so cool." She ran off with Noelle's twins, who were talking her ear off about their own wands, which they had gotten the past summer.

Brenn wove around the crowd in the living room and library, collecting empty glasses and offering refreshments. She was in the kitchen pouring a new round of drinks when her mother joined her.

"Let me help you." Sasha took the knife Brenn handed her and started slicing more fruit. "I must say, darling, you've done a fine job with young Audrey. It seems she fits into your life nicely."

Brenn set the glass she was holding down carefully. "Thank you, Mama. I appreciate you noticing."

Sasha rested the knife on the edge of the cutting board. "I know your father and I don't acknowledge it enough, but we really are quite proud of all you've accomplished. I apologize if we made you feel like you were less than your sisters. It was never our intention."

Brenn braced herself with both hands on the countertop. "I know. And I just—I know that Noelle was your perfect little overachiever, and Cleo was wild, so they took most of your attention. But just because my needs weren't loud, Mama, doesn't mean they weren't there."

"I hear you, darling. And I am truly sorry. You were such an easy child." Her mother came around the counter and smoothed a stray strand of Brenn's hair back into place. She looked directly into Brenn's eyes. "That's not an excuse but an explanation. We are unable to change the past, but I, and your father, will attempt to do better by you from today on."

Brenn leaned her head on her mother's shoulder. "I'm happy to hear that. And I'll try to be more open with you all, for my part."

Sasha pressed a kiss onto Brenn's head. "We can grow together, darling."

∼

ON SATURDAY, Brenn threw the coven an all-day party to say thank you for their help the week before. The entire group, plus Lydia as Audrey's guest, crowded into the Moon House.

There was an incredible feast spread throughout the kitchen and dining room. After they devoured lunch, everyone scattered around the house. Lydia and Junelle were in the living room, watching Brenn's miniatures over and over.

Dani and Aislynn were ensconced on the back porch, discussing weather magic with Audrey. Dani was friends with one of the Vale's weather witches.

"So it's another kind of ward that controls the weather?" Audrey leaned forward in her chair.

"Sort of? The wards are there to monitor, but the weather witches have to actively, like, do stuff." Aislynn looked at Dani.

"The weather isn't exactly controlled by the wards or the witches. More like it's nudged? Like if there is a heat wave or a massive storm system rolling in, they help mitigate that to reduce the impact. And more importantly, and usefully, they extend spring and autumn so we get equal time in all four seasons." Dani typed on her phone. "I just sent you some titles of the books that my friend wrote about weather witching."

Aislynn tapped Audrey's knee. "And Ben sometimes substitutes in that department at the college. I'm absolutely sure he'd be thrilled to introduce you around. The weather you've managed to affect so far is a really strong indicator that your magic will probably settle into that. Those were fucking impressive storms."

Audrey flushed. "Ugh, I don't want to think about those yet." She fanned at her face. "But I would like to talk to both your friend and your husband. How many weather witches are there here?"

The two women looked at each other. "I think we only have three right now, and Radha said Drew is really close to retiring," Dani said.

Aislynn nodded. "I think three is correct. And I don't think anyone in the program at CC is going to stay in the area. So if you do want to pursue that, you definitely will be able to get a job here if you want to stick around."

Nat and Lily were in a spirited discussion of the finer points of monitoring magical energy. Walker balanced her chair on the back two legs as she ferried a steady stream of honey-dipped berries into her mouth, listening with interest as they argued.

Brenn slipped away to sit in the foyer, letting the sounds of her friends, the family she's chosen, wash over her. She felt perfectly at ease, like stepping into a bath that is the exact right temperature. Charles leapt up onto her lap, and Mayhew hopped from the back of the chair onto her shoulder. "This is really, really nice, fellas. Could you have imagined three months ago that I'd have this many people want to be in my life? Forever?" She let out a shaky breath and tipped her head back, eyes closed.

~

"I HAVE one more thing for you." Brenn picked her way through the small crowd around Audrey.

The members of the coven had presented her with several gifts to officially welcome her into their extended circle. Junelle had sewn a pair of brightly patterned pillowcases for her bed, embroidered with a charm for peaceful sleep. Lily had given her a linen-covered journal and brass-barreled pen decorated with etched roses, so she could record her thoughts. Walker and Dani had teamed up to make her a portable starter potion set, much like the one Dani carried everywhere. Aislynn had given her an amethyst ring engraved with sigils for clarity of thought. Lydia had given her a charm bracelet with a charm she'd made herself for steady and precise hands. "So, as long as you have this on, you'll be able to do, like, a perfect wing with your eyeliner," she had explained as she fastened it around Audrey's wrist. "*And* both sides will match." Nat had given her a leather-bound volume that coordinated with the grimoires in the Maren family library for Audrey to start her own grimoire, primed with a spell or ritual from each witch in the coven.

Audrey looked up from her new grimoire. "No, Brenn, this is already too much."

"Whelp, sorry, Charlie, but deal with it." She cleared her throat. "I hope you will find use with these and that maybe we could build on this together." Her voice was stilted, her words overly formal. She held out the divination deck she had painted especially for Audrey.

Audrey slowly pulled the bow out of the ribbon, her eyes shining with tears. "Are your visions back?" Her voice was thick.

"No. Well, yes, they are, but those cards are all directly from me, for you. If you don't like them, or they don't feel right, that's fine, we can—" She was cut off by Audrey crushing her into a hug. Brenn's shirt was damp from tears when they finally pulled apart.

"They're perfect." Audrey sat back down and examined each card in detail.

~

THE REVELRY LASTED LATE into the evening, until Audrey yawned so widely her jaw cracked. "This was really fun, but I need to go to bed now."

Brenn put an arm around her, hugging her close, resting her cheek on the top of Audrey's head. "Night. I'm glad you had a nice time."

Audrey waved goodnight to the rest of the coven. The party started breaking up after she was upstairs, Junelle yawning nearly as much as Audrey had been. Lily's blinks were getting longer and longer. They cleaned up the party clutter, and finally, Nat waved them all out the door. "Go home, you all look like you're going to drop where you stand. I'll help Brenn finish up."

"Really? You sure? Aren't you tired?" Aislynn took a stack of plates from the dining room to the kitchen.

"I'm a night owl, I rarely sleep before three." Nat shooed them out the door with minimal fuss.

When Nat came back into the kitchen, Brenn was washing the rest of the dishes that wouldn't fit in the dishwasher. Nat grabbed a towel to dry, and they worked in comfortable quiet for a while. Once the last dish had been put away, Nat looked at Brenn like she was trying to decide something. "You know, I'm really glad I trusted my gut about you."

"So you did know!" Brenn felt strangely comforted by that realization.

"Yep. Did I ever tell you how I met Arlo and For Whom?" she asked abruptly.

Brenn shook her head.

"So I moved here at the end of June and joined a bunch of clubs and committees trying to meet people. I knew I needed a new coven, so I was trying to get a feel for the people here. Didn't make much headway at first, and it was really frustrating." She draped the damp towel over the edge of a slightly opened drawer.

"I heard those bells at, must have been, two in the morning? So I go outside to figure out what is going on, and there's Arlo and the cart out in the street, right in front of my house. He gives me the spiel and a book."

"What book?" Brenn asked, curious.

"Uh, it was a novel about a witch settling down in a place for good, making her new house a home, finding a community, that sort of thing," she said dismissively. "I've moved around a lot in my life. A lot. And I was just feeling kind of tired. Anyways, at the start of the chapter where the main character finds a coven with an open spot, your business card was tucked in there as a bookmark."

Nat talked louder as she went to the porch to grab her coat. "You were the first piece, Brenn. I needed to meet you to find the path for all of us. I was at Witchery that day to ask Cleo about you."

She put her jacket on, walking back into the kitchen. "And we all know that cart is never wrong." Nat pulled a slim volume out of her pocket. "I borrowed this the day we started looking for Audrey." She offered Brenn back *Middle-Aged*. "I do have to ask—do you think this worked for you?"

Brenn took the book with a grudging fondness. "Nope. I tried a few rituals, but nothing did much. I thought maybe my magic problem was interfering with For Whom. Like maybe it gave me the wrong book?"

Nat flicked the bookmark she left in the book. "So you didn't read from the beginning?" She raised an eyebrow.

"No. Then I just wanted an actionable plan, not theories."

"You'll want to check out this part. Might have saved you some grief."

Brenn dropped the book on the kitchen island. "I will. Walk you out?"

NAT PAUSED IN THE DOORWAY, giving the house an affectionate pat before turning back to face Brenn with a serious expression that made her seem much older. "We, each of us, have our greatest value as the witches we are, not the witches we could be or should be." She gave Brenn a casual wave, then slouched down the path, shoving her hands deep into the pockets of her jacket.

Brenn stared after her, speechless. She went back to the kitchen, sliding onto one of the stools at the island. She opened the book to the page Nat had marked. It read:

'To recap these first few chapters, a successful witch knows the value of practice, goals, routine, attitude, and the importance of taking risks. Part Two of this volume contains exercises you can use to improve your magical prowess on your own.

However, for all we've discussed about these personal steps you should be taking, there is one important component to strengthening your magical mindset that cannot be achieved solely on your own. You need to find a team. No living being in nature is solitary. For some witches, this is a mentor or partner. Others may look to a club of like-minded individuals. For the best results, we suggest joining a coven. The trust and commitment such a group offers is an invaluable foundation for the inner confidence needed to practice your magic at the very highest levels of competence.'

Brenn lay her head face-first onto the walnut countertop. For crying out loud. That damn cart was never wrong.

When she was feeling less annoyed, she got up and flicked the lights off in each room as she walked through the house, closing up for the night. Brenn nestled *Middle-Aged* on a shelf in the library. Her oracle deck sat on the small table in the bay window, gleaming in the light from the street. Sure, she could do a quick reading before she went up to bed. She shuffled the deck gently, pulled a card. It was the first card she'd ever painted—a skeleton key, with a flowing ribbon tied around the stem, showing tiny letters spelling out 'strange, unusual, enough'. Brenn felt a warmth spread in her body, but as she stared at the card, a frisson of unease rippled through her. Something was different about the image on the card, a detail there she hadn't painted herself. She squinted, holding the card close to her face. In minuscule script, on the post above the bit, the key read "Brenn". Oh. She tapped her fingers lightly against her lips, the corners of her mouth curling upwards. She herself was the key? It was a bit cliche, but she was willing to believe it.

Brenn wrapped her deck back in its cloth and gathered Charles Mayhew to go up to bed. She checked in on Audrey, sleeping soundly on her new pillowcases, and wished the Moon House goodnight. She left her curtains open, staring at the nearly full moon, smiling a secret smile. This night, Brenn Maren was absolutely satisfied with the witch she was.

Customer reviews allow independent authors to continue
sharing their stories. If you enjoyed this book, please leave a
review on your chosen platform.

Visit www.felicitykyle.com for information on the next book
in the Tales from Briar Vale series.

Felicity Kyle lives in Western Michigan with her partner and their fluffy familiars. She rewatches Practical Magic twice a year (at least), eats too much chocolate, and actually uses the giant pile of fancy notebooks in her office.

To learn more, please visit www.felicitykyle.com

9 781962 738002